SANCTUARY

SANCTUARY

David J. Lightfoot

Matador
9 Priory Business Park,
Wistow Road, Kibworth Beauchamp,
Leicestershire. LE8 0RX
Tel: (+44) 116 279 2299
Fax: (+44) 116 279 2277
Email: books@troubador.co.uk
Web: www.troubador.co.uk/matador

ISBN 978 1784620 707

British Library Cataloguing in Publication Data.
A catalogue record for this book is available from the British Library.

Typeset by Troubador Publishing Ltd, Leicester, UK
Printed and bound by CPI Group (UK) Ltd, Croydon, CR0 4YY

Matador is an imprint of Troubador Publishing Ltd

This book is dedicated to my daughters, Paula, Sarah and Alison.

Contents

INTRODUCTION

Great speeches can be the catalyst of change. Throughout time there have been occasions when nations have faced threats and had to make dramatic changes. In modern times the threat of invasion by the Third Reich in 1940 made the British Nation fearful and anxious. Winston Churchill was able to engender national resilience and defiance in the face of overwhelming odds. His powerful oratory added steel to the resolve of the people when on 4th June, 1940 he spoke to the masses: "We shall fight on the beaches…". He was not the first leader to galvanise a nation in pursuit of an ideal after judging the mood of the people and appealing to their basic instincts. Hitler roused national xenophobia through the power of oratory at the Nuremburg Rallies. Martin Luther King changed perceptions with his 'I have a Dream' speech. Pope Urban II acted in a similar way nearly 900 years earlier to initiate the First Crusade.

In the seventh century, Byzantium considered itself to be the replacement of the old Roman Empire. This empire included territories in North Africa, Egypt, Palestine, Syria, Turkey, Greece and the Balkans, but big changes were taking place. These eastern territories were swiftly being eroded by Arab armies inspired by the new religion of Islam. The Arabs conquered most of the Eastern Mediterranean including the Holy Land and most of Turkey. Byzantium stopped the Arabs from crossing the Dardanelles and protected the Balkans from conquest.

In the period after the seventh century the old Roman Empire became eroded and fragmented with the remainder of the Byzantium Empire representing the predominantly Christian Greek speaking eastern territories centred on the capital, Constantinople.

The Latin Christian territories of Western Europe were centred on Rome. History shows that it was the Eastern Byzantium territories which acted as a bulwark against the expansion of the Arab armies, protecting the Christianity of Western Europe until as late as the fifteenth century.

In 1095 the Byzantine Emperor who resided in Constantinople, Alexious I Komnenos, made an appeal for western military help against the resurgent Seljuk Turks. They had captured Jerusalem and interrupted Christian routes to the Holy City. Not wanting to fight the Turks in the east and also western armies at the same time, Alexious sought an alliance. He thought that his needs and those of the Western Christians would coincide, and so he asked Pope Urban II for help. Together, they could drive back the hostile forces and go on to reconquer Jerusalem. Alexious did not anticipate that this appeal would result in the fervour and scale of the First Crusade.

Pope Urban ll gave an important sermon at Clermont during a Papal tour of France in the same year, 1095. He used this tour to make strong appeals to western Christians. His sermons had two aims. Firstly, to liberate the eastern churches by supporting the beleaguered Byzantine Empire and secondly to reconquer the Holy Land including Jerusalem. His speech was directed particularly towards the French knights who liked to fight, especially if this violence was sanctified and meant that their sins would be cleansed. As the ecclesiastical leader of the western Christians he had to preach the need for a war when the normal message for Christians was peace. To justify his message the Pope explained that this war was to be a special war, a just war, a holy war. It would not involve violence to anyone except hostile forces who subscribed to an alien creed. The Pope wanted Christians to rise up and march on a crusade to restore their Christian values in areas of the Middle East, including Jerusalem, which were presently held by infidels.

'Take the road to the Holy Sepulchre, rescue that land from a dreadful race and rule over it yourselves, for that land that, as scripture says, floweth with milk and honey was given by God as a possession to the children of Israel'.

(Pope Urban II 1095)

A key aspect of his speech played on the cleansing of sin. Pilgrimage would be an acceptable form of penance resulting in the cleansing of sin. This was a powerful message as Christians at this time were conditioned to think of themselves as full of sin. These sins could be purged by some form of punishment or hardship, in other words a penance. A pilgrimage ranked as a form of hardship where a person had to be disciplined and steadfast in pursuit of their beliefs. Going on the Crusade would give automatic absolution from sin to the participants.

Within twelve months of the Pope's message at Clermont and his subsequent sermons which he gave throughout his tour of France, 100,000 men, women, children, knights and clergymen from all over Western Europe converged on Constantinople on their way to reconquer Jerusalem. The crusaders were filled with an overwhelming feeling of righteousness. The justness of their cause motivated them to achieve the most improbable victories knowing that the hardships they suffered would be rewarded by absolution. They walked thousands of miles, fought battles and were ravaged by diseases. They conquered Nicea, and Antioch, captured Jaffa and negotiated peace treaties at Beirut, Tripoli and Acre. They had to move fast on Jerusalem to prevent the disunited Arab armies regrouping and counterattacking them. This was known as the First Crusade and against overwhelming odds Jerusalem was triumphantly retaken by the Christian armies in 1099.

After achieving their goal many of the fighting men felt that they had done their duty and returned home to Western Europe. Those that stayed helped forge the governance of the city. Amongst these expatriates were a group of experienced French knights, all who had connections to powerful families. They provided support to the

King of Jerusalem, Baldwin II. Their noble pedigrees meant that they were trusted by the king. One of these knights, called Hugues de Payens, was related to Hugh Count of Champagne, a person who financed the building of Clairvaux Abbey. He knew Bernard of Clairvaux who was eventually to become a powerful supporter of Hugues de Payens. As they all came from the same area of France they were known as the 'Troyes Fraternity'.

The main problem in 1119 was the shortage of fighting men. There were insufficient forces to defend the borders and keep order within them. Pilgrims arrived by sea on ships chartered from Genoa or Venice and were then often attacked by hostile forces as they made their way inland to Jerusalem. In response, Hugues de Payens and eight other knights, approached King Baldwin II with a proposal to create a special military order. The aim of this new order would primarily be to protect the pilgrims on routes to and from the Holy City. They became known as the Knights Templar and their emblem was of two knights riding one horse as symbolic of poverty, brotherhood and unity. The King of Jerusalem, Baldwin II, looked on the knights favourably, providing them with a base next to the Dome of the Rock in the former Al-Aqsa Mosque. However, there were so few original knights that they were only of limited practical use in a military way. Suspicions arose about the real intention of the knights. There were rumours about them being deployed to dig up artefacts from below their quarters next to The Temple of Solomon. Any relics or treasure would help to fund the Cistercian Order based at Clairvaux in France. There is no evidence that treasure of any significant intrinsic value was found. It is possible that the Templars inadvertently discovered scrolls written in ancient times, revealing to them information that may have changed the foundation of their faith. For example, the lost knowledge of ancient Egypt transmitted through Moses, King Solomon or the Gnostics. Originally, the Templars had few financial resources and relied on donations for survival, but they had a powerful ecclesiastical ally in Bernard of Clairvaux.

Hugues de Payens left for Western Europe to gain recognition, recruits and revenue for the Templars. They received ecclesiastical recognition at the Council of Nablus in January 1120. Bernard spoke persuasively on behalf of the Templars at the Council of Troyes in 1129 when the Templars were officially recognised by the Church. This resulted in them receiving money, land, business contracts and regular funding. It also provided a flow of recruits from noble born relations who were eager to fight in the Holy Land. At their peak there were between 15,000 and 20,000 Templars with about 10% being actual knights. Seneschals and Commanders/Preceptors managed the regional outposts of the Order. This is where the preceptories or commanderies had been established. They adopted a structure including a Grand Master, the first of which was Hugues de Payens.

'Knights' were the elite force of heavy cavalry and wore white tunics bearing red crosses. They had three horses each and a 'squire' to help them. Light cavalry was provided by the common soldiers of the Order, 'sergeants', who wore brown robes. They were granted one horse. Trucopoles were mercenaries, mainly recruited from the local area. They wore light armour and rode fast horses. They were fast and mobile, able to act as mounted archers. They provided backup for the knights when in action, but in barracks they had to sit and eat at a separate table to the knights. Their status was below that of the sergeants. Religious needs were supplied by ordained priests called 'chaplains' who were dressed in green robes.

Bernard of Clairvaux established the Latin rule by which the Templars would have to abide. It demanded discipline, obedience, moral purity and self- denial. Salvation was promised to all those who fought for Christianity and killing was justified because it involved fighting the battles of the Lord. The Templars started a type of banking system by taking deposits of valuables from pilgrims. They stored the valuables in their preceptories in the home countries of the pilgrims who were given a receipt. Once the pilgrim arrived in the Holy Land they presented their receipt and were reimbursed. The Templars established financial networks across the whole of the Christian world and bought land, farms and vineyards.

They built castles and had their own fleet of ships for transport. However, whilst they were admired they were not particularly liked by the secular knights within the main army.

The Crusaders ruled the Holy City for over ninety years until Saladin recaptured Jerusalem in October 1187. Although there were subsequent crusades in the period from 1187 until 1244 Jerusalem remained under Islamic control. Throughout the 1270's and 1280's men and money were sent to the Holy Land by Popes and western rulers. The position in Palestine deteriorated as the Christian conquests were systematically reversed and companies of knights retreated to Acre. This was the last city and the only remaining port still under Christian control. The siege of Acre lasted from 6th April until 18th May 1291 when it fell to the forces of Al-Ashraf Khalil.

Key: ■ Trebarwith

Trebarwith Beach

Part 1

The journey of our lives is not just about the destinations we have reached. Our wisdom, education and personal growth come from the people we meet, the paths we choose to follow and the lessons we have learned along the way.

CHAPTER 1

Mellifont Abbey

Sholto Kelley woke up, pleased to see narrow shafts of golden sunlight peeping round the edges of the dark cloth which draped across his bedroom window. His room faced east in the small cottage rented by his parents near to Mellifont Abbey, County Louth, Ireland. As an energetic seven year old, Sholto felt pleased that it was going to be another typical day in the summer of 1277. Already he had made plans to take his fishing rod down to the River Mattock. As he joined his mother downstairs in the kitchen he had no way of anticipating that this day would not be typical. His father had already gone out to work at the abbey where he was employed as a stonemason.

At the back of the cottage was an allotment where the family grew vegetables and kept a few hens. Sholto's mother was a good cook and used the produce from the allotment to help feed the family. That morning, around the breakfast table, she agreed that Sholto could go fishing provided that he helped on the allotment during the morning. Digging potatoes and collecting eggs was a small price to pay when the river beckoned in the afternoon. As Sholto collected his fishing rod his mother impressed on him to be back before supper.

Sholto was used to the solitude of this rural environment. There were few other children around, but he never felt lonely because his days were busy. He had learned to occupy himself and was content playing on his own. After spending time fishing, Sholto climbed into the branches of a large willow tree that overhung the river. In this camouflaged retreat he was able to observe a woodpecker building a nest on a tree on the opposite side of the river. It was warm and peaceful. The river gurgled around fallen branches as it made its sluggish way to its confluence with the Boyne. A gentle breeze rustled through the branches of the trees, and in the background was the tapping of the woodpecker's beak. A family of ducks appeared below Sholto's perch and he dropped bits of bread he had been using as bait for them to eat. The chorus of sounds from the cows crowding at the gate of the neighbouring farm suddenly attracted his attention. The herd knew that it was the time of day when they gathered for milking. Sholto was reminded that it was late afternoon. He remembered that he had promised to be home in time for supper. Sometimes he would go to meet his father as he left work at the abbey. It was just a matter of following the course of the river as it ran behind the abbey, crossing a field, and he was at the front entrance. He could tell from his father's face that he was always pleased to meet him. On this occasion Sholto decided to make his way directly home. He retraced his route back to the lane and as he rounded a bend the cottage came into view. Outside was parked a pony and cart. Two men were standing outside the front door talking. They looked solemn. Sholto recognised that one of them was the local physician and he felt his heart beat quicken. This was not usual. Something was wrong.

The events of that day would remain deeply embedded in Sholto's memory. It was not just the shock on learning of his father's fatal accident. It was witnessing his mother's grief and not knowing how to help her. It was the sympathetic features of the abbot as he tried to console them. It was his own personal sense of loss. His father had always seemed so powerful, so indestructible, but now he was gone forever. He could not understand how a day that had been so perfect could turn so suddenly into a living nightmare. These memories disturbed him for years and could return unexpectedly. It was usually something quite innocent that prompted the sadness to return. That day was a turning point in Sholto's life.

Fortunately, Sholto's father had been a member of the Stonemason's Guild. The Guild provided financial support which enabled his dependents to remain at the cottage. The abbot also took compassion on the family arranging for Sholto to make regular visits to the abbey. The brothers taught him how to read and write. They took him to the gardens where he learned about horticulture and they made sure he read the Bible. Gradually, Sholto gained a thorough knowledge of Christian principles and some of the brothers became his friends. His mother was consoled by the welfare that she and Sholto received, but she never fully recovered from the loss of her husband. If only he had been more careful and not fallen from the scaffolding, life would have been so much better. Mother and son were survivors and remained close, supporting each other through the difficult times and sharing the joy on happy occasions.

When Sholto became fourteen years of age he faced an important change. He needed to earn a living to support both himself and his mother. The abbot employed him to assist the monks with the agricultural work in return for a wage. Mellifont Abbey had been built on the banks of the River Mattock to the same plan as Clairvaux Abbey in France. The gardens were more than areas for walking and reflection. They provided herbs which were used for health and medicinal purposes. There were lots of things to learn about plants. Different plants were used to treat different ailments. The plants preferred different treatments; some liked lots of water, others drier conditions, some needed lots of sun and some preferred the shade. This was in addition to the regular tasks involved in keeping the grounds tidy. Sholto felt that his life had gained stability and although the work was hard, it was rewarding. He embraced the additional security the job provided. He was content living a simple life in the place where he was born and near to the people most important to him.

Weeks passed by and the pattern of each working day became a familiar routine, until one sunny day in August. Sholto arrived at the abbey, gathered his tools, and started work weeding the herb garden. Everything seemed as usual except that today was August 20th the feast day of Saint Bernard, founder of the Order. It was a warm summer morning and Sholto could see the east facing wall of the Chapter House bathed in sunlight. Yet there was something different. Sholto noticed that there were fewer monks around the grounds and he could hear the faint sound of singing escaping from the Chapter House. The monks often sang, but this singing sounded different. It was a rhythmic, pulsating sound like the swish of gentle waves breaking on a beach. Intrigued, Sholto abandoned his tools and moved towards the gothic doorway which was the main entrance of the Chapter House.

It was a magnificent doorway flanked on each side by twin pillars of blue marble supporting the cupped hands of the overhead archway, itself richly ornamented with gilt. At the apex was the stone figure of an angel with wings outstretched like a phoenix. Sholto gently pushed open the oak door and stepped inside, finding a discrete vantage point behind a rood screen from where he could see down the full length of the Chapter House. The building was not particularly high, but it had a stone vaulted roof supported by thick pillars. The floor was covered in rich red tiles and the walls were inset with stained glass windows, each depicting biblical scenes. Sholto was aware that the abbot often called meetings in the Chapter House where he sometimes read from the Bible, arbitrated in disputes or explained the rules of the Order.

Today was different because it was a feast day and the abbot was standing before a high table at the end of the room on which was positioned a large carved wooden figure of Jesus Christ. The abbot was striking a drum to a pulsating beat. It sounded like a beating heart. There were over a dozen monks stood in front of lecterns down the left flank of the room faced by an equal number on the right directly opposite them. Each lectern had a sheet of plain parchment draped across it and there were quills next to pots of ink. All the monks wore the habits of the Cistercian order, a dark poncho over a white gown representing opposites, darkness and light, goodness and evil. Sholto observed that the younger monks were positioned near to the door at his end of the room, with the oldest men close to the altar.

The morning sunlight flooded into the Chapter House through the eastern stained glass windows, colouring everything in dappled patterns, but Sholto saw that one particular window radiated pure white light directly onto the figure of Christ creating a spectral effect. Candles sent their flickering light around the walls, their scent snaking insidiously into every portal. The monks on the left flank were chanting a mantra directly towards the monks on the right. "Baphomet, Baphomet," sang the monks in repetitious harmony. "Sophia, Wisdom, Light," replied the monks on the right flank with full vigour. The tempo of the singing quickened in time with the abbot's drum beat. The chanting gained momentum becoming louder and faster with each repetition, until it reached a crescendo. The sound seemed to bounce off the structure of the building with a haunting, resonating echo.

Whether it was the chanting, the smoke, the light or just adrenaline, Sholto felt himself becoming light-headed. Suddenly the chanting stopped and the monks turned towards the figure of Christ which glowed before them. First one, then another started to pick up their quills. They seemed transfixed, but Sholto could see that they were writing on the parchment. One of them was speaking French as he wrote, another mumbled in what sounded like Greek. Then there was darkness until Sholto opened his eyes and was alarmed when he realised that he was in the abbot's chamber.

The abbot was a stern figure and Sholto had seen him walking in the grounds of the abbey from time to time. He always seemed to be alone with head bowed as if in detached contemplation. For many years Sholto had felt daunted by the abbot. This knowledgeable and pious man always seemed so serious and intent as he strolled around the environs of the abbey. His white hair and beard blended with his hooded white robes, and now here he was, in the abbot's room.

Seeing that Sholto had regained consciousness the abbot spoke quietly to him, "I see you decided to join our gathering in the Chapter House."

Sholto felt deeply embarrassed to have been discovered as an uninvited guest and more so as one who had fainted during the ceremony. "I heard singing", said Sholto sheepishly, "I wondered..."

The abbot raised his hand and said, "You heard and saw things that you did not understand. In the words of Jesus 'Nothing is hidden that will not be made known, or secret that will not come to light'. Everyone fears the unknown, so before you go let me explain some things about our ceremony. "

Sholto still felt a bit unsteady so he was quite content to listen as the abbot started his explanation. "Sometimes a building is also an instrument." The abbot looked up at the structure of the ceiling with its vaulted stone surface. "Just like you can hear an echo when you shout in a cave, the Chapter House has been constructed to resonate sound and process light. It is no more an accident that a shaft of light illuminates that statue of Christ than it is that light shines through a shaft onto the sarcophagus of a king in an Egyptian pyramid. Our chanting is designed to empty the mind of unwanted interference. It is a form of meditation aimed at achieving a state of unworldliness. Our senses are adjusted so that we are able to focus on our spirituality. Imagine a muddy pool where the water has been disturbed. When it settles you can slowly begin to see what is at the bottom. When we induce this state we embrace a mystical experience and try to record our thoughts on the parchment."

"What did the monks write?" asked Sholto with a quizzical look on his face.

"Come through the Chapter House and you can read for yourself," said the abbot.

They walked back into the main hall which was now empty apart from a couple of monks replacing the statue on the altar shelf. The parchments lay draped over the lecterns. As they passed each one the same words recurred. Some monks had scribbled 'Faith', some had written 'Hope' and a few had carefully printed 'Charity'. One or two had written these words in French, but to Sholto's great surprise the word which predominated was 'Love'. He could not resist asking the abbot for an explanation.

"Whilst their minds were cleared and they saw the figure of Jesus illuminated by the light from the window His teaching transmitted into their minds," explained the abbot. "Let me refer you to a quotation from the Bible. In Corinthians 13.1.13 Jesus ended with this phrase: '...and now these three remain. Faith, Hope and Love. But the greatest of these is Love.'"

There was silence as Sholto absorbed what he had been told. He thought that it was astonishing that the monks appeared to have a spiritual connection with Jesus.

"They have all read the teachings of Jesus, but the ceremony enables them to connect directly," said the abbot. "We think of the experience as a form of enlightenment. It is a moment when the senses receive a whole cocktail of inputs. This results in sensations which are greater than the sum of each input. It is called a complete experience."

Sholto thanked the abbot for his patience and for the first time recognised an aura of calm, a gentle quietness about the abbot, warmth that he had not noticed before.

"I think you should go home and rest today," said the abbot, "but before you leave I have something important to show you."

The abbot led them to a section of the building where there was a stonemason's mark clearly visible in the stonework of the chapel.

"These are the marks your father made before his unfortunate accident," stated the abbot. "He was a master stonemason and so he knew all about the special properties of buildings. He was given a permanent job here repairing and extending the buildings. He had skills that took many years to develop and we valued his expertise. Please feel welcome to talk to me in the future if you want to know more about Mellifont."

The monks had taught him to read, write and understand Christianity. He was comfortable in the presence of the monks, but now Sholto no longer felt unsettled by the presence of the abbot. His experience in the Chapter House had made a deep impression and he was reassured by the abbot's wisdom and knowledge.

He sometimes came to the chapel and ran his fingers over the mark in the stone which reminded him of his father. It made him more reflective than a visit to his father's grave. He now felt confident enough to discuss spiritual issues with the abbot and he gradually gained a deeper understanding of the Christian faith and values. Sholto had an enquiring mind and often thought about issues concerned with virtue, chivalry, divinity, spirituality, sin, forgiveness and death. Mellifont Abbey housed one hundred monks and three hundred lay brothers. Although he had many questions there was no shortage of people to seek answers.

CHAPTER 2

A Personal Crusade

Sholto's sessions at the monastery acquainted him with the stories coming from the Middle East where the Christian armies were in retreat. He had by now formed clear and strong Christian beliefs. He was conditioned by his environment, but the teaching of the monks intrigued him and he often had long discussions with his mother about religion. He believed that to live as a Christian meant that after death, the human soul would be pure enough to enter a place called Heaven. The soul of a true Christian would be resurrected after death to exist with God. He felt angry about the way Christianity was being attacked by what he perceived were soldiers of an alien culture. These infidels needed to be rescued from their own ignorance, so that they too, could become Christians and enjoy everlasting life.

When he heard that Pope Nicolas IV had called for a new crusade in 1290 to reinforce the Christians in the Holy Land, Sholto talked to the monks about joining this new crusade. They told him that the Pope's call was not being heeded because of a lack of money and the political distractions of many European leaders in countries closer to home. Sholto was now twenty years old, fit and in his prime. He was not a fighting man, indeed he had led a sheltered life close to where he was born, but he was of average build and height, healthy and ready to learn. Working with the monks at Mellifont had ensured that Sholto's life was structured, disciplined and principled. He had a pleasant personality, but was slightly unorthodox in both appearance and behaviour with his long strands of wild brown hair, his blue eyes and impulsive nature. Yet one thing above all others prevented Sholto from leaving his narrow cloistered world. It was his commitment to support his mother who had been unwell in recent times.

Everything changed when his mother died unexpectedly. She had been his confidant. She was the one person who he loved and trusted more than anyone in the world. Her death had left him feeling miserable and vulnerable. They had lived through hard times together. There had been no father to set an example, no husband as breadwinner. Now she had gone there was a vacuum in Sholto's life. He missed the conversations with his mother and he felt increasingly lonely and insular. Her death was so final, so sudden, and so irreversible.

His whole life had been spent in Ireland. He knew nothing else, but he felt that the time had come to change direction. It was unfortunate that the Pope's call for a crusade had come at a time of grieving. In reality, it became the catalyst for change. He felt apprehensive about the prospect of going abroad on a mission to defend the principles of Christianity. There was no mistaking the Christian conviction in which he deeply believed. His anxiety about the unknown world outside Ireland was outweighed by the strength of his desire for change.

Sholto talked to the abbot about his feelings. The abbot told him that it had been his fate that he had come to work at the abbey and that everyone valued his reliability, his resilience and his honesty. However, there comes a time in life when a person has to make difficult choices. Whatever Sholto decided would prescribe his destiny.

"Your decision will be respected by all in our community," the abbot told him. "Take your time and if you decide to go on this crusade we will support you in as many ways as we can. Whatever you decide always remember the virtues we taught you here at Mellifont. You will always be welcome to return here."

Sholto thought carefully about joining the crusade. He felt secure and comfortable at Mellifont with familiar faces as friends, and regular work which he enjoyed. Ultimately, his convictions became overwhelming, driving him to leave. He was not leaving for money, to cleanse his soul or for personal glory. He was going out of concern that his religion was being crushed and he wanted to contribute to stopping this affront. He wanted to learn and to persuade. Eventually he convinced himself and the abbot that it was the right decision to leave.

Feeling sorry that Sholto would be leaving, the abbot wrote a letter of recommendation to an old friend who was now the preceptor of a Templar Commandary in Cornwall. The letter was intended as an introduction to the preceptory where knights were trained prior to leaving for the crusade. As he handed the letter to Sholto he explained that as a person not of noble birth, or from a military background, he would have to gradually work his way into the Order.

"I have suggested that they train you as a squire. This means that you will be assigned to assist a knight," asserted the abbot. "You will be hired by the Templars for a period of probation and will be required to polish weapons and feed horses. If you do well and want to progress there will eventually be an opportunity for you to be initiated into the Order. Do not underestimate the dangers that lie ahead. Squires have to support their knight in battle, so pay heed to the training they give you. It may save your life."

A few days later Sholto left Mellifont. Leaving the cottage where he had always lived was sad, but somehow it no longer seemed the same. He did not want to continue living there on his own surrounded by the memories of his parents. As he closed the front door for the last time Sholto felt that he had to look to the future. To dwell on the past would diminish his spirit. He found it hard to control his emotions as he said farewell to his friends and colleagues. Only the final words from the abbot stopped him from a change of mind.

"Savour your memories, but do not dwell on them," he had said. "Look forward and embrace the future. Use the skills you learn to preserve both yourself and your comrades."

Sholto departed from his homeland in early 1291 in a small fishing boat by way of the port of Drogheda. He caught glimpses of the receding coastline as the boat reached the crest of each wave. He felt apprehensive about what would lie ahead now that he was leaving his familiar homeland. He was determined not to show the fear that he felt as he headed into the unknown. It was a stormy crossing and Sholto was glad when the ship reached the sheltered waters of the Camel estuary four hours later. The port of Padstow in Cornwall had many hostelries and Sholto spent the night in one before following 'The Saint's Trail' across the South West Peninsular. He followed the map given to him at Mellifont and reached the preceptory located near Temple on the edge of Bodmin Moor. It seemed a bleak place, surrounded by a ditch and a stone wall.

Entering through the main gate Sholto saw that there was an inner keep with other buildings surrounding it. He could see that these buildings included a chapel and stables. A large cloistered building appeared to be the living quarters. He could see men training in one part of the courtyard. They wore white tunics with a red cross on the left breast. The clash of metal rang around the yard as attacker and defender practiced their craft vigorously. Sholto felt daunted by all this aggressive activity until he met the preceptor, a tall bearded man, who guided him to a room which formed part of the living quarters.

"My name is Trebighe," he said in a low kindly voice. "How can I help you?"

"I have travelled from Mellifont in Ireland," Sholto replied as he handed the abbot's letter to Trebighe. "I want to join the crusade to the Holy Land and was told that you could help equip me."

Trebighe took the letter and read it in silence before putting it in the pocket of his white tunic. "Follow me," he commanded. "I will show you to your quarters and then we must eat."

They both walked along a cloistered corridor stopping at a store along the way where Trebighe provided Sholto with a green and brown tunic. Further along the corridor Sholto was shown the communal dormitory where a bunk and blanket were allocated to him. Eventually, they entered the dining area where a meal was about to start. It appeared that eating was a segregated activity and Sholto was invited to join the servants and squires on a separate table to the knights. Trebighe took his position at the head of the knight's table and led prayers. When he sat down everyone else followed. Not a word was spoken during the dinner, but Sholto felt renewed now that he had a full stomach. After the meal there was a period of contemplation before Sholto was led to the training area by a knight so large in stature that Sholto felt like a dwarf next to him.

The intensive training lasted for two weeks and in that time not only did Sholto become more muscular, he was changed from a gardener to a warrior. He had learned how to fight with a sword, how to use a dagger and how to protect himself with a shield. The Templars had showed him how to move in defence and how to press home an attack. They discussed military tactics and made sure that he was able to ride a horse competently.

Until now, Sholto had retained idealised thoughts about the crusade and his potential to contribute to the cause. What he had experienced at Temple was not what he had expected and this made him feel uneasy. He found it hard to understand the philosophy of the Templars. They were part of a religious order, but gave the impression that they relished combat. They were a disciplined military force single minded in their convictions, but after two weeks, Sholto had not had a long conversation with anyone. The knights he met were generally courteous, but preoccupied with their monastic way of life. Their prayer sessions started early in the morning and continued throughout the day. Silence was observed at mealtimes. He now knew why the Templars had a reputation for being fearless, and ferocious. Respect for them was widespread, but their insular practices did not win them many friends. Sholto felt content to remain in the role of a squire, and did not seek initiation into the Order. Maybe time would alter his opinion of the Templars, but for now he had doubts about them. In fact, he was beginning to have slight doubts about this whole venture.

Sholto and a couple of other new recruits were accompanied by their trainer to Fowey. He informed them that an English parliamentarian called Othen of Grandson had heeded the Pope's appeal and would soon be leaving for the Holy Land. When they arrived at the port they found that Othon's forces included a contingent of Cornish knights. They were due to board a ship bound for the port of La Rochelle in Western France. Sholto was introduced to one of these knights, a tough muscular individual, who had short cropped hair and a beard. He was called Trevaie and had apparently requested the services of a squire. He had an air of experience about him and Sholto discovered later that he had been to the Holy Land on a previous expedition.

Trevaie was carrying a heavy bag which he dropped with a thud to the ground. He looked directly at Sholto and then walked round him in a circle as if he was assessing an animal at an auction. Sholto stood firm and gazed straight ahead. There was an uncomfortable moment when he thought that he was going to be rejected, but then he heard Trevaie bark a command, "Pick up my bag".

The bag was so heavy that Sholto needed all his strength to lift it. If his suitability was to be based on picking up a bag then Sholto was determined to make a good job of it. Fuelled by the need to impress, he slung it on his shoulder without flinching.

"Carry it across the road and put on that wall," Trevaie instructed. Sholto complied and turned to look back at Trevaie.

"What did you think of my bag?" enquired Trevaie.

"Heavy," replied Sholto honestly. If that was a test of his suitability for the role of squire, it felt very superficial.

"You'll do," shouted Trevaie with a grin. He gestured for Sholto to join him and said curtly, "Welcome to the crusade. Work hard and you will prosper; otherwise you will be unlikely to survive." Trevaie had a feeling that their lives might not last long enough to worry about the finer points of selection.

It sounded an ominous greeting. However, Sholto nodded to show that he understood. He was determined to do his best, but as they boarded the ship, he wondered what kind of man Trevaie would be to work for.

CHAPTER 3

Outward Bound

It was the 1st March, 1291 as the contingent sailed out of the shelter of Fowey estuary. The ship was under full sail as it ploughed through heavy seas. The taste of salt was soon on everyone's lips as spray lashed across the deck. Each and every knight sat bolt upright like statues, singing battle hymns at the top of their voices. They seemed oblivious to the cutting wet spray. Their expressionless eyes were fixed on the horizon. They were assertively spitting out the lyrics as if singing was a way of releasing aggression. Sholto could not help but notice how pugnacious the knights were in contrast to the gentle monks he knew at Mellifont. They sensed that a fight lay ahead and were keen to get involved.

They docked at La Rochelle two days later and Sholto was relieved to set foot on dry land again having suffering sea sickness over large parts of the voyage. The company grouped together and set off on the long overland trek to Marseille in Southern France. They were not carrying supplies of food and had to forage in small French villages. This sometimes involved intimidating local citizens in order to pillage supplies, a practice that shocked him as it seemed to contradict the Holiness of the mission they were on. He had noticed that the brutality of some knights seemed to exceed their commitment to monastic practice. When he showed reluctance to get involved in what he considered to be unnecessary violence, a few of the less illuminated members of the company mocked him as being pathetic.

One particularly unpleasant knight sarcastically accused him of being morally superior. This individual had taken a strong dislike to Sholto. One evening, after an excessive ingestion of some weedy looking herb, he grabbed Sholto from behind and held a dagger to his throat in mock execution. Silence fell around the campfire and Sholto wondered how he could end this humiliation. He remembered that his military trainer had told him that a defence against an attack from behind is to collapse backward onto the assailant. In desperation Sholto tried this and the manoeuvre was partially effective. The two men fell backwards sending pots and pans scattering around in noisy disarray. The humiliation was now reversed and the knight raised his dagger in anger, lunging forward to attack with a face contorted into a malevolent snarl. Just when he thought that his crusade was going to end before it had begun Sholto saw another knight moving his way. Surely he was not going to have to fight off two assailants. To his immense relief he recognised that it was Trevaie, who immediately pounced on the aggressor. He wrenched his arm behind his back forcing him to release the dagger. He then used his boot to grind the bully's face into the dirt.

"If you even look at my friend again I will destroy you," snorted Trevaie whilst aiming a heavy kick into the assailant's ample buttocks.

Disorientated, filthy and bruised, the knight slunk back to his blanket and fell asleep. He never troubled Sholto again.

Sholto had not realised that he had a friend until now.

"Now let us eat and save our energies for later battles," exclaimed Trevaie.

Sholto sat down next to Trevaie and thanked him for his help.

"Never could stand bullies," said Trevaie loudly, so that all could hear. "Especially the ugly ones."

Muted laughter rippled around the camp. Trevaie then settled down to explain that when he had been to the Holy Land previously, the Christian army had occupied more territory. He discretely told Sholto that the military situation in Outremer was bad and deteriorating. They were going to reinforce a beleaguered city and were probably the last hope of survival against overwhelming numbers of enemy soldiers. He explained that the Christians had lost city after city to the Muslims. Tripoli had been the last big city to fall the previous year after one hundred and eighty years of uninterrupted Christian rule. Any male or elderly person who had failed to escape had been massacred. Women and children had been shackled and enslaved. Most of the city had been demolished to prevent it ever falling back into Christian hands. The portents did not seem good and Sholto began to have doubts about the wisdom of their mission.

"I fear we are too late and may be going towards certain death," Sholto sighed. His enthusiasm for this mission was dwindling and he was starting to wish he was back in Ireland.

Trevaie looked straight at Sholto with his steely blue eyes and replied with characteristic directness "All death is certain. We are going to need to support each other. If we stay resolute and work together, we will have the best chance to survive. I am glad that you will be with me as my squire."

Sholto's spirits were raised by this compliment, but he still felt uneasy. "You realise that I am not initiated as a member of your Order?" he demurred.

"No need for squires to be initiates," snapped Trevaie. "Squires are responsible for polishing armour, feeding horses, polishing weapons and supporting their knight. I hope that you can polish better than you can fight!"

"Well, you supported me, and I will gladly do the same for you," smiled Sholto pleased that he could reciprocate the assistance that Trevaie had given him. He had a growing respect for the man and valued his company. Trevaie was totally unpretentious. He was a straightforward, dependable character with firm opinions and a calm, confident manner.

A few days later the force of English knights arrived at the port of Marseille where two large transport ships, called busses, had been commissioned to convey the men and equipment to the Holy Land. The ships had a ramp at the stern for landing forces onto beaches. They were able to carry horses and the provisions needed by the soldiers. It was very warm and Sholto could smell the sweat from the Muslim prisoners who remained chained below deck. Catching a glimpse of the prisoners with their bowed heads and vacuous expressions, Sholto felt a glimmer of sympathy towards their plight. They were needed to provide the necessary propulsion when leaving port, or in a battle situation, or when there was insufficient wind for the sails. Steering was effected through side rudders and navigation by the position of the stars or use of a magnetic loadstone. These ships did not have deep keels and tended to pitch and roll in anything but the calmest conditions. Not the most comfortable to sail in, particularly when the smell of horse manure, mixed with sweat and salt spray drifted across the decks.

When it was time for them to board Trevaie found a place amidships where he thought there would be less motion. Anticipating the hardship of the sea voyage that lay ahead, Sholto had taken the precaution of procuring a few ginger root stems from one of the stallholders who littered the quay. These roots were a sort of tuberous rhizome and he knew that ginger helped to combat motion sickness from his time in the gardens at Mellifont Abbey. Trevaie was intrigued by these remedies which he had never seen before and Sholto offered one to him.

"They help you to travel better," said Sholto. "They can also make you sleepy."

"They don't look very appetising," Trevaie replied as he selected a small root.

Fortunately, the weather remained calm for the voyage, with clear skies, warm sunshine and a following breeze. They passed Sicily and Cyprus under full sail, the red cross of the Templars billowing out unequivocally announcing their presence. There followed a full days sailing helped along by the favourable direction of the wind. A warning shout from the watchman alerted everyone on board that land was ahead. It was now 5th April, 1291, and a month after leaving Cornwall, Sholto got his first glimpse of the last remaining outpost in the Holy Land, the city of Acre. He could see the outline of buildings shimmering on the horizon and a feeling of excitement overcame his misgivings.

As their ship passed between the harbour mole and a structure called The Tower of Flies the skull and crossbones battle flag of the Templar fleet gently fluttered at the top of the mainmast just above the top sail. Sholto could clearly see the chain which could be raised to protect the harbour entrance. Soldiers stood impassively by the winding mechanism as the ship sailed through. The city sprawled out to the north for about two kilometres with its ochre coloured buildings starkly contrasted to the cloudless blue sky. The thick walls of the fortified Templar complex boldly stood on the edge of the sea, to the left of the harbour. Whisps of light grey smoke drifted up from somewhere just behind the port and Sholto caught the faint smell of burning timber. The harbour was full of ships of different sizes, colours and shapes. Ominously, it appeared that more ships were leaving than arriving and they were all full of people, mainly women, children and old people. A man on a passing boat waved to them and shouted "God help you and the city." The knights responded with a rousing battle hymn which they sung with gusto.

They reached a vacant berth and the ramp at the rear of the ship dropped with a dull thud onto the lower quay. Sholto observed that even before the ropes had been secured to the capstans a crowd had formed and were pressing in towards them. Anxiety was etched on their faces. Although there was no panic their desperation was betrayed by jostling and a sea of hands holding up money like little flags. Voices could be heard shouting in Italian, French and Greek. An atmosphere of desperation encompassed the crowd. On this tranquil of evenings there was a sense of abnormality, an all pervading feeling of impending doom.

The crew forced a passage through the frenetic crowds and Sholto, Trevaie and the other knights were led by Othen down the wooden ramp onto the quay. After days at sea they looked slightly drunk as they marched towards the Temple fortress, passing through the stone gateway with its thick wooden doors and into the courtyard. They were greeted by the Master of the Temple, William of Beaujeu, a large, bearded man wearing the white tunic and red cross which symbolised the Templar knights. He was the type of man whose presence commanded respect, and although softly spoken, his words were resolute. He welcomed Othen and his company and it was obvious that he was relieved to see them. William was not a man to waste time with lots of pleasantries and without another word he mounted a large white stallion which reared up in front of the assembly, letting out a snorting whiney. There was a short pause as everyone became silent and attentive.

William spoke in a grave voice "I want to make the military situation clear," he said. "There will soon be a great battle for this city. We are outnumbered and out gunned but we have God on our side. The Muslims can invade our territory, but they will never invade our ideas. We have courage, we have strength, and our loyalty to our Christian heritage is undiminished. As brothers, as Christians, as soldiers, we will live together, pray together and die together. We will never surrender." William raised his arm and Sholto could see that his fist was clenched in a defiant gesture as he spoke the final inspiring words of his address. "Honour all men. Love the brotherhood. Fear God. Respect the king," he exclaimed. A great spontaneous roar of approval reverberated around the courtyard and it was palpable how morale had been lifted.

Taking out his sword, William dismounted, and scratched the ground plan of the city in the gravel. Sholto could now see that the city was surrounded by two thick, high parallel walls divided by defensive towers. William explained that the towers had names including 'The Patriarch's Tower' and 'The Accursed Tower'. In the centre section the two walls were joined by St Anthony's Gate a defensive formation that provided the main entrance to the city. This was a cosmopolitan city with a Venetian quarter, a Pisan quarter and a Genoese quarter. William gave notice that Othen's knights were to be deployed to the northern section of the wall where they were to defend the area between The Templar's Tower and The Gate of Maupas a distance of about five hundred metres. To the south were based the Knights Hospitallers. They had originally provided refuge and care for the travelling pilgrims, but now recruited fighting knights. Their defensive position was in the middle sections of the wall together with some knights from Cyprus. A new military Order called the Teutonic Knights defended further sections supported by Italians. Even the Knights of Lazarus, who were all suffering from leprosy and were based near the port end of the defences, had heroically insisted on defending the city they saw as their refuge.

After William finished his presentation of the plans he explained that although they were at a disadvantage the defence of the city was not without some advantages. "We have control of the sea and can bring in supplies. We can reduce the civilian population by continuing to evacuate those who want to leave. This will relieve pressure on food supplies during the expected siege," he explained.

William spoke with pride when he proclaimed, "We have the formidable resolve, courage and fighting skills of many knights. Go to your posts and God bless you."

He then marched off to the offices at the end of the courtyard without a backward glance. At this point Sholto, Trevaie and their contingent were asked to accompany a sergeant who would direct them to their quarters at the northern end of the city by The Templar's Tower.

As they passed through the streets of Acre Sholto could see that Muslim traders were working side by side with Christians from France and Italy. He could smell the herbs and tobacco smoke drifting around the traders' stalls. Conversations could be heard in a variety of languages, with bargains being struck enthusiastically. The traders did not seem concerned about the danger that was coming. Sholto was surprised at how much at ease the traders from these different cultures seemed to co-exist in the spaces they shared within the confines of the city. He had assumed that it would be heresy to fraternise with people who did not share the Christian culture and religion. The Muslims were supposed to be less than human according to the Pope. In spite of their different cultures all the citizens seemed to be co-operating in exchanging goods, medicines and money harmoniously.

The sergeant led them outside the suburbs to an area near to the city walls where a camp had been set up to house them during the campaign. The tents were close to the shelter of the inner wall as it offered protection from both the sun and any incoming missiles. They just had time to unload their belongings, few as there were, and were about to prepare a meal when the sentry on duty on the wall behind them bellowed a warning call, "Saracens approaching!"

This was not the sort of pilgrimage that Sholto had envisaged when he first set out. He thought that he would be coming to pay homage to the Holy sites, to fight to protect Christianity if necessary, to spread the teachings from the Bible. Now he could see that he was going to be instrumental in repulsing a full frontal attack from a massive Muslim army in a foreign city under siege.

He turned to Trevaie and said, "I don't think we will be seeing much of Jerusalem."

"Not on this trip my friend," replied Trevaie in agreement. "Still it could be worse."

"How?" asked Sholto.

"Thinner walls," Trevaie joked. They both laughed nervously.

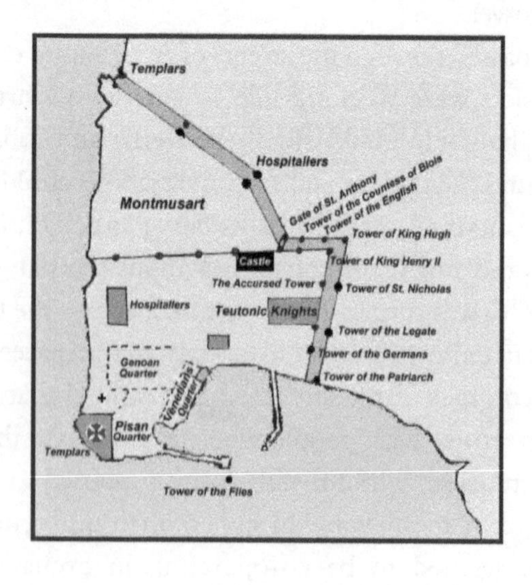

CHAPTER 4

Besieged

Sholto and Trevaie climbed the ramparts and looked out on the flat dusty expanse beyond. In the far distance a cloud of dust darkened the skyline. It announced the arrival of hostile Muslim armies. They were slowly converging on Acre from Tripoli in the North, Damascus in the East and Egypt from the South. These were battle hardened soldiers triumphant after their victories against the Mongols and now confident that they could dislodge the Crusaders from their coastal strongholds. Their leader was an Egyptian called Al-Ashraf Khalil who commanded the feared Mameluk warriors. They were freed Egyptian slaves who had been trained in combat skills and who were merciless towards their foes. They had risen to power in Egypt and were relentlessly extending their influence both politically and territorially. There was no doubting that they were elite, skilled soldiers.

As they got nearer, the sheer size of the attacking armies unfolded. This Muslim army outnumbered the total inhabitants of the city they were here to besiege. Their numbers were estimated to have been 100,000 foot soldiers and 60,000 horsemen. As Sholto and Trevaie watched from the walls the ground trembled with the sheer weight of marching infantry and horses. The air was pierced by the sound of trumpets played by soldiers riding camels, others were thunderously clashing symbols as they marched alongside. The rhythmic beat of hundreds of drummers reverberated around the city walls contributing to the deafening cacophony. The sun glinted off the points of a galaxy of spears and carts rumbled alongside the soldiers throwing up clouds of dust. They carried sections of the dreadful 'black bull' catapults and siege engines. Heat shimmered over the army in a sort of dusty mirage and the musty smells of animals and sweat wafted insidiously over the city. The scene was both hypnotic and horrifying. Sholto was new to combat and he wondered whether his courage would desert him. Seeing the worried look on his friend's face, Trevaie put his hand on Sholto's shoulder.

He said profoundly, "Once the battle starts there will be no time to think, only to act. Standing here contemplating death, but staying whilst daring to live, is a measure of the truest valour."

Until sunset more of the armies arrived, swarming along the whole length of the land in front of the defensive walls like ants. They wasted no time in assembling their catapults and were even beginning to build wooden towers. The defenders assessed their predicament. The poignancy of the address given earlier by the Master of the Temple was fresh in their minds as they realised that their total strength was about a 1,000 knights supported by 14,000 infantry. They had no land army and so could not leave the city defences to confront the Muslim army in the field. This had been a tactic which had stood the Christian army well in the past given their supreme horsemanship. It was not going to be an advantage that they could apply this time.

Al-Ashraf Khalil's tactics were immediately felt as a couple of recently assembled black bull catapults called mangonels, released a thunderous rain of missiles which impacted on the outer wall, followed by projectiles of fire which burst behind them.

"They plan to reduce sections of the walls to rubble and then pour infantry through the breaches in overwhelming numbers," Trevaie mused.

He was an experienced Templar and along with the other military orders these men instilled courage, order and discipline to the defenders. They had enlisted able-bodied civilians to operate catapults and other equipment to back up the men fighting on the city walls. As the sea was behind them the defenders were able to bring in supplies by boat and had already started to harass the flanks of the Muslims using armoured ships. One of the Templar busses had been fitted with a catapult and it was actively lobbing rocks into the camp the Muslims were trying to set up. They had not expected to be attacked from the sea and they had no ships of their own with which to respond. Archers fired volleys of arrows into the camp from the busses inflicting many casualties and damage to the Muslim camp. As darkness fell these initial skirmishes abated and the Muslim army dug in just out of range of the archers. Tomorrow the battle would begin.

They returned to their camp and prepared to eat. They were so hungry that they no longer listened to the vibrations, the hammering, and the shouts from their foes on the other side of the defences. The knights were freed from their monastic way of life when on active service in the field. They lit fires and the smell of roasting hog carcasses soon lifted the spirits of the defenders. Amphoras of wine were supplied to the garrison courtesy of the Grand Master. They would need all their strength to face the coming battle. It was the custom for knights to eat separately, but Trevaie saved some of his wine and discretely passed it to Sholto.

"Try to get some rest Sholto," said Trevaie as he handed his tankard over. "We are going to be busy in the morning."

It seemed a long time since he had left the peace of Ireland, although it was just a matter of weeks in reality. So much had changed and Sholto was worried about whether he had the aggression to perform well in battle. He knew that he would have to expel all compassionate and sentimental thoughts in order to prepare himself for the uncompromising ruthlessness of combat. The wine helped to sooth Sholto's anxieties and he fell asleep.

As dawn broke a bugle sounded the call to arms. Sholto helped Trevaie dress in his protective chain mail armour. Trevaie pulled on his white tunic, and picked up his shield, the red cross of the Templars looking resplendent in the morning light. Sholto followed him to their position on the outer wall, a large dagger thrust between his belt and his green tunic. In one hand he carried a short sword and in the other Trevaie's shield. He blanked his mind to everything except the coming fight. A sort of reckless abandonment of his own safety took over his psychology. Travaie was right. This was the time for action not reflection. He would immerse himself in the aggression, totally focusing on the destruction of the enemy. Sholto knew that he would rather die from his wounds than be seen as a coward.

The Mameluks released a barrage of rocks from their mangonels which thumped into the walls sending sharp chunks of masonry splintered through the air. Burning logs covered in oil whistled overhead and set fire to buildings. The defenders released volleys of arrows against the lines of advancing soldiers killing many and maiming others. Sholto was amazed at the courage and determination the Mameluks showed. Even when injured they continued their attack, if they were able, until they were killed.

"They seem immune from fear, almost like machines," shouted Sholto over the din of battle.

"They are totally committed to their objective, well trained and have their own strong beliefs in the righteousness of their cause," replied Trevaie. "Ultimately they die if you hit them in the right places."

All that day the defenders on the walls held out, inflicting heavy casualties on their enemy. However, the attacking soldiers slowly inched their way to the outer walls using reed screens to both disguise and protect their advance. They looked like turtles. It seemed to Sholto that no matter how many men they killed there were just as many to take their place. Sholto helped Trevaie from their position near The Templar's Tower by firing arrows at the ground troops and dropping heavy stones on to enemy miners who were trying to dig under the foundations of the outer wall. Buckets of hot pitch were brought to the ramparts and poured over the hapless diggers as they burrowed beneath the outer walls. Through sheer persistence, they gradually and relentlessly extended their tunnelling beneath the outer wall.

By the end of the day smoke was rising from buildings in the city that had been hit by burning missiles. Feverish attempts to contain the fires were being made by the townspeople. The outer defences were intact and all infantry attacks had been stopped, but at the price of the lives of many Templar knights. Agonised cries from seriously injured men punctured the air, smoke from the fires drifted across the walls; stretchers were being carried to the makeshift infirmary. Outside the walls, acres of bodies were strewn where they had been slain, their weapons scattered randomly over the battlefield. The smell of blood, decay and death wafted from all directions. Hostilities had now stopped giving the Muslims and the defenders a chance to collect their dead and dying comrades. It was a scene of carnage and desolation. As darkness fell, Sholto and Trevaie slumped down next to their tents exhausted.

After a while Sholto asked, "Have you ever wondered what happens to you after death?" Trevaie was a little surprised by the profound nature of the question and took a while to answer.

"I believe that there is life after death," he said. "The part that survives is not physical though." He went on to recall a time as a child when he had woken up very early one morning and in the glow of dawn light had seen the figure of a woman with a baby. "I thought that I was dreaming," Trevaie reminisced. "I put my head under my blanket and pinched myself to see if I was awake. Then I looked a second time and they were still there, still like a statue."

"Who was the woman?" asked Sholto.

"The figure did not have features, it was just a grainy shape made up of sand coloured dots of light, but I presumed that it was my mother."

"Had she recently given birth to a baby?" asked Sholto. Trevaie shifted his position so that he lay looking straight at Sholto and replied, "I was the only child in my family when I saw the image, but the strange thing was that my sister was born six months later."

Sholto was intrigued by this story and he looked back at Trevaie to ask, "Do you think the image was a vision?"

Trevaie chose his words carefully, "My mother must have known that she was expecting a child at the time, and I had never given having brothers or sisters a thought, so I have often wondered whether her maternal feelings conveyed themselves into my subconscious mind. I suppose you think I am being a bit insensitive", said Trevaie defensively. "I should not be telling you such a mysterious tale on a day that we have faced death ourselves. The incident has always stayed with me because it made me think that perhaps there was more to the world than just the material things."

"It was me who brought the subject up," said Sholto. "Anyway, I once had a similar experience when I was in Mellifont Abbey. The abbot had shown me a stone into which my father had carved his mason's mark. One day when I was alone I was thinking of my father as I ran my fingers over the mark. I did not see anything tangible, but I felt his strong presence as if he was near me yet invisible to the eye."

"How did you react?" asked Trevaie.

"It was a comforting, reassuring presence and I felt inner warmth from the connection," stated Sholto before continuing his philosophical theme. "If we are killed I hope our brotherhood will still be there."

Both men remained silent. Sholto liked to think that death would not just be a black void, like walking through a door and falling into a dark bottomless pit. He preferred the thought of an afterlife where kindred spirits were reunited.

Trevaie felt the exhaustion of the day creep over him and he just wanted to eat and sleep in that order. He stood up and spoke to Sholto like a true friend. "When we have eaten, come and join me for a drink. Let's enjoy the precious time we have. We are alive as brothers tonight; tomorrow we fight to survive as brothers. I believe that you are right when you say that we will remain brothers, dead or alive."

CHAPTER 5

The Raid – April, 1291

The enemy mangonels pounded the outer walls for eight days. Wave after wave of soldiers attempted to breach the defences but were repulsed, causing heavy casualties on both sides. Sholto and Trevaie felt their energy sapping away as day after day they were called into action. On 15Th April their Templar commander decided that a raiding party would launch a surprise night attack on the nearest Muslim positions under cover of darkness. The strategy was to take the initiative back from the attacking army by inflicting heavy casualties on them. By disrupting the Muslims this might cause dissent. If morale was undermined perhaps the enemy would retreat.

Trevaie asked Sholto if he would accompany him on the raid which was scheduled for the following night. "The Muslim camp will be asleep and we will kill them in their nests," Trevaie said enthusiastically.

Although he felt afraid that he would not live up to Trevaie's expectations Sholto felt compelled to go. "Better make sure that we sharpen our blades," said Sholto as he moved to prepare the horses, the armour and the weapons.

The next night he rode alongside Trevaie out through the gate in the tower and across the dusty land in the area between the walls and the enemy camp. There would be no going back now. They had passed the point of no return and they would soon know whether their plan would be a triumph or a disaster. Ahead, smoke drifted up from exhausted camp fires and mingled with the myriad of stars overhead. The air was scented with a mixture of ash and food, like the aftermath of a huge barbecue. They could hear the distant rhythmic scrape of a weapon being sharpened. Occasionally, a horse would snort in irritation as it pulled against its tether. A village of white, pyramid shaped tents littered the landscape. Little did the inhabitants know that death and destruction was about to descend upon their safe haven.

The attack was a complete surprise to the Muslim soldiers most of who were asleep in their tents, but the initiative was lost when many of the horses got tangled up in the guy ropes of the tents and fell, dumping their riders onto the ground. This misfortune happened to Trevaie. His mount stumbled and he fell heavily to become surrounded by a hostile group of Mameluk soldiers. Sholto reeled his horse around and drove straight at the soldiers knocking them over. Trevaie was trying to recover his sword when Sholto spotted a Mameluk soldier running towards him. He dismounted and swung his shield at the soldier. The soldier lay on the ground winded and Sholto stood over him with sword raised ready to strike a fatal blow. The soldier looked up and their eyes met. Sholto saw the fear in the man's eyes and he froze. This was not what he had expected. He had imagined that the Muslims were animals, but here he saw just another man. There was a violent crunch as Trevaie's weapon severed the Mameluk's head. It rolled in the dust like a discarded ball.

Hearing the bugle call to retreat, Sholto grabbed his horse. Trevaie desperately climbed on the horse's back with his arms clasped around Sholto's body as they galloped back towards the city at full speed. There was a gasp of pain and Trevaie's grip tightened as an arrow pierced his back just above the level of his chain mail vest. They sped through the gate in the walls and Sholto knew that his friend had suffered a serious wound. He was straining to give additional support in order to keep Trevaie on the horse. Once safely inside the walls, knights came to help them dismount, but it was immediately apparent that Trevaie was mortally wounded.

Surrounded by his fellow knights, Trevaie took Sholto's hand and his mouth opened and closed, but few audible sounds came out. He didn't need to speak. His firm grip and the look in his eyes confirmed what Sholto already knew. They would always be brothers.

In his dying moments Trevaie fumbled in his tunic pocket. He murmured his final words in Sholto's ear, "Finish my mission."

He handed a small Bible to Sholto who solemnly took it from him. Sholto had learned many things from his friend and commander, but their experiences that night had focussed his emotions. He could see clearly that there was more than just friendship between them. There was a bond which made their relationship much more profound. Sholto felt helpless, realising that Trevaie was going to die. He knew that he was going to miss him so much, but at the same time consoled by the unbreakable bond between them. He knew that his friend, companion and confidant, would always be there in his heart.

The life slowly drained from Trevaie and he died at Sholto's side. Sholto felt great sorrow for his friend and he rested his head on Trevaie's chest in silent prayer. His prayers were interrupted by the Templar treasurer, Theo Haudin, who had been summoned to take part in the burial of the fallen combatants. Theo walked purposefully towards Sholto. He wore the white Templar tunic with the red cross, above his chain mail vest. He strode close up to Sholto who saw that he was a man with a weathered, gaunt face. Sholto stood his ground resenting the insensitive intrusion that this man had perpetuated. As Theo spoke he could smell the musty cocktail of meat, and mulled wine on his breath. Obviously, a man with access to the cellars thought Sholto!

"You have been given a precious object by our brother. Do not take it out of this city without speaking with me first," he commanded. Theo moved away looking back at Sholto with a look of menace. Sholto could not understand the reason for this seemingly inane remark. After all, it was not as if he would be going anywhere soon, trapped in this besieged city. Certainly not alive anyway. Witnessing this incident a knight came over to Sholto and advised him to be careful.

"That is the treasurer of our Order. He knows the price of everything , but can sometimes overlook the value of things that are priceless. It may not be easy, but avoid conflict with him if you can," advised the knight.

There was little time for grieving because the next day the effects of the miners could be felt as two breaches were made to the outer walls. Sholto helped the defenders thwart the attack although they were now short of fighting men, and were exhausted and battle weary. The attackers now held the gap between the outer and inner walls. The Mameluks were seen filling in the defensive ditch dug to protect St Anthony's Gate. They were using earth, bits of wood and dead bodies. At sunrise on 18th May the Muslim armies launched an all-out attack at all points along the defensive walls, but the focus was on St. Anthony's Gate where they flooded across the ditch that they had filled in the day before. They came on foot and some riding camels. The attack was heralded by the sound of trumpets, drums and crashing symbols. Al-Ashraf Khalil had received reinforcements to replace his dead and wounded soldiers, so could press home this relentless attack backed by full resources.

In the fierce battle that ensued the Master of the Temple was killed and the effects of the mining finally caused the collapse of The Accursed Tower. The defenders braved wave after wave of the attacks, until they were unable to secure the perimeter of the city. Now that the outer defences of the city were penetrated, Sholto retreated with Othen's surviving knights from their defensive positions. It soon became obvious that an orderly retreat was becoming impossible due to the speed and ferocity of the attack. The Christian military orders were compelled to break ranks. Inevitably, they were forcibly separated as each individual became embroiled in fierce hand to hand fighting within the confines of the city streets. Discipline evaporated and the battle turned into a rout as every man had to look out for himself.

The members of the civilian population who had not been lucky enough to evacuate earlier were running, panic stricken towards the port. Rubble littered the streets, buildings were ablaze, crackling in the shimmering heat. Charred sections of timber and roof tiles rained down, smoke and dust polluted the air. In the streets soldiers fought at close quarters, the clash of steel from their swords, the groans from the dying, the cries for help from desperate civilians added to the mayhem. At the port a flotilla of boats was hastily evacuating civilians who had survived the gauntlet from the city. Most of the boats were overloaded and some had capsized. Those in the water looked up helplessly having spent their money on fares, as unscrupulous captains charged extortionate fees to civilians who were ready and able to pay.

Sholto navigated his way street by street. He knew from the position of the sun which way to head. Eventually, he could see the port where Othen was trying to rally survivors from his contingent of knights. As he reached the end of a street a group of Mameluk soldiers appeared. Sholto quickly darted into an open doorway which gave him access to the interior of a wrecked apartment. He entered only to be confronted by a terrified Muslim woman protecting her two young children. The family looked like ghosts, covered in dust and ash which was still falling from the smouldering rafters of the apartment. The woman's hair was covered by a scarf and she stood in front of the children trembling. She had fraternised and traded with the Christians in the city and she knew that her family would not be spared by the Mameluks if they were taken prisoner. Most likely, the children would be taken as slaves and would never see their mother again. Sholto placed his sword on the ground and stretched out each arm with his palms facing the family trying to calm them. He retrieved his weapon gesturing the group to follow him. There was an awkward pause as the woman assessed her options, but then she quickly turned and followed Sholto, her decision made. Sholto looked out furtively, but there was no way they could reach the port down the main street. The woman pointed to a rear door and Sholto could see a church across a patch of rough ground. He escorted the family out and through the church. The fortified Templar quarter lay just beyond. If they could reach the Temple it would provide them with a sanctuary.

Just as they exited the church a group of Mameluk soldiers approached from the north end of the building. Sholto led his little group of refugees to the side of a large house that was burning ferociously. The soldiers closed on them and their situation looked hopeless. Sholto drew his sword in defiance, but just when confrontation seemed inevitable, fortune turned in his favour. Large blocks of masonry from the building suddenly collapsed on the soldiers, burying most of them in a heap of rubble. The surviving soldier made a grab for the woman who shrieked in fear, as she tore her arm away leaving only the sleeve of her dress in the Mameluk's hand. Sholto attacked the soldier with fury severing the assailants arm above the wrist.

The Mameluks had a justified reputation as ruthless warriors and Sholto was about to discover why. Instead of backing away the soldier advanced like a robot. His eyes were fixed in a sort of murderous stare and he lunged at Sholto ignoring the blood pumping from his wound. He was brandishing a sharp dagger in his remaining hand. Sholto deflected the powerful blow with his shield but the dagger swept downwards and penetrated his leg just above his knee. In desperation the woman charged at the Mameluk distracting him sufficiently to enable Sholto to force the blade of his sword through the Mameluk's throat. The soldier fell to the ground writhing like an eel in his death throes. Blood pumped out of his mouth and turned the dusty ground red. Sholto picked up the dagger and together the bedraggled party staggered to the huge doors of the Temple where the guard hastened them inside. The huge wooden door boomed shut behind them.

It was only now that Sholto became aware of the pain from the gash in his leg. He was weakened from the loss of blood and could not walk unaided. As he slumped to the ground, a feeling of relief flooded through him. The joy of survival easily trumped the physical pain from his injuries.

A chaplain wearing a green gown appeared from a side door and escorted the woman and her children to the refectory where they were provided with food. He returned to where Sholto had dragged himself to a step built into the wall of the Temple, his leg still slowly oozing blood. Sholto leaned on the chaplain as they crossed the courtyard to where they entered a room furnished with a large rectangular table. He lay on the table helped by the chaplain who cut his clothing away to reveal a deep cut forged by the sharp blade of the dagger. The chaplain then carefully, cleaned and stitched the wound using a hair from a horse's mane. He then wrapped a tight cotton bandage around it to protect the wound from infection. Thanking the chaplain, Sholto moved to get up, but the pain in his leg was acute and he collapsed back onto the table.

"Can we see the port from here?" asked Sholto.

"Let me help you to the window," replied the chaplain. "Then you need to eat and rest."

Sholto watched sadly as amidst the chaos Otto de Grandson managed to load the last remnants of his English army onto three Venetian vessels and they immediately put out to sea. How he longed to be reunited with them, but this was now impossible from his location in the besieged Temple complex. The chaplain assisted Sholto to the refectory where he was provided with cushions and a plate of bread and vegetables. The family he had rescued were eating at a long table, their clothes still covered in dust, but grateful for the hospitality.

The woman's brown eyes fixed on Sholto and she began to speak softly. "My name is Jasmin. You have saved our lives and I thank you. I pray to Allah that He will look after you all your life. My children are called Zak and Sabira," she added, pointing towards the pair, busily devouring every scrap of food on their plates.

On leaving for this crusade the last thing Sholto expected was to be granted Allah's protection, but as he looked across at Jasmin, her solemn face radiating sincerity, he felt compassion towards her that he had not expected.

Sholto smiled as he spoke. "My name is Sholto. I was not aware that you understood English."

Until arriving in the Holy Land his only religious experience had been restricted to Christianity. His faith in God remained strong, but his view of religion was changing. He had come to realise that people of other religions were not as alien as he had first thought. He may have saved Jasmin's life, but in another way she had enriched his own.

Jasmin told him that her husband had been evacuated to Cyprus before the siege where he hoped to earn money to buy a passage for the rest of his family. They had not understood how little time was left to survive in Acre and the price of a passage on a ship had risen to exorbitant levels once the captains realised they had a strangle hold on the market.

Regret tinged with sadness flooded over Sholto. Regret that the conflict between religions had become so bitter and divisive. Sad that he had been so short-sighted. He was concerned about the personal plight of this foreign family, but was unsure of what he could do to help them.

"It has been good to meet you," Sholto said.

Although he had not been in this country long, his experiences had given him greater perspective. He was beginning to understand that people with other beliefs were not that different. Since leaving on the crusade his views had mellowed. He now appreciated that those he had once regarded as aliens were human after all.

After the meal the chaplain took Sholto to a small room with just a bed and a candle placed on a little bedside table. It provided a flickering light that sent shadows around the walls. There was a complete change of clothing neatly folded on the end of the bed. Sholto undressed and as he did so the small Bible that Trevaie had given him dropped to the floor with a dull thud. Events had been so traumatic that he had never thought to look at it. As he opened the little Bible Sholto could see that it was hollowed out and that it contained a sort of necklace. It appeared to be a chain on which hung a key. The key was round at the top like a small coin.

It portrayed a horse carrying two riders on one side with an image of The Temple on the Rock on the reverse. The stem of the key was a type of Egyptian ankh, the symbolic key to life, except that the round part at the top showed the symbol which displayed the seal of the Templars. The chain of the necklace was threaded through a small ring on the top of the round section of the key.

Feeling exhausted Sholto put the Bible on the bedside table and even though his leg ached with a deep pain he fell asleep and did not wake until the next morning. When he awoke he felt the presence of someone in the room. He turned and was startled to see Theo, the Treasurer of the Temple, looming over the bed. Theo spoke slowly and deliberately, not requiring any response to his deliberations. His moorish breath drifted over to Sholto as he outlined their predicament. The attackers had overcome all defences except for the Temple fortress. The deputy commander had asked him to organise evacuation from the port on one of the last remaining boats still operating. The Muslims were digging to undermine the walls which were becoming weaker by the day. If negotiations failed the fortress could not hold out indefinitely. He was instructed to load the boat with all the treasure from the Temple and fill the rest of the boat with as many women and children as possible.

Theo glanced towards the little table beside Sholto's bed. "I see you have found the key," said Theo looking towards the table.

Before Sholto could reply Theo continued, "Let me tell you something about our history so that you will understand better what I have to say. Our Order was established by a French knight called

Hugues de Payens as a military order. The aim was to protect pilgrims on the road to Jerusalem, but there were only nine knights altogether. They had the support of King Baldwin II who was aware that their real purpose was to excavate beneath King Solomon's Temple in Jerusalem. It was a sort of treasure hunt. They tunnelled for seven years and during that time uncovered many ancient scrolls. Our scribes have deciphered some of the scrolls. I met with Trevaie after your group arrived in Acre because I knew he was a man I could trust from his previous visit to the Holy Land. He agreed to take a chest containing two of the undeciphered scrolls back when he returned to the West, where they could be examined in safety. I gave him the Bible with the key to remind him of our agreement, but almost immediately we came under siege."

"So that is what Trevaie meant when he said he wanted me to complete his mission," Sholto interrupted. "He wanted me to replace him as the courier to return the scrolls to the West."

"I suppose that you expect me to give you the key back," said Sholto looking at Theo suspiciously.

"It does not matter that you have never been initiated into our order, you have served us well these last few days and I know that Trevaie would want you to fulfil his mission," retorted Theo.

"You agree for me to return the chest?" said Sholto, "I do not see a way to get away from here."

"There is a way," said Theo leaning forward. "It will mean leaving with me tonight. Your mission is to escort the chest back to your monastery in Ireland where there are brothers who can read the texts."

There was a pause during which neither man spoke and then Theo continued "We will take on supplies in Cyprus and continue to Western Europe with an escort." He turned to leave as Sholto raised himself to speak.

"I accept the mission, but have one request."

Theo spun round with an inquisitive look on his face. "What is it?" he snapped.

"You mentioned evacuating the women and children. Well I want a place found on the boat for the woman and her two children I saved from the Saracens."

"But they are Muslims," snarled Theo.

"It matters to me that they finally escape from here," pleaded Sholto.

Theo let out a deep sigh of resignation. He simply had more important matters to deal with.

"I will be concentrating on loading the Treasury, but you will have to pass the captain when boarding and his orders are for Christians first," stated Theo as he strode from the room dropping a bag of gold coins on the bed. "To cover your expenses," muttered Theo as he departed.

Sholto swung his legs over the side of the bed and tentatively tested his injured leg to see if it would hold his weight. The leg was sore, but he found that he could walk if he distributed most of his weight onto his good leg. Proving his mobility came as a great relief. He knew that any delay in departing would probably be fatal given the state of the hostilities.

Later that day Sholto was given custody of a small metal chest containing the two ancient scrolls by the deputy commander of the Temple. The chest was rectangular in shape and had a carrying handle on the curved top. A metal clasp secured the lid to the sides and it was here that a keyhole was located. Sholto tried the key and the chest opened revealing the rolls of ancient texts which Theo had told him about. The deputy commander stamped the chest with the Templar seal. He was a tall man with an easy going conciliatory manner, a personality which he was going to need if he was to negotiate a truce with Al-Ashraf Khalil.

"Meet at the West Gate at midnight. Theo's party will be there. It is going to be a tense evacuation so be careful," said the deputy commander. He smiled weakly, squeezed Sholto's arm before returning to his quarters.

Apart from the chest Sholto's only other belongings were a solid gold cup which he had found during his retreat through the city and the dagger taken from his attacker. It was quite an elaborate weapon with what looked like a ruby embedded into the hilt. He intended to use the cup during the forthcoming sea voyage.

CHAPTER 6

Dangerous Exit – May, 1291

Just before midnight on 19th May, Sholto headed for the West Gate as he had been directed. He entered the courtyard where the refugees from the siege were sleeping rough. There was a full moon which cast shadows everywhere, but after a few nervous minutes straining to see through the gloom he saw Jasmin and her two children huddled against the wall to the left of the courtyard. He walked directly to them and sat down next to Jasmin without exchanging a word of greeting.

He leaned towards Jasmin and whispered; "If you were to remove your headscarf for one night would it destroy your beliefs?"

Jasmin was taken aback by this sudden question and indignantly answered with a question of her own "If you were not to wear a red cross would it destroy yours?"

Given the dire circumstances, Sholto felt frustrated by this remark and found it difficult to supress his irritation. Although he knew he could not raise his voice he decided to come straight to the point. "You can all leave here with me tonight, but you will have to look like the Christians. If you stay you will almost certainly die within days and your children will be enslaved. Is it worth dying because of something you are wearing?"

There was a pause and the shadow of a cloud crossed the moon making everywhere quite dark for a few seconds. In that moment Jasmin had made her decision. Her dark hair flowed down across her shoulders and she stood up with the children.

"We have chosen to live," she whispered quietly.

Sholto was struck by how beautiful she looked without the headscarf, but he was still worried about how her Arabian appearance would be greeted by the crew of the ship. They arrived at the West Gate and the escapees were ushered through with just a nod of recognition from the guard. A group of about twenty people, men, women and a few children were crouched on the rocks. Sholto noticed that they were Western European in appearance. A mixture of Venetians, Genoese, and Pisans from the sound of their language. They all shared the tension generated by their precarious position. Nearby could be heard the sounds of music and voices from the Muslim camp. The glow of their camp fires could be seen all too clearly. They had surrounded the Temple and occupied the port, but they did not control the mole or The Tower of Flies. They lacked boats and so Templar snipers sailing in galleys had been able to kill anyone who moved on the unprotected harbour walls.

The sea stretched out in front of them caressing the rocks, the silvery trail of the moon reflecting on the gentle swell. It felt exhilarating to regain a sense of space and freedom. They sucked the sea air into their lungs, liberated from the hot confines of the Temple whose stark walls reared up behind them. A boat was secured by an oar wedged between two rocks and the crew were helping people aboard. This boarding was precarious with the movement of the boat and the slippery rocks. Sholto was limping, slightly lame from the wound in his leg. Nothing mattered more than leaving this doomed place and Sholto was relieved that the weather was calm. Jasmin realised to her dismay that the bearded boatman helping people aboard looked like the same man who had charged such a large fee when her husband was trying to book them a passage to Cyprus just a couple of weeks ago. Sholto hoisted the children aboard and started to help Jasmin.

"You can board," he said to Sholto. Pointing at Jasmin he continued, "She stays."

This was no time to start an argument and so angrily, Sholto grabbed the collar of the boatman's tunic with one hand and with the other he pulled a gold coin from his pocket and held it in front of the boatman's nose. Looking menacingly into the boatman's eyes he snorted, "She is boarding with me."

The boatman's objections seemed to evaporate as soon as he saw the gold coin. Ignoring the confrontation as if it had never happened he looked up at the night sky and whispered, "Look lively everyone, climb aboard, hurry along now."

Without further delay they took their places, pushed away from the rocks and smoothly glided out to sea with just the faintest splash from the oars. Soon they came alongside a larger Templar transport ship. Sholto took the precaution of threading his belt through the handle of the chest. He would need to use both hands to climb aboard the larger vessel. Everyone climbed the primitive knotted ropes that hung like pieces of threadbare washing down the side of the vessel. Grateful to be aboard, they took their place on the main deck. The exertion was extremely painful for Sholto and it was only through desperation that he managed to climb aboard. Now, sitting on the deck with his chest by his side, he caught a glimpse of Theo fussing with the Treasury wares. He decided to be discrete and rest his aching leg. Placing his arm across his raised knee Sholto was disconcerted to see that his hand was shaking slightly. There was a rumbling and clunking sound as the ship weighed anchor and the crew took up the oars heaving the ship into motion, following the line of the harbour mole.

They slipped like a shadow past The Tower of Flies and into open water where the order was given to hoist the sail. As Sholto looked back at the receding silhouette of the Temple he caught sight of a tall solitary figure on the battlements. He could not be certain, but he thought it looked like the deputy commander of the Temple. He held this brave, honourable man in the highest esteem.

Everyone felt drained, but it was too uncomfortable to sleep soundly. Sholto told Jasmin stories about life in Ireland and she translated them to the children. They were very interested to hear about his travels in England and France, places which seemed strange to them. Eventually they all fell asleep.

As dawn broke the following morning the ship berthed at

Limassol in Cyprus. This is where Theo had arranged for water and provisions to be loaded and the civilian evacuees to be taken off. Sholto looked at Jasmin who was pale and bedraggled after the trauma of the last couple of days. Her attraction to Sholto was not just her physical appearance, but her demeanour. She had remained calm in the most dangerous situations, been brave at times and intelligent with decision making when under pressure. He could not help it, but he had not expected to feel so sorry now they had to part. His heart told him to stay with her, but he knew this was not going to be possible. He smiled at her and slipped the dagger with the emerald handle into her hand.

"Until you meet your husband you may need to use this," he said. "When you are safely reunited it may be quite a valuable item."

Jasmin said nothing. She gently touched Sholto's arm. The look in her eyes said more than any words could convey. A tear welled in her eye and trickled slowly down her cheek. Her hand softly brushed his face. Then she turned and left with the children. She did not look back. The last sight that Sholto saw of her was with the children leaving the port amongst a crowd. Suddenly, they were gone and a wave of sadness flooded over Sholto and he felt hollow and empty. Of all the traumatic things that had happened recently his rescue of Jasmin and her children had lifted his spirits. Now that they had gone Sholto knew he was alone and he had time to reflect. He thought about Trevaie, another lost friend. He remembered his childhood in Ireland and the sorrow when his father was killed. He recalled fond memories of his mother and the friendship of the monks in Mellifont Abbey. His parents had departed, his friend had been killed, Ireland was a long way away, and his injuries a constant reminder of the conflict. It would have been easy to slip into depression. Sholto never saw Jasmin or the children again, but the memories of those few dramatic days when all their lives were at stake never left him. He looked around at the activities on board the ship and he decided to look forward. He was heading home and this thought lifted his spirits.

The ship took on food and water together with a contingent of

Templar knights. The vessel left immediately after the loading had been completed. After a short stop at Marseille, they spent two days at sea, sailing through the Straits of Gibraltar and north into the Bay of Biscay. Fortunately, the weather remained favourable and Sholto was glad to relax whilst giving his leg time to heal. It was late afternoon when the ship passed between the impressive grey stone towers which guarded the harbour entrance to the inner port of La Rochelle, in Western France. It felt a long time since Sholto had first passed through this port on his way to the Holy Land. So much had happened in such a short time frame.

The two towers provided a deep water, narrow entrance to the busy quaysides. They were linked to a curtain wall that protected the city from naval attack. The buildings of the town hugged the borders of the quay, and many boats were moored around the circumference of the port. Traders had set up stalls between the fishing nets and stacks of empty boxes. Containers of freshly caught fish were being hoisted ashore from the holds of little fishing boats. Men sat on benches mending nets, chatting in French, as greedy seagulls screeched overhead. The smell of fish and salt pervaded the air as the crew secured the Templar ship to heavy stone bollards.

As if on cue, a covered wagon pulled by two horses appeared, entering the harbour area through the elegant stone arch that separated the town centre streets from the harbour. The driver was a tough rotund man with a red face half covered by an ostentatious moustache. He shouted for the captain. "Bon soir. Où est le capitaine?" Sitting next to him was the preceptor of the local temple. Theo strode off the ship and Sholto could hear him conversing in French with his brother knight. A few minutes later Theo's precious cargo was being unloaded under the vigilant gaze of the Templar knights, supervised by the local preceptor of the Temple.

Meanwhile, Theo asked Sholto to follow him. He had noticed an English ship called 'Red Rover' was in port and he knew the captain, a Cornishman who had crewed on Templar ships many years ago. After days at sea Sholto felt a little unsteady. He had become so accustomed to the motion of the sea that although he was now on land his body simulated the movement of the ocean and he hoped his swaying was not misinterpreted. His leg still felt sore and he was limping slightly as he carried the chest containing the scrolls along a cobbled section of the quay. Theo directed Sholto to the gangway of the 'Red Rover'. Paint was peeling off parts of the hull and the effect of wind and salt had bleached the entire structure. On board, Theo was greeted by the captain, a man called Redvers. After a brief conversation Theo introduced Sholto to the captain.

"Redvers is sailing for Fowey on the morning tide," said Theo handing a pouch of coins to the captain, who took the payment without a flicker of expression. "This captain is a friend of the Order and can be trusted to take you to England," Theo continued. "If you find someone who can read the scrolls, and if they have anything interesting to say, be sure to let me know. Especially if it affects the Treasury," he quipped with uncharacteristic humour.

Sholto thanked Theo for helping him to escape and they parted on good terms. Theo hurried off to supervise the unloading of the Treasury and Redvers directed Sholto to a vacant starboard cabin. This accommodation offered more comfort than that which Sholto had become accustomed to on his recent travels. It contained a bunk, a chair and a table.

"I hope that you can make yourself comfortable," smiled Redvers. "The weather is set fair."

They left La Rochelle on schedule and set a north westerly course. Redvers invited Sholto to join him for a meal after the evening watch had been sounded. The prospect of good food was incentive enough and Redvers seemed an affable fellow. So that evening Sholto found himself at the captain's table. A member of the crew brought in two large plates loaded with fish and crab. Sholto had brought his gold cup and the captain filled it with wine. Redvers noticed the slight shake in Sholto's hand as he held out the cup, but he remained discrete and ignored it, although he knew the cause. He had seen the same effect on other men who had been in combat and knew that only a period of convalescence would cure the problem.

"What shall we drink to?" asked Redvers.

There was a short pause. Sholto felt safe and more relaxed now that he knew he was getting nearer to home and he was beginning to reflect about his survival. He was convinced that his life at Mellifont had been an important preparation for the trials he had endured at Acre.

Sholto lifted his cup and answered, "To obedience."

Their vessels clinked solidly as if they were proposing a toast.

"Do you think that freedom could be more important than obedience?" enquired Redvers quizzically. He was intrigued to hear how Sholto had fared in the company of the Templars, having crewed on their ships himself.

Sholto took a long sip of his wine and thought carefully. The question had triggered conflicts in Sholto's mind making a short answer impossible.

"I was indoctrinated with Christian values in a monastery where the monks taught me everything I knew. I saw the world in that restricted way because I had no other perspective. I was inducted with the virtues which the monks held to be important and obedience was one of them. Freedom was not an issue at that time because I felt safe and secure within the family of the monastery. I took it for granted. In Acre with the Templars the value of obedience stayed strong and I followed the commands given to me. In that perilous situation discipline and structure were essential to preserve your own life and that of your fellow warriors. I had the freedom to abandon the cause and run, but this would have been my prison."

"Why? Asked Redvers, "Most people would understand if you withdrew from a hopeless situation."

"I was free to choose and I chose to stay because that meant that if I survived I would not be perpetually haunted by my conscience. I would rather have died honourably than lived as a deserter."

"So you think that freedom is an illusion because your conscience denies any real choice?" exclaimed Redvers.

"Freedom is a double edged sword," Sholto replied. It is good if you have the discipline and framework of values to make wise choices. Freedom is not an excuse to behave selfishly. There is no virtue in making an unwise choice only to be trapped by regret. The monks taught me that the power and glory of all creatures consists in their obedience to the will of God, not in their freedom. That is why I survived with my integrity intact, and that is why I proposed obedience for our toast."

Sholto was feeling the soothing effects of the food and drink, which he feared were loosening his tongue. More wine glugged into Sholto's cup as Redvers extended his hospitality.

"What the monks did not give me was a perspective of religions so that I could compare and evaluate them," Sholto continued. He recounted his experiences during the battle for Acre, as Redvers listened carefully. "When I saw Jasmin and the children I had immediate empathy with them in their plight. Religion never entered into it, I just knew within myself that I could not leave them. It was like an instinct. Nothing that has happened has altered my values or my belief in God which I acquired at the abbey. However, I no longer think of the Christian religion as the only passage to Heaven. Anyway, that's what I think, but tell me why you decided not to stay with the Templars."

Redvers took a deep breath and shrugged his shoulders.

"I still respect them, but I felt that their rituals were suffocating me. I did not want to live in poverty, to avoid women, to be regulated as to when to eat or pray or even speak. I became more and more disillusioned. Then on one expedition we stopped over at Fowey where I met a special woman. It was an instant attraction and after a short time I knew that I wanted to stay with her. When it was time for my ship to leave I could not bring myself to abandon her, so I chose to stay in Fowey. When my family grew I took the opportunity to buy this boat and now I make a living as a trader. One day I hope that my young son will join me in the business."

"Did you worry that you were losing your direction when you left the security of the Templars?" asked Sholto.

"The values and disciplines which the Templars taught me are still there," said Redvers. "I shared their sentiments and respected their Christian beliefs. On this ship every member of the crew has been recruited by me and they know what standards of behaviour I expect from them. You can leave your cabin door open without any fear that your goods will be stolen. The crew work as a team, they are loyal, self-disciplined, reliable, hardworking and honest. These are the virtues that matter to me and I connect them with my Christian teaching. My crew may not all believe in a God, but they all embrace the Christian code of behaviour. This gives them a framework which coaxes them into a cohesive pattern. Gradually, I have seen that these virtues have facilitated a bond between the crew. They share a spiritual connection which goes beyond work. I believe that people have an inbuilt spiritual instinct that can be activated by knowledge of the Christian virtues, although I realise that there are other catalysts. We do not all need organised religions with their priesthoods, symbols, and rituals. Individuals find their own triggers with which to activate their spiritual potential and I agree with you that no single religion has a monopoly."

Sholto never expected to have held such a profound discussion with this captain who he had only met the day before, but he was really glad that they had talked. It had helped him to a deeper perspective about his life.

"I do not think my experience in Acre caused me to lose direction," said Sholto thoughtfully. "It did result in a readjustment of my spiritual awareness though."

"Talking about directions, what are your plans when we berth at Fowey tomorrow?" Redvers enquired.

Sholto explained that he intended to follow 'The Saint's Trail' which he had travelled along on his outward journey. He knew that he would need to buy a passage back to Ireland from the boats that connected with Padstow.

"You are limping already and with that chest to carry you could use some transport," advised Redvers. "When we berth I am expecting to unload a few barrels of French brandy onto a cart. The drayman is a trusted acquaintance of mine and he will be making deliveries at Callywith, near Bodmin. He will then proceed to

Temple for an overnight stop at the preceptory. He will eventually return by way of St Austell with a load of peat. With your agreement, I will ask him to give you a lift to Temple. You will be able to break your journey. It will provide you with a restful sanctuary and it will be less strain on your leg."

It was not what Sholto had been planning, but he knew that it would save him finding a horse and navigating in an area he did not know very well.

"Thank you. That would be a big help to me," said Sholto cheerily. Soon afterwards he bade Redvers good night and returned to his cabin.

It was near the end of May and the next morning dawned warm and dry. A few low white clouds clung to the tops of the surrounding hills as the 'Red Rover' berthed at Fowey. It was a bustling port lined with warehouses and numerous inns. Ships were loading tin, copper and china clay from the mines and quarries near St Austell. Sholto found himself sitting on the delivery cart with his Templar chest on the seat between himself and a drayman called Travis. Seven barrels of French brandy were secured on the back of the cart. Travis was of medium build and height; he was strong with muscular arms and had the confident air of an experienced operator. Taking out an old, battered hat from his pocket and adjusting it on his head of tangled blond hair he jerked the reins and off they went with a jolt.

Redvers waved and shouted to Sholto from the deck of his ship, "Don't lose your direction."

The cart lurched along the rutted road that led northeast towards Bodmin with Sholto fondly thinking about his return home to Ireland. Travis seemed glad to have some company and he interrupted Sholto's thoughts by asking about his travels overseas. Sholto thought it expedient to change the subject to Travis's work. Mercifully, Travis was pleased to talk about his trade. In fact nobody ever usually asked anything about his work, only about how much discount they could negotiate on a barrel of brandy. It appeared that most working people in Cornwall were in the habit of avoiding paying the King's Duty if they could and Travis was no exception.

"I have an arrangement with Redvers for the trips after he returns with brandy," boasted Travis. "The French always cross through the stem of the number seven on the manifest. Redvers makes a small alteration and the seven becomes a four and that is what goes in the Custom house book back on Fowey harbour".

"What if you get caught?" asked Sholto. "I have heard that people are hanged for less."

"Hanging or transportation are the usual sanctions for evading tax, but few are caught because there are too few customs men. Those that there are don't know the area like us locals," laughed Travis. "The price of brandy is eighty percent more expensive than in France so I reckon the King gets a fair share. My customer gets his six barrels at a reasonable price, Redvers gets a ready market, and I get sufficient return to make it worthwhile running the business. None of us see it as dishonest, more a fair method of redistributing wealth from the rich to the poor."

Sholto thought about this informal system for a few moments before asking Travis about a discrepancy. "I thought you said that you were carrying seven barrels!"

"We share the other barrel with the Preceptor of the Temple and his men in exchange for an overnight stay," said Travis in a matter of fact way. Noticing Sholto's raised eyebrows he quickly added, "I presume it is used for culinary and medicinal purposes."

By the time they had delivered the six barrels Sholto had received a thorough education in the brandy business and was looking forward to a rest at Temple preceptory.

CHAPTER 7

Temple Retreat

As Sholto and Travis approached, Temple preceptory slowly revealed itself amongst the deep slopes of Bodmin Moor. The grey stone buildings bathed in the warm glow of the late afternoon sun, contrasted against the lichen green of the moor. They could see the glint of steel and hear the shouts of Cornish knights who were training in the courtyard. The main building was frequently used as a refuge by pilgrims from Ireland on their way to and from the Holy Land via Padstow and Fowey. It was thought to be safer than navigating the reefs and currents around Land's End. It was not by chance that this trek across the Cornish peninsular had been called 'The Saint's Trail'. Sholto noticed that there seemed to be a lot more knights than pilgrims populating the preceptory and a shudder ran through his body as the memories of Acre flooded back. The trauma of battle still haunted him, but he was heartened by the thought that he was on his way home.

Travis pulled up at the stables and started to detach the cart, giving the horse a chance to rest after the day's work. A tall, bearded man was approaching them covering the ground quickly with long strides. He wore white robes bearing the emblem of the Templars. Around his shoulders was draped a white cape fastened with a single black stud at the front. He carried a short bladed sword which hung from a black belt buckled around his waist. Sholto recognised the emblem on the buckle as being the two knights on one horse. The same symbol as was on his Bible key. He discretely nudged Travis to gain his attention and he responded by looking up.

In a low voice Sholto whispered, "Better start unloading your cargo quickly."

"Good to see you again," said Trebighe shaking Sholto's hand firmly. He nodded towards Travis, "I see you have met my beverage supplier."

"Sholto is returning home from the Holy Land," Travis interjected. "He was recommended to travel with me by Captain Redvers."

"I know who he is," said Trebighe turning to scrutinise Sholto with eyes that seemed to penetrate his every thought. Then after an awkward pause and to Sholto's surprise he said directly. "You fought alongside one of our knights in Acre?"

"I was Trevaie's squire until he was killed by the Saracens," replied Sholto. The memory of his friend still left him feeling sad, but he tried not to show any emotion.

"Come with me to the church where I will find accommodation for you," said Trebighe warmly.

"The usual arrangements for me?" interrupted Travis who was feeling detached from the conversation.

"Yes, please leave the delivery in the kitchen storeroom . I will return to meet you there shortly and will sign your paperwork," instructed Trebighe.

Travis trudged off and Trebighe lead Sholto along a downhill path which meandered through a small graveyard to the granite arch which dominated the side entrance to the preceptory chapel. The inside of the chapel was a mixture of granite pillars and white painted plaster. It would have been cold and plain except for the coloured patterns which were generated by the sunlight shining through the beautifully crafted stained-glass windows on the western elevation. At the front of the chapel was an altar covered in a cloth illustrating a lamb in a pasture overlooked by a large human eye. They walked through the choir and into a little side chapel where a candle burned in a niche built into the wall. There was no furniture just a large cross in front of a few cushions which Sholto presumed were to kneel on when praying. Set into the wall were two doors side by side although one was much bigger and wider than the other. Trebighe opened the larger door which led to a room with only one high window providing just enough ambient light to see the layout of the furniture. The room was sparsely furnished with book shelves, a chair and a table, a wardrobe and a single bed.

"Try not to go through the wrong door or you will end up in the crypt," said Trebighe with a wistful look on his face. "The chapel will not be used in the evening until the weekend. Although the room is basic you will not be disturbed."

"I do value your hospitality," said Sholto. "However, I intend to continue my journey tomorrow as I want to get back home. Also I promised Theo, The Treasurer of the Temple in Acre, that I would deliver this chest to Mellifont Abbey in Ireland." Sholto took out one of the gold coins he had been given by Theo and offered it to Trebighe. "Will this cover my lodgings for the night?" he asked.

Trebighe looked at the coin and shook his head saying in a grave voice, "You have already paid for your lodgings with your courage and so we are glad to be of help." He turned to leave and as he reached the door he looked at Sholto. "I will be in the hall of the Manor House about an hour from now and I would be pleased if you would join me. I have some news from Acre which I think you should hear."

In the Manor House Sholto found Trebighe seated at the end of a long wooden table in a room which was adorned with hunting trophies. Deer heads, stag antlers, shields and swords festooned the stone walls. Behind Trebighe was a large fireplace which had smoke blackened stones and piles of logs, fuel for cold winter days. As Sholto took his seat next to Trebighe the ambient warmth of the summer evening and the glass of brandy supplied by his host helped him to relax.

The news Trebighe had heard from Acre was depressing. After Sholto had escaped, the temple fortress had held out for another ten days. The Templars had tried to negotiate a safe passage out by sea, but the Muslims had broken faith with this agreement and the Templars had fought for every inch of the compound. On the last day more than one hundred Muslim soldiers had broken into the temple building and were battling hand to hand with the surviving Templars. The effects of the constant pounding and undermining of the walls finally took its toll and the whole building collapsed killing everyone inside, both attackers and defenders. The Muslim commander, Al-Ashraf Khalil, had poisoned every well, killed or enslaved every inhabitant, and reduced the city to rubble. He had been reported as stating that never again would a Christian army be allowed to invade their lands.

Sholto recounted how he had fought with Trevaie day after day resisting the invaders from the walls of Acre. He described how Trevaie had been killed, his rescue of Jasmin and her children and his injury during the retreat to the temple fortress. Finally, how they had escaped with Theo by boat loaded with the treasury of The Temple. Trebighe listened with ever furrowing brows.

"The crusades were an inspiration for all Christians and now I fear that control of the Holy Land and Jerusalem is lost forever," he lamented.

"Trevaie was a brave, kind man," said Sholto sadly. "He taught me about honour, chivalry and brotherhood and was a great credit to your order. The conflict in Acre altered my views. It made me appreciate that chivalry was not the property of one religion. Our enemies showed equal measures of it in their own way. We were divided by religion and had different cultures, but we shared the capacity to be compassionate, to be honourable, to be brave and to exercise wisdom. We were fighting about material acquisitions like ownership of land and cities. The fight was about which religious belief system would predominate, about political control, and empire building. We were not fighting about what we had in common because this was something deep within us. Ironically, the conflict provided a perverse scenario where our mortality and spirituality, the things we had in common, were displayed in the most divisive circumstances."

Trebighe listened patiently to Sholto's heartfelt proclamation and after some reflection he spoke with conviction. "Spirituality and materiality are not mutually exclusive? They are two sides of the same coin and one cannot exist without the other. Humanity is the sum of both aspects."

"Perhaps, you are right," said Sholto slowly. On reflection, my experiences in the material world have stirred my spiritual thoughts, so there is a link! I have learned that wisdom is more important than wealth. In fact they are opposites. When you spend your wealth you have less of it. The more you use wisdom the more you gain. Sorry to sound so philosophical," said Sholto apologetically. "Each time I accept hospitality I seem to end up becoming more and more opinionated. Maybe the brandy has loosened my tongue! It is just that I feel so lucky to be alive after seeing so many friends die violently." Lowering his voice Sholto continued, "The trauma of battle returns to me without warning, triggered by the most unexpected things and I then I hear the voices and see the faces of people…." His voice trailed away and he swallowed a sip of brandy to steady himself from betraying his emotions.

Trebighe placed his hand on Sholto's shoulder and told him, "What you feel is what many others also experience. Only time and rest will ease it. Why don't you stay for one more day and give yourself a short convalescence before continuing with your journey. Borrow one of our horses and hunt rabbits or go fishing on Bodmin Moor. This will give me time to find someone to escort you back on the trail to Padstow and give you a chance to test your leg."

Sholto's instincts told him that he needed to leave the next day, but a day out hunting appealed and he thanked Trebighe for his considerate proposal. A short break was what he needed. He had been horrified when he noticed that his hand still shook when he held the glass of brandy. The moor would be a quiet place to convalesce.

"I think I will take your advice and use the time to recuperate," Sholto sighed. He was vaguely worried about his leg. He had always taken a pride in his agility and he had convinced himself that his physical impairment would just be temporary. The wound was taking longer to heal than he had anticipated and he was starting to think about life with a permanent limp. A day on the moor would test his mobility.

A feeling of relaxed contentment descended over him having made his decision. He was glad to be safe amongst friends. On this occasion he would allow his heart to control his head. He would deliver the chest to Mellifont as he had promised. One more day was not going to make much difference and an escort would be very reassuring. Sholto resigned himself to extending his stay at the preceptory. He had no way of knowing that the decision to wander on the moor would change his life.

CHAPTER 8

Trebarwith Strand

Two and a half miles south of Tintagel is a narrow inlet called Trebarwith Strand. It is situated at the seaward end of a deep valley which forms a gash in the surrounding farmland. In 1291 access was by a narrow track which clung to the valley wall. The gradient was so steep that careful navigation was essential. High above sea level, at the landward end of the track, was a slate quarry. Carts brought slate down the track to a little rocky quay where it could be loaded onto small boats. Sand from the beach was taken back to the top of the valley to improve drainage on the surrounding farmland. Sweating teams of labourers worked the route six days a week.

Built into the left hand side of the valley on a narrow plateau, overlooking the quay, was the harbourmaster's office and stables. The wooden buildings joined the cliff at one end, rising above the entrance to a natural cave which ran along the line of a fissure in the rocks. During construction of the harbourmaster's office, the entrance to the cave had been widened to give sufficient headroom for people to pass through. It became incorporated into the cellar in the part of the building which was used as an inn. 'The Strand' provided refreshment, mainly to local farm workers, the drivers, labourers and crews from visiting boats. The cellar of the inn linked to the cave and was divided from it by a stout oak door. It was possible to pass through the cave and arrive on the beach below the high cliffs. This proved to be very convenient for the landlord to supplement his income by indulging in occasional smuggling. It was a way to preserve his family's standard of living at a time when the king had been organising more efficient tax collections. Wars against the Scots and other military campaigns were proving to be very expensive.

The landlord was called Edward Denke. He was a rotund man, his face etched by exposure to the elements, with eyebrows that seemed bleached in contrast to his weather beaten face. His mop of grey hair festooned his head making him appear slightly unkempt. He owned a boat which he moored by the quay. When he made fishing trips he left the management of the inn to his wife, Jane Denke. She was a convivial hostess with an infectious laugh and a good sense of humour. Jane had always lived locally and was respected in the community, her well rounded figure still appealing to the eye.

Their daughter, Jade, assisted in the business, sometimes working in 'The Strand' and sometimes accompanying her father on fishing trips. The family kept a few chickens and grew vegetables on a section of land at the side of the Inn. Working outside meant that the elements had turned her skin golden brown, a colour which matched her hair. Everyone worked hard and their survival depended on supporting each other, especially during the winter months. In the summer she occasionally visited the neighbouring Trebarwith Farm. This farmland extended to the edge of the towering cliffs which reached up behind the inn. The farmer, George Lursk, and the Denke family had been friends for years. Jade would take fresh fish to the farm and would return with milk. It was during these visits that Jade had formed a relationship with George's son, Mathew Lursk. They had known each other since childhood, but during their teenage years their friendship had developed into affection and they were frequently seen walking, hand in hand, through the village. Now nineteen years old, Jade had set her heart on marrying Mathew and was looking forward to starting a family.

Mathew regularly visited the market in the nearby town of Wadebridge. Sometimes he went with his father to take cattle to the auction and at other times he went alone to collect supplies. It was on these visits that Mathew had met a girl who managed the animals at the auction. As they often worked together preparing the stock, Mathew had increasingly enjoyed her company. Apart from her physical attraction he admired her skills tending the animals. She shared his interest in animal husbandry and enjoyed hearing about life on the farm. This affinity developed until Mathew found himself longing for his next visit to the town.

Jade had sensed that Mathew had been less attentive towards her and had asked him what was wrong. Eventually, she managed to prise a confession from him that he had feelings for someone else. She felt shocked and hurt knowing that the person she had committed herself to marry had allowed himself to fall for another woman's charms. Mathew had tried to explain that it was just something that had happened. It had not been planned. He tried to reassure Jade that she would be certain to find someone new, but the shock and pain of the breakdown of their relationship had put Jade's life on hold. Some days she felt angry, and some days she would find it hard to control her feelings when something reminded her of Mathew. It was only now, a few weeks later, that she had decided to start to take control of her emotions and begin to rebuild her life.

A coastal path snaked up the steep side of the valley behind the inn giving rise to the most spectacular views. Half way up the path Jade scanned the sea. The sun was gradually sinking below the horizon leaving a pink glow in the darkening sky. When the tide was out there were plains of glorious sand at Trebarwith Strand, but once the tide turned it came in fast completely covering the sandy beach. Jade watched the tide flooding around the rocks below her. A quarter of a mile off shore a large grey rock rose out of the sea. It looked like the head of a gigantic monkey that had waded out leaving only its head above the waves. Plumes of spray showered off the outcrops of grey granite as the Atlantic swell thundered against it. Seabirds swooped around the crevasses, their mournful calls echoing all around. In the fading light Jade could just see her father's little boat at the side of a lugger that was hove to. She swiftly retraced her route to the inn and descended the steps from the office at the back of the bar. As she reached the last step she saw George Lursk, the farmer. As on previous occasions he was already in the cellar waiting with two lighted torches. They looked at each other and as George passed a torch to her she smiled in recognition. They did not indulge in conversation, partly because of George's awareness of the sensitive nature of his son's relationships. George unbolted the oak door and they made their way through the narrow passage soon reaching the exit where the sea was framed by the mouth of the cave.

Edward knew that time was tight. The captain of the lugger was on route to Bristol and did not want to stop any longer than was necessary to make a quick cash sale during this brief rendezvous. The transfer of three casks of French brandy, was completed with smooth efficiency. It was an informal transaction seamlessly executed. Edward pushed his boat away from the hull of the lugger using his oar and turned towards the shore. He raised his single sail to take advantage of the on-shore breeze and it billowed obligingly. Immediately, the boat responded with a powerful surge through the waves. Edward had to synchronise his arrival at the entrance to the cave in Trebarwith Strand with the water at the right depth and the light just sufficient to enable him to navigate close to the rocks. Ahead he could see two flaming torches side by side. The lights gave him the position of the cave entrance and the signal that all was well. If the flames had been one above the other he knew to head back out to sea. There was little margin for error and the manoeuvre required careful seamanship.

George was now positioned at the right side of the cave entrance with Jade to his left. The tide was lapping at their feet as Edward used his oars to row stern first towards them. The keel of the little boat gently beached on the sand, its bow caressed by the incoming tide. Quickly, Edward lowered a long wooden plank. Working together, George and Jade guided each cask as they rolled down the plank beyond the surf and into the cave. The couple then pushed the stern of the boat as Edward pulled on his oars. Mercifully, the boat was soon reclaimed by the incoming tide. Edward rowed back out to the safety of deeper water and in less than five minutes the boat was bobbing innocently off shore, its primary fishing role restored.

It was a routine that had been well rehearsed. Always done when the tide was right and the fading light made the boat less conspicuous. Arrangements of times, dates and places were made in the watering holes which festooned the Cornish coast. Local people knew that Edward last paid duty on a cask of brandy ten years ago and it had still to run dry. They were careful to remain silent, content to pay lower prices, loyal to their neighbour.

Moving the casks through the cave was exhausting. The floor rose quite steeply and it soon gave way to a slippery, uneven rock surface. Crystallised minerals hung in dripping icicles from the roof and quartz veins streaked like flashes of lightening across the walls. There was just enough headroom to stand upright, but the sides were narrow. The sound of the sea breaking against the rocks was amplified in the confined space. The taste of salt was on their lips as they laboured with the casks. It was dark, damp, dismal work with just the light from the two flaming torches to guide them in the darkness. Jade hated this part of the job. At least the unpleasant, claustrophobic conditions stopped her thinking about the mess she felt her life was in. They both knew that they were near the end of the cave when the rocks became drier, the echo of the sea had become a distant pulse, and the chisel marks of the miners appeared on the walls.

The last of the customers had left the bar by the time the pair of smugglers had stacked the three casks inside the cellar underneath 'The Strand'. Firmly securing the oak door from the inside the bedraggled pair climbed the short flight of rocky steps that led to the door at the back of the office. They walked through to be greeted by Jane Denke, their mission completed.

The following morning was bright and sunny as Edward escorted Jade to the stables where a mule was being hitched to a small cart. After returning from his fishing trip during the night

Edward was intending to get some sleep before resuming his work around the inn. Jade stroked the mule's distinctive white mane as she listened to her father. He explained that a delivery of slate had been promised to a friend who needed to repair a leaking roof in the village of St Breward, on the edge of Bodmin Moor. On top of the slate rested a bale of straw which had been hollowed out to conceal a couple of pigs' bladders. They were bloated and Jade knew that they were filled with brandy. They were intended for the landlord of the inn in Blisland. This was the place where Jade could expect to exchange her mule for another animal strong enough to travel on the return journey to Trebarwith. She set off, glad to be gaining the freedom of the countryside, released from the routines in Trebarwith, liberated from the sad emotions of the recent past. Driving the cart up the track that led from the valley with the breeze gently blowing her hair, Jade enjoyed a sense of renewal.

CHAPTER 9

Moorland Rescue

The next morning Sholto awoke to hear the clash of steel as the knights continued their program of training. For a few seconds he felt disorientated, alarmed to think he was in Acre, before reassuring reality flooded back. He had been travelling for so many days that he was glad he had agreed to stay at Temple for a little bit longer. The servant at the stables had prepared a dappled grey stallion for him to ride and was full of assurances as to the good nature of the beast.

"If you want fishing, ride out in a westerly direction along the track," said the servant as he emphasised the direction by pointing. "After about a mile you will see a crag on your right upon which there is an unusual formation of rocks. Keep following the road until you reach a bridge over a fast flowing river. Cross the bridge and the land is flat. Follow the river until you find a place to fish. It is about three miles altogether," said the servant advisedly.

Sholto mounted the horse and with a jocular smile he shouted to the servant "Thanks. I hope to be back before evening. If not, you had better organise a search party!"

The weather remained settled and Sholto breathed deeply, sucking in the fresh morning air. There was a blue sky with only the odd fluffy white cloud drifting by on a light breeze. It was warm and dry, just the sort of day to relax with a little fishing expedition and a picnic.

It was immediately apparent that much of the moor was covered in grass and marshland. The landscape was coloured in a mix of yellow ochre and lichen green. The sunlight glistened off small, boggy areas where reeds were prospering in the moist peat. Here and there, dark hills betrayed the original mountains which had been eroded after millions of years exposure to the elements. Now the highest contours remaining were the granite outcrops called Tors.

Before long, Sholto was on the track which wound its way around the south west side of the craggy outcrop of granite known as Carbilly Tor. Near the summit was a symmetrical pile of rocks which looked as if they had been placed one on top of the other by a giant hand. This natural feature gave the impression of an artificial sculpture, but was a distinctive landmark. Sholto crossed the bridge and followed the meandering path of the river upstream until he came to a raised bank. It was getting hotter and so he decided to tether his horse to the wizened trunk of an old oak tree. He was able to take in the view whilst having a drink from the leather flask which he had filled with water at the church. The shade from the tree was welcome shelter from the sun. Ahead, the river flowed under another bridge about a quarter of a mile to the west. This was a stone clapper bridge providing a crossing for the long undulating road linking St Breward with Blisland. A plume of smoke drifted lazily into the sky from a farm some distance to the north. Beyond the farm Sholto observed a high Tor rising loftily above a lot of undulating moorland. There were sheep and wild ponies grazing in the warm sun and in the distance a little cart was trundling along the road leading to the bridge. Although it was still far away, Sholto could see that it was led by a mule with an unusual white mane. He leaned back on the grassy knoll next to his horse and with his arms behind his head he watched a fluffy cloud with a dark patch drift across the sky. Sholto remembered from his time at sea that it resembled a cave within chalk cliffs. He felt so warm and comfortable that he started to doze.

He suddenly jerked back awake feeling the vibrations as his horse scraped its hooves on the ground and bellowed as it tossed its head in a sort of tormented dance. He went to calm the animal, but something definitely seemed to be unsettling it. Sholto had heard stories that animals can sense things before humans, but he had always regarded this as fantasy. However, the horse was clearly troubled so he decided it would be a good idea to move on. He mounted the horse ready to continue on his route. As he looked towards the river he saw the cart and the mule with the white mane. This time it was much nearer and just approaching the bridge. A young woman was driving the little cart which contained a bale of hay. The woman had long brown hair which fell to her shoulders. As the cart jolted along the path her hair tossed from side to side. She wore a green tunic with long tight fitting sleeves. The top few laces on her tunic were undone revealing glimpses of her ample breasts. Her long skirt was fastened with a belt around her waist and her feet were placed astride of the shafts which attached to the mule. The woman directed the animal along the pathway, pulling the reins from side to side to keep the animal in line. Sholto was stunned by how attractive this peasant looked as she drove the cart over the rutted path, like a voluptuous warrior queen.

Any lustful thoughts that may have formed in his head were soon dispelled as two men suddenly appeared from below the bridge and grabbed the halter attached to the mule bringing the whole cart and its contents to a shuddering halt. The woman stood upright and lashed the reins to break free, but one of the men grabbed her arm and dragged her unceremoniously off the cart. For a moment Sholto watched incredulously as this act of highway robbery unfolded, but then a tide of anger took over as he remembered his own experience at the hands of a bully.

Without any thought as to his own safety he rode at speed directly towards the bridge. It never crossed his mind that he might not be able to control the situation. Seeing him approach, one of the thieves twisted the woman's arm up her back and pushed her roughly against the side of the cart. The other stood in the road before the mule and menacingly unsheathed his sword. Sholto dismounted and walked purposefully to within a yard of the man. It was only then that he remembered that he had no weapon of his own.

"This is not a good plan," snarled Sholto. "Your thieving is not going to happen. Go home if you want a future."

"She be the thief," snapped the thug, in a heavy Cornish accent. "Smuggling brandy she be doing."

Sholto took another step forward and replied sharply, "Whatever she is doing, it is not your business. Let her go." He was in no mood for explanations or justifications.

"Or else?" snarled the thief with an arrogant smirk. "You have no weapon, and I saw you limping. It is you who should go home."

"I don't need a weapon to deal with the likes of you," retorted Sholto angrily.

The thief's face became contorted in rage and without another thought he blindly lunged towards Sholto, his sword raised maliciously. The clapper bridge was constructed from slabs of granite placed across columns immersed in the river bed. The narrow confines of the area leading up to the bridge restricted movement. Sholto anticipating the assault, sidestepped the onslaught and landed a fierce blow on the back of the thief's head. The blow knocked the thief off balance and he crashed heavily onto the granite slab at the start of the bridge. There was a sharp crack, like the sound of someone stepping on a dry branch as the thief's neck snapped on impact. He let out a gasp before collapsing, completely immobilised, and died on the bridge in front of the mule. Sholto picked up the man's body and threw it into the river.

There was a moment of inertia as everyone contemplated what had happened. Sholto moved towards the other thief who was still pinning the woman to the side of the cart. As he neared them the thief swung the woman round and pushed her forcefully into Sholto who caught her firmly around the waist to stop her falling. Momentarily, they were clasped in an embrace, her body pressed against his. She felt so soft, slim and curvaceous that Sholto had an impulse to maintain their embrace. His thoughts were interrupted by the thief who had retrieved the horses previously hidden in a bend of the river just downstream from the bridge. The woman released herself from Sholto's arms and leaned on the side of her cart. She felt shocked, violated, and humiliated. This day had started so well. She had been feeling so much better before this crude interruption. Her anger suddenly boiled over and she spat on the ground.

Addressing the thief her face was like thunder as she shouted at the culprit of her misfortune. "You stupid fool, was it worth your friend dying for a bladder of brandy?"

The thief ignored the comments as if the words he had heard were a foreign language. He did not look left or right, but remounted his horse without a word. As he left he looked vengefully over his shoulder towards Sholto and said ominously, "When Troy hears about this, you will regret what you have done."

Sholto could see that the woman was trembling. She was clearly upset by her ordeal. He quickly tied his mount to the cart and after helping her aboard he started to drive the mule forward across the bridge.

"My name is Sholto, where were you heading?" he asked. The woman told him that her name was Jade Denke and that she was delivering the hay to the stables next to the inn at Blisland.

"It is about two miles up the road," she said rather sheepishly. "I sometimes make this journey to help my father when he is busy."

"Those two rogues tried to rob you for a bale of hay?" asked Sholto with a hint of suspicion in his voice.

Jade spoke quietly. "They belong to the Lamphill gang, and I think Troy is their leader. They are a ruthless, cruel gang, who try to control the trade in smuggled goods. They protect you when you trade under their umbrella in return for a commission. Otherwise they resort to intimidation."

"Are you smuggling something?" asked Sholto.

"My parents operate a business about twelve miles north west from here, Jade explained. My father has a fishing boat, but fishing is a hard, dangerous job and so a bit of extra trading helps the finances. Everyone does it around here. I am carrying some duty free brandy to a customer in Blisland."

"I would have thought that smuggling was just as dangerous as fishing?" Sholto replied. "Your father could go to jail if he gets caught."

Jade gave a wry smile and continued. "Whenever the authorities impose high rates of duty smuggling is inevitable. Rich people know how to avoid their taxes and receive knighthoods. Fishermen use their initiative to evade taxation and receive jail sentences. It can be dangerous, but it's more virtuous than being in debt."

"So the thieves were after the brandy because you are not part their scheme," said Sholto. "Now I understand, but where is it?"

Jade pointed to the bale of hay. "There are two bladders filled with brandy in there."

"Bladders?" enquired Sholto.

"Pigs' bladders," Jade replied with a cheeky smile. "They make strong, flexible containers and are easy to hide!"

"I hope you washed them thoroughly before you filled them with brandy!" said Sholto in an attempt to lighten the atmosphere.

Their laughter echoed over the moor. In these circumstances mirth was in short supply, and it quickly evaporated to be replaced by a more sober mood as they both contemplated the possible consequences of their actions. Sholto felt shocked at the violence that he had unleashed. He had never been an aggressive person. The conflict in Acre had made him battle hardened, and the changes in his behaviour worried him.

Having broken the ice the remainder of the journey to Blisland was uneventful. They unloaded the hay, delivered the brandy and Jade received her usual payment without a word to anyone about their ordeal. One hour later they were heading out of Blisland on the track back to the river, a fresh mule hitched at the front of the cart. Although Jade was by now much more composed, Sholto was aware that she remained nervous because she periodically turned and looked furtively over her shoulder as if checking to see if they were being followed.

In an attempt to reassure her Sholto reminded her that the delivery was complete. "You are safe now. Those thugs got what they deserved. I don't think they will bother you again today." Outwardly he sounded confident, but privately he felt uneasy.

Reflecting for a while Jade sighed with a sort of sad resignation. "We are both going to have a problem with them because they belong to the Lamphill gang. They are unforgiving, violent, and totally lacking humility. They intimidate people in order to maintain credibility and I fear that they will try to exact revenge on both of us for what happened today."

Sholto realised that he could not just abandon her to continue her route back to Trebarwith unaccompanied whilst she remained so vulnerable. He decided to ask if she wanted him to accompany her on the journey home. Knowing that women were not permitted to stay at the preceptory, he explained that he would have to call back at Temple to return his horse and collect his belongings. This would mean a small detour.

Jade felt guilty that Sholto had become implicated in her troubles, but on the other hand she was afraid for her life if the gang intercepted her on the way back. His presence made her feel secure and she liked his direct and unassuming manner. She would be glad to spend more time with this gallant stranger.

She turned towards Sholto and said, "I am already indebted to you for saving me this morning, but if you would accompany me back to Trebarwith I would be very grateful."

"Well that's settled," Sholto replied as he swung the cart to the right, heading in the direction of Temple. "Consider me to be your escort."

It was now late afternoon and they were about two miles from Temple. Jade was intrigued to discover more about this stranger who had rescued her and her cargo from the hands of the robbers and asked Sholto where he was working. He had time to give a summary of the mission he had been on to the Holy Land and how he was staying at Temple before returning home to Ireland. He avoided any mention of the chest containing the scrolls or the treasure that was moved from the Temple Fortress in Acre. Jade listened with growing dismay at the ordeal that Sholto had suffered. She was sad that he had survived Acre only to be confronted by criminals in Cornwall. Before she had time to say anything she caught the distant, but unmistakable sound, of hooves pounding the track. They were being followed. Looking back, Jade caught glimpses of a group of four horses, the heads and shoulders of the riders rising and falling as they vigorously whipped their mounts in pursuit of the two fugitives.

"I think The Lamphill gang is on our trail," confirmed Jade.

They entered the grounds of the preceptory just ahead of the gang and were making their way to the stables when the four sweating horsemen raced past them and surrounded their cart in the stable yard. Sholto jumped down from the cart as Troy, the leader of the group, a scruffy individual with an old injury that formed a red valley down his cheek, addressed him.

"You killed Haden and must pay," he shouted to Sholto.

The thief who had been at the bridge glared at Jade who was still sitting on the cart and snarled, "She is a thieving whore who will get what's coming to her."

Jade said nothing, but made a rude gesture in his direction. Realising that it would be futile to reason with the members of this gang as they seemed obsessed with vengeance, Sholto shrugged his shoulders.

Looking at Troy he said, "I have more respect for the creatures that crawl over the moor than I have for you and your gang."

Troy turned crimson, his face contorted like a screwed up bag, and he moved to draw his sword, but before he had pulled it from his belt the bolt from a crossbow smashed through his arm and the sword fell to the ground with a metallic clatter. Troy screamed with pain and clasped his shattered arm. The servant who had been working at the stables walked out from the shadows of the stable block whilst reloading the crossbow. Then Trebighe's deep voice vibrated around the yard and everyone turned to see him approaching with a battle axe in one hand and a large dagger in the other.

"I do not tolerate trespassers on my land. You have one minute to leave before my brother from the stable releases another bolt."

"He slaughtered our mate," bellowed one of the gang stabbing his finger in the direction of Sholto, "We want justice."

Trebighe laughed. "You think you are going to be judge and jury on our land?" He was now standing shoulder to shoulder with Sholto. This man is one of our brothers and he is under our protection."

The problem that this gang had was that their lust for violent revenge was greater than their collective intelligence. However, they had belatedly come to realise where they were. It had dawned on them that it had not been wise to have violated a Templar preceptory where knights were in training. Nevertheless, this realisation was insufficient to overcome the seething anger of the thief from the bridge and he moved towards the cart gathering his weapon from a sheath on his back. Trebighe swung his axe which had a blade on one end and a pointed spike on the other. The spike smashed through the man's upper thigh breaking his leg and severing the muscles. The thief bellowed like a mad bull, his leg broken, bleeding and limp. His groans seemed to galvanise the rest of the gang as they realised that they were no longer assassins, but being assassinated. Like startled deer, they turned and fled. A trail of blood stained the cobbles of the stable yard marking the scene of the conflict.

Trebighe looked over towards the servant with the crossbow, "So our training is not without its uses," he mused. "Thank you for saving our guests."

They all looked up at Jade who remained seated on the cart, her brown hair dropping onto her shoulders and her breasts barely contained within her blouse. Her attraction was hard to ignore even in this monastic setting and Trebighe was worried that she would be a distraction to the brothers.

"Get the lady a shawl," Trebighe instructed the servant. "Take her to the kitchens. She will need refreshment."

He turned to Sholto who was bending to pick up the discarded sword, "Let us go to the church where we can talk."

Once in the privacy of his room within the church Sholto explained the sequence of events which had unfolded that day on the moor.

"You seem to be doomed to rescuing distressed females," said

Trebighe remembering what Sholto had told him about Jasmin in Acre. "The criminals will not trouble you again today, but they are stupid and without chivalry. Our order believes in acting nobly, but they are possessed with a full complement of deadly sins. It is likely that those members of the gang who are still able bodied will continue to hunt you down. Their credibility in the protection business depends on a reputation for fear and intimidation."

Sholto sat on his bed with his chin resting on his hands. "What is your advice?" he asked.

"Well you cannot stay here with the woman, and yet you are duty bound to return her safely home." Trebighe frowned as he thought of a solution. "If you leave now and head north on the main road towards Exeter after about five miles you will come to a village called Trewint. Just through the village is another called Fivelanes where the carriages stop on their way to Exeter. Take the first left turning and within half a mile you will come into a village called Penpont. You should be able to find a room there at the inn. After an overnight stop you will have plenty of time to travel to Trebarwith by way of Davidstowe and Slaughterbridge. This means that you will not have to cross the part of the moor near the Lamphill woods which is where the gang have their base."

There is one problem though," Trebighe sighed. He was thinking about Sholto's mission.

"You are concerned about the scrolls in the chest," said Sholto anticipating what Trebighe was going to say next.

"Exactly, I would advise that you leave the chest here for the time being, after all this is a Templar estate. When you are back in Ireland you can send your archivist here or contact me and I will arrange safe transportation to Mellifont with one of our brothers."

"Is there anywhere secure here?" enquired Sholto.

Trebighe gestured for Sholto to follow him and they both left the room together with Sholto carrying the chest. Trebighe lit two candles from the church altar and passed one to Sholto. He opened the smaller door which was next to the entrance to Sholto's room and they descended a short flight of stone steps to the base of the crypt. There was a musty smell of dust and decay. Shadows darted around the stone walls as the flame from the candles flickered around the arches and the low stone vaulted roof. The crypt was the size of a large room and supported the choir area of the church immediately overhead. Scattered around the walls were four stone tombs covered in dust. The whole crypt gave the impression that it had been unvisited for years. Trebighe still carried his battle axe and after inspecting the tombs he selected one which was inscribed with 'SEPULCRUM PROTI MARTYR' and using the axe as a lever he started to prise open the lid.

"It's come in handy today," he said with a wry smile as he put pressure on the weapon. "This is the tomb of Saint Protus to whom the church in Blisland is dedicated," Trebighe gasped. "He was burned to death centuries ago and his remains sent to rest in this tomb."

Sholto help him slide the heavy lid which moved grudgingly with a deep, grating sound.

"Just as I thought," said Trebighe peering into the tomb, "Martyrs' tombs only contain ashes so there is invariably lots of space available for other items."

"Are we desecrating a grave," Sholto remarked, his brow furrowed with concern.

"Desecration is when there is no respect for the dead," replied Trebighe. "Saint Protus would forgive us disturbing his resting place if he knew it was for a good cause."

Sholto still felt a little uneasy about this operation, but he placed the chest inside the tomb next to a cloth which held Saint Protus's remains. They closed the lid which slid back into place with a dull thud.

"It will be safe there for the time being," said Trebighe reassuringly as they both retreated from the crypt.

Back inside the church Trebighe wrote a receipt for the chest and stamped it with the Templar's seal. "The holder of this receipt can use it to gain access to the preceptory for the purpose of retrieving the chest," explained Trebighe. He folded the receipt and inserted it into a leather pouch.

As he put it in his pocket, Sholto noticed that the symbol of the Templars was embossed into the leather cover of the pouch. Two riders on one horse reminded him of Trevaie. The two men walked back to the kitchen where Jade was finishing a plate of pork and apple.

"A rare person and an even rarer moment," Sholto remarked, realising that Jade was probably the only woman ever to have eaten at the preceptory.

Jade took hold of Trebighe's hand and shook it. "Thanks for what you have done today," she said warmly. Then she turned to speak to the servant who had been at the stables, "Thank you too".

"I wish you both luck on your journey," said Trebighe as he and Sholto embraced. "Give my regards to the abbot when you get back to Mellifont Abbey."

None of them could have foreseen that within a week Trebighe would be relocated to Cyprus where he would die, with honour, during a battle involving invading Turks. Meanwhile, deep in the crypt, the chest and its contents remained hidden as life went on as normal in the preceptory at Temple.

CHAPTER 10

Overnight Stop

The mule had been fed and watered at the preceptory, but it was weary, and by the time that Jade and Sholto arrived outside the inn at Penpont it was getting dark. The 'Ring O' Bells Inn' was situated near the Norman church. Its tall granite tower standing like a sentinel in front of the backdrop of hills which formed the edge of the moor. The innkeeper, a man with a round, ruddy face and belly as large as a beer barrel was not very accommodating. He wore a white apron which made him look like a penguin and stood in the entrance with hands on hips insisting that his inn was full. From the raucous noises coming from the bar it seemed as if it was full of drunken men. Sholto extracted one of the gold coins from the depths of his tunic pocket and showed it to the innkeeper. The sight of the coin changed his stance from obstruction to construction almost instantaneously.

"There is space in the barn, if you don't mind spending the night with the beasts," he said with unconvincing conviviality.

Sensing his customer's hesitation he quickly added. "Freshly baked bread, pork and ale for breakfast, make no mistake." His newly found hospitality only thinly disguised his insincerity.

Spending the night in a barn was not an attractive proposition. To travel on in the dark would be dangerous and the mule needed resting. There was little option, but to accept this dubious offer and so Sholto drove the cart into the barn and started to unhitch the mule.

"Let's hope the beasts are better company than the innkeeper.

Clearly money is his priority, make no mistake," whispered Sholto borrowing the innkeeper's phrase.

The barn was divided into bays so that the horses could be tethered and groomed individually. There was a supply of fresh straw piled against one wall. Jade found some blankets used for covering the horses and by piling clean straw into the back of the cart she made a reasonably comfortable bed. She looked across the barn to where Sholto was inspecting the wound on his leg. His injury was still sore and Sholto had sat down on a bale of straw to bathe the wound with water. Jade was shocked to see the extent of the injury and was concerned that Sholto had somewhere comfortable to sleep. Sholto began searching for somewhere to set up his own bed when Jade interrupted him.

"When you told me about your fight in Acre I didn't realise how seriously you had been hurt," she said. "It would be much more comfortable for you on the back of this cart".

Sholto hesitated. He was not used to female company and had never slept next to a woman before.

"Don't you want to sleep next to a smuggler?" she asked conscious of his unease.

This was an invitation that Sholto had not been expecting, although he knew from their travels that Jade could be very direct. She was warm and convivial, but did not waste words on triviality. He looked over to where she was perched on the cart; her long brown hair dropping to her bare shoulders and without further hesitation climbed aboard to join her.

"I expected to be spending the night in the chapel," said Sholto, reflecting on his arrangement with Trebighe. "I never imagined that I would sleep next to a smuggler on the back of an old cart. Fortunately, you are the most beautiful smuggler that I have ever seen."

Jade smiled at the compliment as Sholto hung his sword on the side of the cart. She looked towards him and said, "I suppose that you think smuggling is evil?"

This was a question that Sholto had not thought about so his response was intuitive.

"Well, I suppose it is a form of dishonesty." He lay back on the hay with Jade leaning towards him resting on her elbow, her eyes looking directly into his.

"I think the King is more dishonest", she whispered, "because he is already rich and tries to make himself even richer by imposing high taxes on hard working people."

Sholto could feel the sincerity of these words burning into him as he focused on Jade's lovely blue eyes. "I understand what you are saying as to why people smuggle, but it is difficult to justify one dubious activity by comparing it to another."

"So you do think it is evil," Jade persisted.

This was the type of conversation that Sholto sensed could lead to discord. He decided to try and divert the drift of their dialogue.

"There may be times when a little dishonesty can be justified in order to avoid unreasonable demands," he said slowly. "It is easy to judge people when you are not in the same position. Tell me about your life in Cornwall, it can't have been easy."

There was a brief silence before Jade responded. She lay back on the straw and looked up at the timber beams which formed the roof of the barn. It was warm and comfortable lying next to Sholto and Jade felt reassured by his presence after the trauma earlier in the day. Memories of her time with Mathew drifted back and the pain of the break in their relationship returned. Her eyes filled with tears as she started to tell Sholto about the person she had known since she was a child and grown to love.

"We knew each other so well," she said. "I didn't expect that he would leave me and go off with someone else. Maybe we started to take each other for granted. I was looking forward to settling down and starting a family. It felt like I had been betrayed."

Sholto could see that Jade was vulnerable. Obviously, her emotions were still raw and he felt sympathetic towards her. He slipped his arm around her shoulders and gently pulled her towards him. She turned her head towards him and their lips met. After the stress of battle, the pain of injury and the loss of friends, lying with Jade was so comforting. He felt passion rise within his body, but was uncertain of how to proceed. Feeling embarrassed he decided that honesty was the best option.

"I have never been with a woman before," he said quietly.

Putting her finger on his lips, Jade snuggled up closer so that her body pressed tightly against his. "There's nothing to know that nature won't take care of," she whispered.

Her body was soft and warm, her curves so exciting to explore and her kisses so sensual, that the pressures of the outside world receded as quickly as an ebbing tide. Jade felt secure with her rescuer. Her unhappy memories evaporating as she lay with Sholto on the cart, their bodies entwined.

The next morning Sholto woke up early. Jade lay next to him, her arm draped over his chest. Although it was early, Sholto felt renewed as the pleasant memories of last night returned. The stress and tensions of conflict which had haunted him had receded and instead he felt exhilarated and positive. He stretched his arm out and noticed that his hand did not seem to be shaking. Whether it was the fact he was lying down or wishful thinking he could not be sure. As Jade stirred he leaned over and kissed her on the cheek. Her eyes opened and she raised herself onto her elbows as the appetising smell of newly baked bread wafted into the barn.

"I originally intended to go straight back to Ireland you know," Sholto said as he moved off the cart. "Now, I am glad that I let Trebighe persuade me to stay."

"Perhaps fate brought us together," replied Jade. "Sometimes circumstances have a way of working favourably. Fortune was certainly on my side yesterday."

They followed the smell from the oven and found that the ruddy-faced innkeeper was as good as his word. He had produced breakfast of white bread, carvings of pork and two mugs of ale. Suitably fortified the couple embarked on the last leg of their journey to Trebarwith. Even the mule seemed to have become revitalised after his night in the barn and they made good time on their travels. By early afternoon Jade turned the cart onto the steep downhill track which led to Trebarwith Strand and home.

As they reached the bottom of the valley Sholto noticed that the land had widened allowing a torrential stream to gush over the rocky ledges and on to a sandy beach beyond. He found the view of Gull Rock with the surf breaking around it majestic. Above and to their left was the narrow plateau cut into the cliff about thirty feet above the rocky part of the beach. Sholto saw the inn which also doubled as the harbourmaster's office perched on this terraced balcony of land. The cliff on the opposite side of the cove dropped steeply into the sea with its lower sections sculptured into shelves after centuries of wind and waves had eroded the rock face.

Outside the inn a solitary figure could be seen sitting on an upturned boat repairing a net. He was wearing the distinctive yellow apron and leggings worn by fishermen. When the cart appeared around the last bend of the track the figure stood upright, motionless, staring expectantly at the approaching cart. Jade immediately recognised the fisherman as her father. He was a distinctive man, his lined face adorned by bushy eyebrows that seemed bleached in contrast to his weathered features. On his head a floppy hat covered strands of unruly grey hair. Jade waved vigorously and her father raised his hand in recognition.

CHAPTER 11

House Arrest

The cart stopped outside the Inn and Jade jumped down and ran straight to her father. She had always been close to him and they embraced affectionately. Her father frowned and Sholto heard the concern in his voice as he spoke.

"You have been away longer than your mother and I expected. It is a great relief to see you back safe and sound," he said.

Excitedly, Jade gestured towards the cart where Sholto was still seated, before introducing her companion. "This is Sholto. He risked his life to save me from The Lamphill Gang when I was crossing the moor. They chased us and threatened us. That is why Sholto escorted me home."

Jade stepped to one side and her father walked over to the cart holding out his hand in friendship. "Edward Denke," he pronounced, "Thank you does not seem enough to convey my gratitude for what you have done. Come inside and tell us what happened."

Sholto climbed down from the cart and tethered the mule to a post from which a sign hung displaying a picture of a grey rocky island in a stormy sea. Written across the bottom of the picture in bold letters was 'THE STRAND'.

Seeing Sholto looking at the sign Jade's father shouted over, "I created it myself to attract attention to the inn. It is rather crude, but an effective use of vegetable dyes!"

Sholto smiled and followed father and daughter into the inn. Hearing their entrance Jade's mother appeared from a door at the back of the bar. Sholto was struck by the strong family resemblance. The mother was obviously older, but with the same twinkle in her eye.

"We were getting worried about you," she said as she gave Jade a hug. "In fact, we were just about to send out a search party."

"Well fortunately, I'm alright," Jade replied. She looked over her shoulder and smiled at Sholto. "This is the man who rescued me when I was crossing the moor."

"I just happened to be nearby at the time," said Sholto modestly as he introduced himself. "I am pleased to meet you Mrs Denke."

"You can call me Jane if you like," exclaimed Mrs Denke looking a bit puzzled. "Please sit down and tell us what happened before the customers start to arrive." She knew that once the men started bringing the slate down the track they would be calling in for refreshments!

They found seats around a long wooden table and both Jade and Sholto described what had happened on Bodmin Moor, each adding their own experiences. Jade's parents interrupted periodically to clarify their understanding of various details. When the story came to the end everyone sat back and there was a pensive silence. Jade's father wore a worried look on his face and was stroking his chin nervously.

"When I was outside mending the nets earlier, I saw two men arrive on horseback. I presumed that they were hunters just passing through, but there was something slightly suspicious about them," he remarked.

"In what way were they suspicious?" asked Sholto.

"They did not speak to each other although they were side by side and they appeared to be rather furtive. They were more intent on surveying the buildings than enjoying the scenery. Neither of them passed the time of day with anyone and I noticed a crossbow protruding from a saddlebag on one of the horses. That is not a weapon normally used by hunters around here."

Nobody spoke as Edward leaned back and placed his fingers on his temples. "Thinking about what you have just told me concerning the events on the moor yesterday, I now think that there could be a connection with those hunters. They could have found where Jade came from by talking to the landlord in Blisland. Perhaps I am being too reactionary after listening to your story. I hope that I am wrong, but it is possible that they belong to the gang and have come looking for you."

"Are they still around?" asked Jane anxiously looking towards the window.

Edward spread his hands in a gesture of ignorance. "I need to find out," he sighed.

Edward left the table and went out to deal with the mule. On his way back from the little hut which was used as a stable he noticed one of the men sitting on a rocky ledge on the cliff opposite. He picked up a broom that was leaning near the front door of the inn and started to sweep the path as a pretext to see behind the building. Sure enough he caught sight of the other man perched high on the cliff behind the inn. Both men carried their crossbows and it was obvious that they were watching the building. Edward finished his chores outside and casually entered the inn through the front door. Jade was talking to her mother. Sholto was checking the receipt for the chest which he was glad he had hidden back at the preceptory. The leather pouch emblazoned with the Templar seal lay on the table in front of him.

Edward beckoned for Sholto to come to the window and glancing towards the cliff opposite he said quietly, "I am afraid that we do have unwanted visitors."

Sholto sat back down at the table while trying to think of what to do next. It was going to be a dangerous exit when either he or Jade left the safety of the building. His training told him that the best tactic would be to attack the assassins when they least expected it. The problem was that they were geographically separated and despatching one would very likely alert the other. He was not familiar with the landscape and could not hope to surprise the men in the dark. Sholto knew that he could not stay inside for ever. It was like being under house arrest and his mission was to return to

Ireland. He put the leather pouch back in his pocket as his predicament sunk in. He was surprised by his feelings, but he felt devastated at the thought of having to leave Jade behind. Maybe Jade was right when she said that fate had brought them together. It was not just the intimacy of last night; Jade had filled a void in his life. He enjoyed her company and hated the thought of her being hurt by these violent gangsters.

Turning to Edward he spoke slowly. "Normally, I would leave alone to try and draw the threat away from you. I have to return to Ireland as part of my mission, but I have a dilemma. I do not want to leave without Jade. Neither do I want to put her in jeopardy. It may have been just a short period of time that I have known your daughter, but it has been a deeply emotional time. We have experienced intense, dangerous situations by virtue of this gang and I think that this has accelerated our feelings for each other. I want to stay with your daughter, to look after her and to protect her from these criminals."

Sensing that something was amiss Jade broke off her conversation with her mother and the two of them came over to join the men. Looking at her father's forlorn expression she knew what the problem was without the need for further explanation. She knew that The Lamphill Gang were back and would not rest until their lust for vengeance was quenched. Before she had chance to say anything Edward put his arm around her shoulders and spoke kindly.

"Your friend has to leave for Ireland and he wants you to go with him. Unfortunately, you are going to be in danger whether you stay or leave. What is important is what you want. How do you feel about leaving with Sholto?"

Jade had grown fond of Sholto. She knew that something special had developed between them. She admired his courage and his honesty. He had shown tenderness towards her which she needed after her heartbreak with Matthew. Sholto made her feel valuable and desirable. She felt happy in his company and did not want to lose him.

Moving to position herself next to Sholto she took his hand. Looking into his eyes she said, "You have been so kind to me. You have made me feel happier than I have felt for a long time. I would be so sad if you were to leave me behind. I know there is danger ahead, but I trust you and my heart tells me to go with you."

Jane looked across at her husband and shrugged her shoulders. She knew that she would have to accept the inevitable, but she could not see how any departure could be made safely.

"Are you sure the men are waiting for them?" she asked in horror.

"I fear for their safety if they leave the sanctuary of this inn," Edward asserted with obvious dismay. "If they are part of that Lamphill mob they will be intent on restoring their fearsome reputation."

He walked over to the large stone fireplace with its blackened bricks and store of logs piled in the hearth. Leaning on the mantelpiece he stared at Sholto as if evaluating his worthiness as a suitor for his daughter. He had known Sholto for less than a day, but on the other hand Sholto had saved his daughter from thieves when he could have turned the other way.

Edward finally spoke, confirming something that everyone in the family already knew. "Apart from my work as a fisherman and innkeeper I have some experience as a smuggler."

Aware that workmen from the quay were now beginning to enter the inn, Jade put her finger on her lips.

"Not so loud," she said in alarm.

Ignoring her Edward continued. "I can use my boat to transport the two of you into Padstow harbour. Boats regularly leave Padstow bound for Ireland."

As Jane moved to serve one of the slate labourers, Edward addressed Sholto quietly so as not to attract unwanted attention.

"We love our daughter dearly and of course we will miss her when she leaves. We would have liked to have become more acquainted with you. Unfortunately, this is not going to be possible just now. However, your actions have already proved that you are a man of integrity, and most importantly our daughter says that she wants to be with you. You can count on our full support."

Tenderly, Sholto put his arm around Jade's waist and pulled her closer to him.

"You have my word that I will do my best to take care of your daughter," he said sincerely.

Edward asked Sholto and Jade to accompany him into the room at the rear of the bar where they could talk in complete privacy. The room was lined with wooden panels and in the centre was a strong table covered with miscellaneous bits of fishing gear and a set of scales. Edward explained that he would leave the quay in his boat on the high tide during the night.

"The strangers will be watching the quay closely and will be prepared to intercept if you try to leave that way," he explained emphatically.

Leaning over the table Edward outlined the details of his plan.

"The tide will be coming in at first light tomorrow morning. Before it completely covers the sandy beach I will hold the boat as far inshore as I can. The two of you will need to sprint across the beach and then wade the short distance to the boat."

"How will we get out of the inn without the gang seeing us?" asked Sholto.

Edward strode over to where there was a door discreetly built into the wood panelling of the room. Taking a large key from his pocket he turned the lock and opened the door. A draught of cold, damp air which smelled faintly of a mixture of seaweed and ale wafted through the opening.

"Let me show you our special exit," said Edward beckoning Sholto to follow him.

The door led to a flight of steps cut into rock. The stacks of casks and barrels stored around the room clearly identified this space as the cellar. At the opposite end of the cellar Sholto saw that the rear wall was rock. Edward opened an oak door built into the face of the rock and pointed to the entrance of what appeared to be a cave.

"At low tide you can climb down to the beach at the other end of this passage avoiding the quay in Trebarwith. That cave has seen many barrels of brandy pass through," Edward confessed with pride. "We call it 'The Strand' because it is the fine link that keeps us solvent!"

Remembering his discussion with Jade about the ethics of smuggling the previous night, Sholto decided that avoidance was the best policy regarding this issue.

"We may need a glass of your spirits if we have to creep through there," he said with a wry smile.

"Just remember to be on the beach at first light so that the tide and my boat will be in the right place," replied Edward sternly. "When you emerge from the cave the cliffs will screen you from the area around the quay. Once you venture further out onto the beach there will be a point where you will become exposed to observation from anyone watching from the rocks. You will need to move fast and remain vigilant when covering this short, dangerous section."

They all returned to the upstairs room and Edward went through the whole plan again making sure that they all had the details clear. Finally he embraced his daughter.

"I hope that when you return this gang will have found someone else to intimidate," he said sadly.

It was now evening and workers from the quay were calling at the inn before making their way home. Edward joined his wife to say goodbye as he needed to prepare his boat if he was to catch the tide. Jane was busy serving the influx of people jostling for service at the bar. She was very concerned, knowing that Edward had worked out a plan of escape. She had heard odd bits of the conversation between him and the others. She did not know the details, but anticipated that members of her family were going to be at risk. Her work at the bar demanded that she would have to wait before she could learn more. Edward tried to discretely reassure her that he had taken all the risks into consideration, but the bar was too public an area for a private discussion. They both knew that this was not the time or place to win acceptance of the arrangements. Edward also knew that he could count on her support in an emergency. It was not that he wanted to take Jane's consent for granted. He always valued her opinions and respected her intelligence, but the current circumstances dictated decisive action. If the escape plan was to work he had to move without delay.

"Jade will tell you all about my fishing trip after the inn has closed," he said with a wink. "See you tomorrow."

Jane continued to work with professional detachment, hiding her inner feelings. The discretion of the landlord determined the time when the inn closed rather than any statute. It could not come soon enough for Jane. The usual routine was that most customers had drifted home by 10.30pm. Tonight, she had made sure that the door had been locked to new customers at 9.00pm. Jane had gently ushered everyone out by 10.00pm.

In order to avoid suspicion Edward intended to follow most of the normal practices prior to a fishing trip. There was a damaged area of the sail that needed patching, nets to be loaded, hooks and pots to be stacked on the deck. He busied himself, conscious that unseen eyes were watching his every move. By the time darkness fell he had left on the rising tide.

CHAPTER 12

Journey's End

Although they both felt apprehensive about the early morning escape plan, Sholto and Jade enjoyed their evening together at the inn. Jade had produced bowls of pottage made from leeks. This had been followed by a mixture of fish and dark rye bread, washed down by a tankard of ale. By the time that Jane had joined them they were feeling very relaxed as they related the escape plan to her. Jane listened uneasily as the details of Edward's plan unfolded. She knew that the couple could not stay indoors indefinitely and so she resigned herself to supporting them in any way she could.

"Take these blankets into the room at the back and be ready for when I call you," she said.

"I will keep a lookout tonight in case those horrible men show themselves. You both need to try and get some sleep."

There was limited space in the wood-panelled room at the back of the bar because most of the area was occupied by the large table. The couple knew that they would have to make an early exit at dawn and so they remained dressed, ready for an immediate departure. Sholto had been feeling shabby in his green tunic and old brown breeches. His tunic was stained and a rip had appeared on the left side of his breeches. He was looking forward to replacing some of his old clothing when they arrived in Ireland. He still had some of the gold coins that Theo had given him. As he lay next to Jade the blankets helped to soften the hardness of the floor. There were cushions to use as pillows and their clothes helped to insulate them.

It was still uncomfortable though and Sholto was finding it hard to sleep. He kept thinking of the green fields and the river where he used to fish in Ireland. How good it would be to show Jade the places where he had lived. He imagined being reunited with his friends at Mellifont.

Eventually, his thoughts turned to his mission. In the back of his mind he was worried that if things went wrong in the morning nobody would know where he had hidden the chest. If he did not return and Trebighe was posted to some foreign land the chest would be forgotten. He considered leaving the pouch containing the receipt with the Denke family. The problem was that he had promised the Templars that he would take personal responsibility for the safe delivery of the chest. The Templars were secretive about their business and they would not look kindly on outsiders becoming involved in their affairs. In any case he did not want to put a burden on the family. These thoughts were making it impossible to get to sleep. Ensuring that he did not waken Jade, Sholto quietly shuffled off the floor and went to the big table. He made his decision. He would hide the pouch in the cave with directions as to the whereabouts of the chest. It was not a perfect plan, but it offered a modicum of insurance in case he lost his life in the morning. If he reached Mellifont he would tell the abbot about the chest. Presumably, the abbot would appoint an emissary to collect the chest. Sholto would arrange with the Denke family for the emissary to call at 'The Strand' so that he could retrieve the receipt from the cave. The weakness of this idea was the possibility that someone else might find the pouch by accident.

On the table was an old candle which Sholto lit. Amongst the various items littering the table was a quill and a small pot of black ink dye. There was nothing handy to write on and so Sholto ripped a section from the lining of his tunic. He picked up the quill and carefully dipped it into the ink pot. He remembered that Trevaie had taught him how to use a cypher when they were together in Acre. At that time he never imagined that he would need to use it. Dredging the details of the cypher from the recesses of his memory he carefully drafted a message. Ensuring that the ink was dry he put the cypher in the leather pouch containing the receipt for the chest and placed it in his pocket. It would be most unlikely that any ordinary person would be able to decipher the code, therefore protecting the exact location of the chest. Satisfied with his strategy Sholto stealthily snuggled back under the blankets where Jade still lay asleep.

Lying in the dark, Sholto knew that there was the additional problem of the necklace and key inside the little bible. It was essential to keep these personal items safe. He turned this worry over in his mind without conclusion. Exhaustion finally intervened and eventually he drifted into a shallow sleep. He dreamed he was back in Acre, under attack and with the same sense of doom that haunted him during his time there. The dream came to an abrupt end as Jane shook them awake. Sholto wearily rubbed his eyes. It did not seem very long since he had fallen asleep, but outside dawn was breaking. It was time to leave, to be liberated. They both hoped to make a new life away from the intimidation and the threat of violence. Jade had already been awake when her mother came into the room. She was happy to go to Ireland, or any other place, as long as she could remain with Sholto. The excitement and anticipation of the pending adventure had overcome any lingering tiredness she felt.

"I will be thinking of you," Jane whispered as she hugged her daughter. "Please take care. I am going to miss you. Especially when it comes to delivery time," she added after an emotional pause.

"I know you will take care of our daughter," she said looking towards Sholto who was busy rummaging through his pockets.

Whether it was his dream or just the urgency of the occasion Sholto felt a sense of foreboding. He knew that they would have to rush across the beach and wade through the surf to the boat. He did not want to be weighed down any more than was necessary, especially if they came under attack. He decided that his sword would be more of an encumbrance than a help when speed was more important and so he decided to leave it leaning against the wall.

Taking out the Bible that contained the key to the chest, he placed it firmly in Jane's hand. "This is a precious possession. I would be grateful if you would look after it for me until I return from Ireland. In the meantime, I will let you know if it needs to be passed on to anyone else," he said cupping her hand between both of his.

He then turned, and accompanied Jade into the cellar. They opened the oak door and entered into the cave. Immediately, the salty smell of the sea enveloped them, sharpening their senses. Jade had a lighted torch which flickered off the low roof of the cave and made her blue tunic shimmer like water in a pool. Sholto looked up and saw a little crevice in the rocks just above his head which looked a bit like a collection box and he discretely took out the leather pouch from his tunic pocket and slid it into the opening. It fitted neatly onto a smooth lip of flat rock.

"Hurry up," said Jade as loud as she dared realising that Sholto was not immediately behind her. Her voice echoed round the confined walls of the cave.

"Right here," replied Sholto as he caught up with her. His injured leg was still causing pain when he exerted himself, but adrenalin drove him on.

Jane closed the oak door and returned to the wood-panelled room. She looked around the room where her daughter had been safe only moments before. It was empty now, hollow, like standing in a vacuum. She wanted to cradle her head in her hands and cry, but as tired and anxious as she was, she went to the door of the inn and looked towards the beach.

Meanwhile, Jade led the way through the narrow passage. They rounded a bend after which the cave suddenly opened out and natural light poured through a narrow rectangular cleft in the rocks. It was just a shallow drop down from a flat rock onto the sandy beach. Jade's father had estimated the state of the tide accurately because the entrance to the cave would have been flooded at high tide. After scrambling off the slippery rock the fugitives ran together towards the sea. In front of them they could see the fishing boat, stern to the beach bobbing up and down on the swell with Edward heaving on the oars to maintain his position.

There was a rocky outcrop some way to their right which had been providing cover for a member of the gang. Out of the corner of his eye Sholto noticed the movement of a figure dressed in dark clothing, camouflaged against the grey rocks. The figure levelled a crossbow and recognising the danger Sholto pushed Jade so violently that she sprawled flat out into the sea. The bolt from the weapon hit Sholto in the chest with tremendous force and he fell on the smooth carpet of wet sand at the edge of the sea. He tried to get up, but could not move. He wanted to speak but his body would not respond as searing pain invaded his every sinew. Then he felt a sudden release and the pain evaporated. Sholto felt himself involuntarily elevated above the beach, weightless, ephemeral. It was as though he was conscious of his surroundings, but physically detached from them. He could see Jade kneeling, resting his head in her lap. He could see her father fighting the swell as he beached the boat on the sand. He felt no fear, or pain, as he drifted over the ocean towards where he could see Trevaie beckoning to him. It was like experiencing vision through the lens of a camera as it slowly, but steadily, zoomed out from the beach. As the land receded from his vision he joined Travaie. A little further in the distance was his mother. They both smiled at him as they all floated ever further from the earth towards an infinite horizon. The affection he felt for Jade was still there and he was conscious of her feelings towards him. Sholto felt a strong conviction that one day they would be reunited, and this was a comfort as he passed into the unknown dimension of the spiritual world.

Jane had witnessed events on the beach from 'The Strand' with abject horror. She had always felt nervous about the plan Edward had devised, but she had been unable to think of a better alternative. The shock of seeing Sholto executed on the beach and the spectre of her daughter's grief stung her into action. Gripped by a furious impulse to avenge the violence inflicted on her family, she grabbed the sword that Sholto had left leaning against the wall and rushed headlong down to the place where the men had left their horses tethered. Anger mixed with a numb sensation seethed through her. Sickened by the stupid, unnecessary violence that had been unleashed, she wanted to wreak revenge on the perpetrators.

It wasn't as though she hadn't anticipated that there would be trouble. True to her word she had stayed up last night to check if she could see where the two men had positioned themselves. She had looked through the windows, but could not see them. Then undeterred by the risk to herself she had decided to go outside the inn. There had been no sight of the men, but their horses had remained tethered to a tree near the end of the track that ran down the valley. Jane was not an impulsive person, but on this particular night she made a bold decision. Moving stealthily she had quickly reached the horses. Although it was dark she had managed to locate the straps which held the saddles in place and untied the buckles. She calculated that if there was to be trouble tomorrow, then the gangsters would be denied a quick departure.

Satisfied that he had extracted retribution, the assassin who had killed Sholto appeared scurrying around the rocks at the top of the beach. The Denke's neighbour, George Lursk, was guiding his horse and cart along the track that ran to the quay. As usual he was delivering milk to the inn. Suddenly, the dark shape of the criminal appeared, darting across the track like a jackal. The farmer's horse reared up in fright and the cart had to pull up sharply. The farmer stood up on his cart and was about to shout at the man when he saw Jane, sword in hand. She was approaching the tethered horses. The assassin saw the woman too, but completely ignored her, passing her by as if she was invisible. Feverishly, he untied his horse, pulled its head round with the reins, and attempted to mount the horse with his foot in the stirrup. The whole saddle came off the horse under his weight and he was dumped onto the ground, landing with a dull thud. Disorientated, the man started to get up, but before he could regain his footing Jane charged at him and with all her strength she pushed the weapon into his chest. A demonic look of rage momentarily crossed the man's face and he clutched the sword with both hands before collapsing in a heap beneath the hooves of his agitated horse. Jane looked up and saw the second criminal returning down the cliff path that ran behind the inn. He raised his crossbow and fired. She stood frozen to the spot as the bolt headed straight at her. Her life was saved only by a piece of good fortune. One of the mounts, unsettled by the violence, moved and the weight of its body knocked her to one side. The bolt whistled past embedding itself in the tree to which the horses were tied.

Responding to the seriousness of the situation, George impulsively pulled out a pitchfork from the rack of tools on his cart and advanced to the path on which the second criminal was standing. Seeing the raised pitchfork, and not having time to reload the bow, the thug retreated up the steep path. George pursued him knowing that as the path reached the top of the cliff it continued along the border of an open field. On the right of the path was a steep grassy ledge with clumps of thrift growing precariously on the slope. The ledge fell away for a few yards after which there was a sheer drop of over one hundred feet into the sea.

Reaching the point where the path reached the summit of the cliff the criminal decided to make his stand. He took another bolt from his belt and was in the process of loading his bow. George was within range of attacking the thug and without delay threw his fork like a javelin. The man ducked to one side and the fork narrowly missed his left shoulder. This sudden movement dislodged the gravel on the edge of the path and the man lost his footing. He started to slide down the grassy ledge feet first, clawing with his hands at clumps of vegetation. He groped with such desperation that he succeeded in clutching a clump of thrift with one hand. This tenuous grip prevented his body going over the edge of the cliff. His bow lay on the grass a few feet to the left.

The criminal looked up, fear and panic in his eyes, and spoke to the man he had intended to kill only moments before.

"Help me," he implored.

George lay down on the path and glared at the stricken man. He did not feel inclined to do anything, but some primeval sense stirred him into action. Picking up the discarded bow, he lengthened the reach of his arm by extending the weapon towards the man. The man moved to grab the bow in desperation. His movement was too much for the clump of thrift which came out of the ground, roots trailing in the air. The man let out a final shout as he slid down the grass and over the edge of the cliff, causing an avalanche of gravel to fall with him. His cry trailed away as he dropped towards the black rocks which glistened below in the morning sun. His body was never recovered.

Jane was still standing next to the body of the gangster she had slain when George, drenched in sweat, finally descended from the cliff. He took her in his arms and tried to console her. Her face was ashen and she was visibly shaking. Her angry impulse had now been expended to be replaced by numb shock. She had felt possessed with vengeance. Now that the red mist of fury had subsided, she felt empty and stunned. If she could have rewound time she would not have let herself repeat such deadly actions. Trying to remain rational she pointed to the beach.

"My husband and daughter are still down there, but those criminals killed her friend," she said weakly.

"We'll go to them in a minute," George replied. "First we need to remove this body from view."

He helped Jane to her feet and led her to the milk cart which still straddled the track.

"Lead the horse to the stable by the inn and I'll join you there in a minute," said George firmly.

The gangster laid where he had been slain, his eyes vacant, an empty hollow shell, testament to a wasted life. George recovered the sword and wrapped the body within one of Edward's discarded fishing nets that he found dumped nearby. He made sure the two horses were secure before re-joining Jane at the stables. Together, they walked straight down over the rocky approach to the beach. Before them they could see the rocky island and the fishing boat anchored at the edge of the sea. Edward, helped by Jade, was pulling Sholto's body across the flat wet sand leaving tracks which led back to the boat. They looked round in alarm at the sound of the approaching couple.

"It is alright, the danger has gone," George said quickly. "Both assailants are dead."

Looking at Jade's tearful face he said gently, "Go back to the inn with your mother, I will help Edward now."

Jade was in no condition to argue and without a word she meekly returned to the inn with her mother. Jane did her best to calm her daughter, but Jade was inconsolable. She had been so happy, excited to be starting out on a new life with Sholto. Suddenly, all that had disappeared, cruelly replaced by grief and emptiness. The inn looked the same familiar place and yet to Jade it seemed different. Different because Sholto was no longer there and would never return. How could this have happened so suddenly?

On the table rested the little Bible containing the necklace and key. As Jane glanced up her eyes focussed on it. Sholto's last words flooded back with haunting clarity. "This is precious, I would be grateful if you would look after it until I return." Now he would never return and she would need to ensure that the book would be preserved. She picked up the Bible and put it in Jade's hand.

"Sholto would want you to keep this," she whispered softly. She knew from that moment that the Bible would remain with the family for ever.

Later Edward recounted the whole tragic story to his friend and neighbour. George agreed to allow the family to bury Sholto's body in a corner of one of his fields where there was an open view across the Atlantic Ocean. It was a sunny, west facing plot, where Sholto could be laid to rest facing towards Ireland. The family had a granite headstone ENGRAVED which read

SHOLTO KELLEY
1270-1291
'Gave his life for a friend'

They all agreed that it would be imprudent to involve the authorities in these tragic events, with their invasive questions, enquiries, courts and bureaucratic practices. It was far better to remain discrete and avoid official intruders. No one wanted the spotlight to fall on Trebarwith. This was the traditional way that Cornish people preferred and it felt justified under the circumstances. Edward had taken the gangster's body, still wrapped in the old fishing nets, and deposited it at sea. The body, weighed down by the nets, swirled round and round, deeper and deeper, until it disappeared from sight. It was unmourned, unforgiven, unwanted, and unclaimed.

Sholto's burial was attended only by the Denke and the Lursk families. They had taken the vicar of the parish church of St Materiana Tintagel, into their confidence and he presided over a short private, ceremony. After everyone had left only Jade remained sitting next to the stone, holding the necklace which Sholto had left, looking out to sea, thinking of what could have been.

George included the two gangsters' horses with his own livestock at the monthly cattle auctions in Wadebridge. The Lamphill Gang never troubled the family again. It was not known whether the gang had been destroyed by depletion, or whether they felt fully avenged by Sholto's death. The family were just content to be clear of them. The normal routines of life gradually returned to 'The Strand' and the Denke family, but not for Jade. She discovered that she was with child. On 17th March, 1292 she gave birth to a baby boy. Jade regularly visited the neat little grave in her neighbour's field, always fondly remembering her short but eventful relationship with the man who saved her life.

In his brief life, Sholto had made both a physical and a spiritual journey. He had started on the crusade with ideological certainty, but had become more and more disillusioned. The experience of battle, of human suffering, of bereavement, of corruption, and of different cultures had been a harsh education. It had left him feeling less certain and had softened his rigidly held beliefs. His view of religion had been dramatically adjusted. His mind had matured and his beliefs evolved. He had always remained a true Christian, but had come to the conclusion that no one religion had a monopoly of the truth. He had recognised that people were equally regarded by God whatever their creed. After the lonely journey home he had felt fortunate to have met Jade. Having survived the ordeal in Acre, only to be intimidated in Cornwall had been unlucky. Jade had given him new hope and aspiration that had been missing in his life. Now his body lay at rest in a Cornish field. He lived on in Jade's memory and his spirit was rekindled in their son.

Jade treasured the little Bible. While nobody in the family understood the significance of the key it strongly reminded Jade of her time with Sholto. On the day she gave birth she had insisted on wearing the necklace. Later, she looked fondly at her baby boy and she saw the same blue eyes looking up at her that she had seen with Sholto.

"You look just like your father," whispered Jade." You can have the same name – Sholto. Sholto Denke."

The significance of the symbol on the key was never recognised, but it was inherited by Sholto Denke who ensured that it remained in the custody of his family. The story of what happened at Trebarwith Strand in 1291 was retold and became embedded in the family history. No member of the family could have predicted that six centuries later another tragic and dramatic event would occur in the same cove. A time shifted coincidence which would challenge the family to further evaluate their stewardship of the cherished necklace.

LURSK AND DENKE FAMILY CONNECTIONS (13C and 14C)

	Trebarwith Farm	**Trebarwith Inn**
1291	George Lursk + Wife	Edward Denke + Jane Denke
	Son – Mathew Lursk	Daughter – Jade Denke
	Mathew Lursk + Wife	Jade Denke +Sholto Kelley
	Daughter – Charlotte Lursk	Son – Sholto Denke
1310	Charlotte Lursk* + Sholto Denke	

*Charlotte inherited Trabarwith Farm from her father Mathew Lursk. After marrying Sholto Denke the family name changed to Denke.

The double - sided 13C Templar Seal

Part 2

Sometimes the bad things that happen in our lives put us directly on the path to the best things that will ever happen to us.

CHAPTER 1

Cheshire 1890

James Cartwright was looking forward to seeing his brother again. The trip back from Cornwall on the 'Mersey Rose', a square rigged, three masted Barque of 550 tonnes displacement, had been routine, but he had been away for more than three weeks. Sea trips were always tougher in the winter months. Sometimes the vessel would be unable to leave port because of adverse weather conditions; storms, gales, and fog were the usual problems. Often the trip became longer than scheduled as the ship could only average about 12 knots under calm conditions. It was now Christmas Eve, 1890 and this was the last trip of the year for the crew of the 'Mersey Rose'.

A light breeze was blowing from the north making the temperature feel cold with a threatening grey sky which extended in all directions. A few flakes of dry snow fluttered across the Mersey estuary, dusting across the deck. Slate coloured waves slapped against the hull as the boat moved with the rising tide at a steady four knots. James felt relaxed as the ship navigated along the estuary with the cranes and warehouses, a familiar and reassuring sight. They passed the Port of Liverpool and an hour later after navigating between the buoys that marked the deep water channel on the Cheshire side of the estuary they were safely berthed at Saltport, Runcorn. The cargo of china clay from the Cornish quarries now ready to be loaded onto barges for the final leg of their journey along the Trent and Mersey canal to supply the potteries in the Midlands.

James had always had an ambition to go to sea although his

family had traditionally been involved in dairy farming on the fertile Cheshire plain. After leaving school at fourteen he had found work on the barges which plied the River Weaver. The barges, called Weaver Flats, because of their shallow draughts, transported salt from the mines at Winsford to Runcorn. James had often watched the boats at Saltport and sometimes chatted with the crews of the sea going vessels before returning to his barge wondering what life would be like at sea. Still only seventeen years of age he was given the chance to enlist on the 'Mersey Rose' as an apprentice. He spent the first year cleaning, painting and polishing, but he also studied and established himself as a regular deckhand. He had never been very studious at school but he loved working at sea and this is what motivated him to learn the theory of his trade.

After his third year he was given the chance to work with the first mate where he learned navigation and qualified as a certified seaman. James worked well with the captain of the 'Mersey Rose', an ageing seaman who was respected for his knowledge and experience. Captain Stansby liked to operate an orderly ship. He was strict, but fair and consistent in his dealings with the crew and they responded with loyalty and hard work. Officers and crew referred to him warmly as Captain Stan for short.

It came as a surprise when James heard that Captain Stan had summoned him to his cabin. He had just finished packing his bag ready for disembarkation and was due to meet his brother William on the quay, and so he hoped the call would be a brief one. James entered the cabin where the captain's large frame was casually draped in his black, leather upholstered chair. On his head was perched a seaman's cap that pressed down on tufts of white hair which bushed out untidily. His grey beard framed his rugged features making his tanned skin seem even darker brown in colour. He was smoking a small cigar and the cabin was filled with a fog of aromatic smoke. Captain Stan was a gregarious character, always pleased to share a joke and chat with members of his crew. James sensed that today he seemed a little lethargic and there was sadness in his eyes. The captain gestured for James to sit down on a wooden chair next to a table covered with shipping charts.

"I heard that you plan to spend your leave ashore this time, but I've some important news for you before you go," said the captain in his familiar gravelly voice.

He frowned as he looked at James. "The next trip in January will be my last one."

"Your last trip?" repeated James. He could not disguise the surprise and dismay he felt at this unexpected announcement.

The captain dropped James's wages on the table and held out his hand to wish him a happy Christmas. "It's been good working with you, but my time has come to retire. I need to spend longer periods at home caring for my wife," explained the captain. "Her health has been deteriorating." Captain Stan was not a person who was predisposed to discuss his private affairs whilst at work.

"Sorry to hear that she is unwell," said James sympathetically. "I had no idea that you were considering retirement."

He shook the captain's hand whilst bending over the table to pick up his wages with the other hand. Their heads were closer now. The captain had a very firm handshake which was typical of his solid and reliable personality.

"We will miss you," said James. "The whole crew will miss you. Nobody was expecting you to retire just now."

Captain Stan turned his head and blew out a fresh cloud of smoke. "I had not intended to retire just yet, but sometimes circumstances tell you when the time has come." He then leaned forward purposefully, "I spoke to the owners about my retirement and they have accepted my recommendation that John will replace me as captain after our next trip to Cornwall."

This was another surprise, but James was relieved that it was John Kenyon, an officer he knew and respected who would eventually become the new captain.

"There is one other matter," added the captain as James readied himself to leave. "The owners are happy for you to become first mate."

James felt stunned. On the one hand he felt flattered to be

considered for the position, but on the other his inexperience made him feel apprehensive. The duties of the first mate involved planning each trip, routing, navigation, timings and the safety implications. It was a skilled and crucial position.

"But Captain, I have only worked with John Kenyon over the last few trips," James replied. His words rolling out hesitantly as he considered the extra responsibility the job would carry.

"Some people do two hundred trips and are never ready to take the job on," the captain growled. "You'll be competent, and I have no doubt that in time you will become an excellent first mate."

"Well I have been fortunate to have had a good teacher," said James sincerely.

James thought for a minute and then responded without further hesitation. This was a good opportunity and he would be foolish to turn it down.

"I would be honoured to accept the position. Have a good Christmas," he said to the captain as he opened the cabin door to exit.

"Just make sure you're back on 2nd January to take on the next load," said the captain. "We have a contract to deliver salt to a customer in Cornwall."

As James approached the gangway which linked the ship to the dock he waved goodbye to John Kenyon who was on deck. The prospect of being the first mate of the 'Mersey Rose' and still only twenty one years old was going to take time to sink in. Still, it was something good to celebrate as 1891 approached.

This year, James had been invited by his older brother, William, and his wife Jayne, to spend Christmas at their house in Wharton, near Winsford in Cheshire. James usually stayed aboard the 'Mersey Rose', in the cabin provided by his employers. The crew were a closely knit team and after a time they had become almost like a family. This was fine for most of the time, but this was Christmas and he was pleased to be joining his brother. Sometimes James envied the settled life that William enjoyed, but after a short time ashore he always looked forward to returning to sea. There was something compelling about the space and freedom of the ocean. It taught you to respect the power of the sea, to cope with the unpredictable weather patterns and to plan each voyage carefully. Nature was something that you could never underestimate or take for granted. The sea represented a vast lonely place where you had time to reflect in relative isolation. It was also a place where you were vulnerable to the elements and were often reminded of your mortality.

William had travelled to meet James with a horse and trap from the farm where he worked. From where he was positioned he had a clear view of the 'Mersey Rose', her black painted hull rearing up above the level of the dock like a monstrous whale.

Seeing James sauntering down the gangway William raised his arm and shouted, "Over here!"

"Sorry to keep you waiting," James said excitedly throwing his bag into the cart. "I just heard from the captain that I am to be promoted."

"Well that sounds a fine way to end a voyage," William replied as he turned onto the main road. "I can see that you are in good spirits. There is plenty of ale at home. Your news gives us a good excuse to celebrate with some liquid refreshment!"

The snow was still threatening to fall, but had not become heavy enough to cover the roads. The brothers were so involved in their conversation that they had completely disregarded the weather until their safe arrival at William's house. Now they noticed that the surrounding fields were dappled a mixture of green and white. Their breath hung in the air like mist as they spoke. Jayne had agreed to cook them all a meal with a goose the farmer had gifted to William in recognition of his hard work. When they entered the building the brothers were pleased to be met with the tasty aroma of the cooking drifting from the direction of the kitchen.

William Cartwright had never been as ambitious as his brother, content to follow in the family tradition of farm labourer. He had worked for the farmer at Moulton Hall Farm for a long time and was treated well. Recently, he had achieved a reputation as a skilled wheelwright. The tenant farmer paid rent to the squire for the use of the farm and sub-let one of the small houses on the edge of the farm to William and Jayne.

William was of slightly heavier build than James although their faces did show a family resemblance. Their parents had instilled the same values into their sons. Learn a skill, work hard, be honest, and reliable. Happiness and success will follow. The words of their father sometimes returned like an echo at times when crucial decisions had to be made.

Never staying anywhere for very long, James had a few female friends, but had not formed any serious relationships. Most of his friends were also his shipmates. By way of contrast, William had met Jayne at Moulton Hall Farm where she had started working as a milkmaid. He was repairing a broken wheel on a cart and had noticed the pretty, blonde haired girl walking towards the cowshed followed by the farmer and the squire. He had seen the girl before and was waiting for a chance to talk to her. Thinking that the other men would make off in different directions, he had followed to see what was going on. To his disappointment the squire stayed with the girl as she disappeared into the cowshed. The squire looked a little tentative about entering the cowshed and William heard the farmer reassuring him.

"Jayne will show you the process," explained the farmer in a cheerful voice. "I'll be back in a few minutes."

Apparently, Jayne had been asked by the farmer to demonstrate milking techniques to the squire. She had sat down on her milking stool in preparation to milk a large black and white cow. Feeling a little self-conscious she had neglected to tell the squire where to stand. Unfortunately for him the beast had no regard for status and suddenly arched its back letting out a trumpeting blast of methane before releasing the contents of its bladder in the form of a polluted waterfall. A tidal wave of urine swamped the poor squire's expensive shoes.

William witnessed the squire marching out of the cow shed, red faced, his feet swamped, muttering, "That filthy beast has ruined my new leather boots." He had jumped on his horse and ridden off at speed, too angry and humiliated to see any humour in the situation.

William entered the cow shed to see Jayne, her face flushed with embarrassment. The two farm workers looked at each other with pensive, serious expressions. Their frowns reflected this unexpected drama which they anticipated could end in bad consequences. The serious looks did not last long. Spontaneously, they both become convulsed with laughter.

"I hope he didn't mean you were the filthy beast," William had joked before introducing himself.

That incident had been two years ago and William and Jayne had been together ever since. The last twelve months had been difficult for them. Jayne had been expecting, but sadly, she had suffered a miscarriage. The emotional scars were taking time to heal. Now, on Christmas Eve, she had put her culinary skills to good use preparing a superb meal of goose, potatoes and vegetables for the three of them.

The house was not very big with just two rooms upstairs and a kitchen and lobby below. There was a sink in the kitchen and a tin bath was propped against the wall next to it. A roaring log fire was burning in the hearth which was where the cooking was done. The toilet was in a small building outside. The three family members sat down in the kitchen around a wooden table. Cooking smells drifted around the house making James feel ravenous after his travels. They ate heartily, the Cartwright brothers catching up with events since their last meeting and Jayne asking about life at sea and the ports that James had visited. It was such a convivial atmosphere that James was able to fully relax. The warmth from the fire was welcome after the sea journey and they drank and talked until the early hours. Eventually, William and Jayne decided to retire for the night. As he stood up William leaned over the table and spoke to his brother.

"After the Christmas break I've had a special request from the farmer at Moulton Hall Farm to complete work on the squire's cart. The job has to be completed urgently because the cart is to be used as a stage for the band during the New Year's Eve celebrations at the

Manor House. I have to repair two broken wheels and you can help me if you like."

"Why doesn't the squire just leave the cart in position at the Manor House?" asked James.

"The plan this year is for a hog roast at the Manor House. I am told that the squire will drive the cart with the band aboard and the villagers will follow behind. The whole procession should arrive at the bridge over the River Weaver in time for fireworks as the clock strikes midnight," explained William.

Although the ale was clouding his thoughts James still had the presence of mind to make an enquiry, "If we fix the cart will we get invited to the celebrations at the squire's Manor House?"

"Not only that, but I'm told that extra pay is due for completing the work promptly," replied William with a glint in his eye.

"Consider me another pair of hands," smiled James.

Jayne had prepared the rear bedroom for James to sleep in, but after he was left alone he fell asleep, slumped untidily on the fireside chair. During the night he had a strange dream. He had been in a large cave, dark and wet, but at the far end was a light where a horse stood with two riders. The rider at the front held the reigns with one hand and was pointing to somewhere in front of the horse with his other hand. James couldn't see what the man was pointing at, but his mouth moved as if in a silent movie. The man's face looked strained and his body language displayed anxiety. He had the demeanour of someone concerned to attract attention towards an unseen object in the direction in which he was pointing. James wanted to follow but felt immobilised, his legs were like lead and his energy was totally sapped.

The next morning over breakfast James felt slightly hung over, but he accompanied William and Jayne as they walked into town. They intended to visit their parents during the day and spend the evening at home. Traditionally, the evening was spent playing games like charades, cards and dominoes. The exercise and socialising soon cleared James's head and took his mind away from his dream, but from time to time it returned. He felt slightly disconcerted by it and found it difficult to supress it.

As the days passed the vividness of the dream faded and as he set off for work at Moulton Hall Farm with William, he was looking forward to meeting his brother's workmates. The pair returned at the end of the day with a joint of pork, courtesy of the farmer, and the promised invitation to the festivities at the Manor House. The work had been hard, but the rewards made it worthwhile.

CHAPTER 2

Leaving Liverpool

James had enjoyed the warmth of his welcome during his visit to the town of Winsford. The New Year celebration had been the best he could remember. It was with some sadness that he bade farewell to William and Jayne on Friday 2nd January, 1891. Yet, he loved the freedom that his job gave him and he felt comfort in the prospect of returning to the lonely, open spaces of the sea.

"Make sure you bring back some more tasty stories from the South West when you return," shouted Jayne, as James trudged towards the River Weaver. "Try to find a woman to make you happy," she added with a twinkle in her eye.

James pulled up the collar on his merchant seaman's coat as there was a cold wind blowing. He knew that he could hitch a lift on one of the Weaver Flats which would take him back to Saltport fifteen miles away. The preparations for the next trip were preoccupying him as he arrived at the port in the early afternoon. The 'Mersey Rose' needed to sign a crew of ten as the rigging on her three masts demanded strength and skill when under sail. The ship was always kept in good condition with her black wooden hull and white superstructure. Yellow streaks of rust ran down the hull from the anchor and from the deck bollards. Thick ropes attached to the ship extended to the bollards on the dock. On the stern 'Mersey Rose' was painted in red just above the name of her registered port 'Liverpool'. Her bows and stern were higher than the midships section of the hull and between the foremast and main mast was the open hatch cover. A gangway provided access to the middle decked area of the ship where there was a small gap in the rails. Overhead a crane was preparing to lower rock salt through the open cover and down into the hold. Captain Stan was always meticulous about distributing the load equally and ensuring the cargo was secure.

In the part of the ship between the main mast and the mizzen mast were the white-painted cabins, each with a round porthole window. The wheelhouse was located above the two rows of cabins. Stair ladders ran down to the deck from doors located on both the port and starboard sides of the wheelhouse. The lower cabins accommodated the crew members. The remaining cabins at deck level were reserved for the captain, first mate, and any occasional passenger. Access to all the cabins was from watertight doors which faced towards the stern section of the ship.

Most of the crew already knew each other as they lived nearby and regularly signed with the company for the return trips of the vessel to Cornwall. However, on this visit James learned that they would be carrying a passenger. Looking at the manifest he was surprised to see that the passenger was a young woman called Coral Byford.

Coral was a twenty two year old student from the University of Manchester. She was part way through a research project about medieval legends. Her father had been a History lecturer and when she was young her family had lived in Tours, France for a year. Her father had been seconded to work on a project in the History Department of the university. At the weekends Coral's father took his family on visits to museums, chateaux, and sometimes to a royal castle. One particular trip always reminded her of when she first caught the history bug. She was about ten years old and the family had stopped to visit Chinon Castle in the Loire region. A guide was explaining how Phillip II had imprisoned leading members of the Knights Templar in one of the towers. The Grand Master of the movement, a man called Jacques Molay, had been taken from the tower and burned to death for heresy. The most powerful memory was when she was shown writing carved by Jacques and other condemned prisoners in the stone wall of the tower. She had run her fingers over the carving. Here was firm evidence that history was about real people. People who had lived long ago, suffered and died. Coral felt empathy towards them as fellow humans and had a passion to find out more about their lives, their beliefs, their heresies.

After the family returned to England her father had become ill with cancer and had died. Not long afterwards her mother was killed in a riding accident. There had been some sad, dark days, but Coral knew that her parents would have been proud of her academic achievements. It was fortunate that she was of an age to reside at the university which was like a second home.

At the university her professor had introduced her to the legends of King Arthur. She was intrigued by these strange stories and had been trying to extract historical fact from embroidered romance. Coral was a meticulous researcher and spent long hours reading, until she found evidence to corroborate the stories left by historical sources. Who was this chivalrous king called Arthur who had been immortalised in Sir Thomas Mallory's book published in 1485, *Le Morte d'Arthur*?

Her professor was now in Cornwall examining recent archaeological evidence retrieved from the area around Tintagel. He had been an inspiration to Coral. His knowledge of the subject was impressive and his enthusiasm in the lecture theatre was infectious. He made history come alive with stories of expeditions, his photographs and actual relics. In tutorials, he had been so approachable, so easy to talk to, that he was like a friend. When he asked if she would like to join him in what he described as 'King Arthur country' she readily agreed. She knew that she would miss her friends, but she expected that this would only be a limited expedition.

It was once the excitement of this compelling invitation had died down that Coral started to investigate the practical transport options. She knew that it could take many days to reach North Cornwall by road, especially in winter. She would be carrying some of her books which would make her rucksack heavy. She did not relish the prospect of carrying it about during the inevitable overnight stops in dusty public houses. It was a conversation with the university bursar that gave her the inspiration to travel by sea after he told her about the salt trade between Cheshire and Cornwall.

Now, as her carriage approached Runcorn she brushed back her long brown hair and tied it back to stop the wind blowing it across her face. The shipping company had told her to be ready to board no later than three o'clock and a quick glance at her watch showed that it was that time now. Coral was a very punctual person and she had made arrangements to leave Manchester in plenty of time to cover the thirty miles to Runcorn. She could hardly contain her frustration at the delay caused when the carriage hit a deep rut. It had taken over an hour to replace the broken wheel, but now the carriage was passing under the towering railway bridge which linked Runcorn to the Lancashire side of the Mersey estuary. Five minutes later she was on the dock struggling to harness her heavy rucksack. The coachman seemed concerned for her safety and although he meant well, his assistance was actually an unwelcome interference. It was a task best completed by the wearer. An impatient shout from one of the other passengers diverted his attention and Coral was relieved when he returned to the carriage.

She walked towards the 'Mersey Rose'. Captain Stan was pacing anxiously around the deck muttering about the tide waiting for no man or woman. He too was a very punctual man and did not take kindly to having his plans disrupted. Coral preferred to keep a low profile and she climbed the sloping gangway carefully. She wanted to avoid tripping and inviting a spectacle. Once on board, she was met by James who moved to help her remove the burdensome rucksack. Feeling the weight of it he couldn't help but wonder how she had managed to cope with it on the journey from Manchester.

Captain Stan was in no mood to provide a warm welcome and without glancing in the direction of his guest, he barked a stark command. "Show her to her cabin and get back up here fast. It will be high tide in fifteen minutes."

"Is he always so charming?" asked Coral.

"He'll be fine once we get out of the port," said James, showing Coral into her cabin. "I'll check you are alright later when you have had time to settle in."

Coral surveyed her little cabin with its wooden bed, built in table, cupboard and wardrobe. One round porthole provided the only natural light and it was locked shut. There was a misty view of the dock through the accumulated film of salt that covered the glass. An oil lantern hung on an 'S' hook from the ceiling and some old orange floats decorated the wall nearest the door. It was rather a dreary cabin and Coral felt grateful that she would only have to spend one night in there.

A chorus of shouting from somewhere outside ended abruptly as the ship gave a sudden lurch when the crew cast off the last of the ropes. Operating from this far up the River Mersey needed careful seamanship. The vessel had a shallow draught, but it was fully laden. They slowly edged away from the quayside and entered the River Mersey at a point called Runcorn Gap. Here the river was three miles wide and the Lancashire coast was clearly visible on the starboard side of the ship. It was Monday 5th January. 1891 and the 'Mersey Rose' was underway on her voyage to Padstow with its cargo of salt and one intrepid passenger.

The ship passed Birkenhead where the river flowed at the narrowest point on its route to the sea. George's Dock, in Liverpool, was just ahead on the starboard side. James could see grey clouds scurrying overhead, threatening to fill in the clear blue patches from which shafts of sunlight played hide and seek with the cloud. Ahead, there was a bright ambience which announced the vastness of the open sea with Wallasey on their port side and Crosby on the starboard. James looked up at The Red Ensign flapping from the top of the mizzen and remarked to John Kenyon, the first mate.

"It looks like we're going to have a following north westerly wind."

John frowned as he replied, "Yes it will help, but I'm worried about the barometer reading."

James checked the barometer and sure enough he could see that air pressure was falling dramatically.

"We should be able to keep ahead of bad weather once we start heading south," he said hopefully.

The ship navigated along the deeply dredged Queen's Channel out of the estuary and after passing the last lightship they turned to port following the main shipping route south. The crew energetically hoisted the top sail on the main mast, and the staysail jibs from the foremast giving the ship momentum from the following wind. The bows ploughed through the swell sending back a moderate spray that glistened on the deck like dew. James was on first watch and he could see the darkening shape of the North Wales coast on the port side of the ship stringing out beyond the Dee Estuary. The distant Welsh mountains shrouded in scurrying cloud. Further to the south he could see the intermittent beam from 'The Skerries' lighthouse warning of the treacherous rocks on the tip of Angelsey.

It was now five o'clock on this boisterous January night. Standing on watch when it is dark could be lonely. Tonight there were few stars, but the wind was keeping visibility good and sometimes it was possible to see the twinkle of lights from the shore. James often reflected on the lives of the people in the distant towns as they passed in the dark, five miles offshore.

Captain Stan joined him about an hour later to check their position. "I always know we are well underway when I see the 'South Stack' light," he remarked.

"The barometer has dropped," said James "Do we need to adjust our sails?"

"I'll keep an eye on the weather until next watch, you can check if our passenger has settled down," replied the captain as he looked down to check the compass bearing.

Moving around the ship was a little precarious at the best of times. The lights were dim, and this evening there was spray on the stairways. It needed a firm hand on the rails to adjust for the pitch and roll of the ship as it cut through the swell. After reaching his cabin James collected some biscuits and with care navigated his way through the gloom to the passenger cabin. He knocked on the door. A faint voice called, "Come in." Coral was lying on her bed feeling slightly queasy.

"I've brought you some ginger biscuits," said James. "I thought you might need something to help you settle for the night. It's unfortunate that it is so noisy and unsteady."

Coral thanked him and pointed to her large rucksack.

"I've got plenty of food in my bag, but I just don't feel hungry. I will be glad when we reach port because the motion of the ship is making me feel a bit sick. When do you expect we will arrive at Padstow?"

James leaned on the cabin wall and thought carefully.

"Under normal conditions we should arrive tomorrow afternoon. The weather conditions aren't good, but we have a professional crew who should get us through on time. Have you got to meet someone?"

Coral hoisted herself onto her elbow and said casually.

"I plan to head for Camelford where I expect to join a colleague from the History Department of Cornwall University. He is renting a couple of rooms at a coaching inn called 'The Stonemason's Arms'. If it is too late to get transport, I will stay the night in Padstow."

James moved to the door and noticed the books escaping from the top of the rucksack. "It looks like you have a whole library of books in there. What are you studying?"

Coral took a deep breath. She felt better talking to someone.

"As part of my History degree I am studying legends and North Cornwall is where King Arthur's castle is reputed to be situated."

"I have read about King Arthur and the Knights of the Round Table. I always thought the stories were fictional. Do you think Arthur was a real person?" asked James with a note of incredulity in his voice.

Coral was used to scepticism related to her subject so she replied without feeling irritated by the question.

"Well that's what we're investigating. Sometimes research shows there was a real person, but over the ages their identity has become altered and obscured. Sometimes the stories represent an idea or a concept that the author wants to communicate. For example a person may be writing about splicing grapevines, as a way of explaining interconnections between family genealogies."

"It sounds complex," said James before adding after a pause, "but interesting. If you need anything you will find someone is always on watch in the wheelhouse. Just be careful to hold the rails firmly because of the heavy swell."

Taking a bite out of the ginger biscuit Coral propped up her pillow and thanked James for taking the trouble to visit.

"I'm hoping that it will be calmer tomorrow so that I can come out for some fresh air," she said optimistically.

James made his way back to where Captain Stan was checking their course. The wind had increased and rain and spray were driving relentlessly across the decking.

"It's turning out to be a dirty night," observed James as he stood beside the captain.

"Too right, and by the reading on the barometer it's going to get worse." The captain's gravelly voice had a hint of concern in its tone. "I'll ask the lads to replace the main sails with storm jibs."

James climbed down the stair ladder and made his way to his quarters. John Kenyon was just leaving his cabin on his way to relieve the captain and start his watch.

"I hope you can get some rest with this turbulence," he said. "It looks like it is going to be a long night!"

James bade him good night just as the bows plunged through a heavy swell. The ship shuddered and a deep groan made it sound as though every bolt was straining. It was difficult to get into bed with the vessel pitching and rolling. Once installed James fell asleep oblivious to the crashing waves and howling wind. He was tired after a busy day and he knew that he was on first watch the next morning.

CHAPTER 3

Storm at Sea

It had been one of those nights of light, unsettled sleep filled with flitting dreams, each portraying a distortion of recent events. In his subconscious, James was on a ship that was vibrating under a thunderous onslaught from huge waves. A violent concussion jolted James awake. As he re-orientated himself to reality he knew immediately that something was wrong. The movement of the ship felt laboured and abnormally sluggish, as though the sea had taken more control than the crew. An ominous creaking made it sound as if the vessel was groaning in pain. Suddenly, there was a sharp crack, followed by the sound of splintering timbers. A deep thud resonated through the hull as the foremast snapped and crashed onto the deck. These were sounds that James had never heard before and a shiver of fear ran through him.

He dragged himself up the stair ladder to the wheelhouse where John Kenyon was struggling with the wheel to keep the ship on course. The foremast lay snapped like a twig across the deck, held on board only by the remains of the rigging. There was a risk of it causing further damage if it became snagged below the waterline. Members of the crew were fighting to secure the mast on the deck against the constant swirling mass of water washing over the vessel. Although it was now dawn, the white crests of the enormous waves contrasted sharply against the glowering sky. The wind raged around the ship, whining stridently through the rigging. Visibility was poor with shrouding spray driving relentlessly across the immediate field of vision. In the wheelhouse John grimly held the wheel, his face strained, staring ahead as if frozen to the spot. He felt as though the damp and cold had seeped into his every joint.

James checked the barometer which was still falling. "Storm Force 10," he shouted.

John gave an almost imperceptible nod, "Better call the captain."

There was no need for a call. Woken by the commotion on deck Captain Stan fought his way into the wheelhouse feeling every one of his sixty years. Alarmed by the loss of the foremast he urgently set about assessing the extent of their predicament.

"What was our last position, John?" he yelled above the crescendo of the storm.

"Caught a glimpse of the North Light on Lundy about half an hour ago," John shouted back. So we must be about ten miles North West of Hartland Point."

"The wind is still strengthening and has veered more to the west," James commented.

The captain stroked his chin, concern for their safety evident from the frown furrowed across his brow. He tapped James on the shoulder and pointed to the compass.

"Take the wheel and try to keep her bow to the south west. When the ship peaks on each wave John and I will check for the Hartland Light. If we can navigate within five miles of the shore we will try to ride out the storm in a more sheltered position."

Another turbulent hour passed before their vigilance was rewarded.

"Hartland Point Lighthouse," shouted John excitedly. "We seem much nearer to the coast than I expected though."

"It's the strength of this gale and the loss of the mast," grumbled the captain, more to himself than anyone else.

As if to confirm his thoughts the ship ploughed into a deep trough and as its bow came up a monstrous wave crashed over the whole ship. The vessel shuddered and immediately they were horrified to see that the main mast had been stripped away leaving only a splintered stump and a few twisted lengths of rigging. They were now at the mercy of the storm. They knew that the westerly direction of the wind would drive them towards the North Cornish coast. Only the storm jib on the mizzen mast remained intact. Captain Stan stared into the gloom surrounding them, their predicament lying heavily on his shoulders. Suddenly he turned, his decision made.

"Gather a couple of the crew and try to cut away that rigging before it gets entangled around the rudder. Then ask everyone to come up here please," he barked to John. Then he quickly added, "Don't forget the passenger."

James, who was struggling with the wheel, felt shocked that he had forgotten about Coral. The poor girl must be terrified, he thought. The captain reached into the locker and brought out a distress flare.

"Let's try to alert the coastguard," he shouted. "In the meantime, if we can get to more sheltered waters we can deploy the sea anchors and heave to until the storm passes."

***

As the storm raged over the high, rugged cliffs of the North Cornish coast George Denke was struggling to rescue one of his sheep. Most of the flock had been gathered the previous day into a sheltered pen. This unfortunate animal had trapped its leg in a thicket of gorse. Its mournful bleating carried across the fields by the gale. George had worked all his life on Trebarwith Farm, but this was one of the worst storms he could remember.

The farm had been in the Denke family for generations. As far back as anyone could remember there had always been a farmhouse in the sheltered fold of the land cradled amidst the sloping fields. The present building had been reconstructed from the stones of the previous farmhouse sometime in the eighteenth century. George had been born and brought up on the farm and now it had been bequeathed to his stewardship.

The Denke's had always been a close family. George had listened to stories from his grandparents, who, in turn, had learned them from their own ancestors. Although he listened politely, he did not always concentrate fully and some of the details remained muddled. Over time the stories may have become increasingly vague, but they still contained elements of truth. One story that had embedded itself into his memory concerned a boy who had lived in an old smuggler's inn down in Trebarwith Strand. The boy had married into the family and had brought with him a necklace to which was attached a key. When he had shown interest in this story his mother had shown him the necklace. George had been struck by the distinctive symbol on the key, two riders on one horse. It made him think about the importance of sharing during hard times. The necklace and the hollow Bible in which it was kept, remained a treasured possession of the family and George preserved it carefully. There had also been some vague talk of an old gravestone at the edge of the farm, but George had never been clear as to its historical significance and had taken little interest in it.

A few years ago George had married Catherine, a girl from nearby Tintagel. They both shared the work on the farm and enjoyed life together. George had inherited the same characteristics as his ancestors. He was hardworking, honest and reliable. He was also a man of routine. Catherine often joked that if invaders were spotted off shore during an afternoon, he would ignore them until he had completed the milking!

Out on the farm this morning it was cold and wet with a penetrating wind gusting in from the sea. Fortunately, the fields on this part of the farm fell away from the cliff edges which bordered them, affording a modicum of shelter from the westerly gale. Even so, George was glad of the protection that his waterproof jacket and leggings gave him. As he struggled to release the distressed sheep he glanced towards the sea and caught a glimpse of a vessel amongst the angry grey waves. She was near Tintagel Head. Two of her masts lost, drifting helplessly, towards the Otterham rocks just off Trebarwith Strand. As he finally extracted the sheep a flare shot up from the stricken vessel momentarily illuminating the grey gloom of the sky. In answer another flare soared into the sky from the direction of the coastguard station at Willa Park near Boscastle.

Farming was a job which suited George's careful organisational skills. It took most of his time, but he was also a member of the North Cornwall Volunteer Life Saving Brigade. This group of local volunteers were organised and trained under the jurisdiction of the coastguard. When there was an emergency the coastguard at Willa Park alerted a network of rescue stations along the relevant part of the coast. Each rescue station had equipment stored for emergency rescues. The equipment included a Manby's Mortar, a device used to shoot a line from shore to a wreck, flares, floats, and medical supplies. The volunteers organised observers at intervals along the track a ship was taking until they were sure where to gather in order to effect a rescue. On this occasion, George knew that the call would most likely go to the station based at Trebarwith Strand. A rough estimate of wind and tide predicted that it would be the closest location from which to mount a rescue.

Having returned the sheep to the flock in the pen, George hastily returned to the farmhouse and informed Catherine of the situation. Then he wound his way down the steep path that provided the quickest route to Trebarwith Strand. As he approached 'The Strand', a rebuilt hostelry on the site of a former smuggler's inn, he could see other members of the group assembling. He was greeted by Jake, the inn keeper.

"Have you received a call from Willa Park?" asked George.

Jake shrugged his broad shoulders. He was a tall heavily built man and could sometimes be forthright.

"Nothing," answered Jake. "I saw the ship earlier and have been trying to contact the members of our group."

"When I saw the ship I decided to come straight down," explained George.

"You are going to be needed. It is not going to be an easy rescue if she goes down here," Jake replied. His face wore a worried frown.

***

Coral and the ten crew members huddled in the wheelhouse where their plight was summarised by Captain Stan.

"We are about a mile from Tintagel Head. This is a violent storm with winds in excess of force ten. It shows no sign of easing and is blowing us inshore assisted by the tide. We have lost two masts and our two sea anchors are not holding us in position. My officers inform me that within an hour we will drift with the swell towards the Otterham rocks. They are offshore from a place called Trebarwith Strand. The coastguard has acknowledged our distress flare, but I fear that the ship will be lost, because we are unable to control her movement."

Nobody spoke and a shocked silence enveloped the gathering as each person considered their predicament. Coral's voice was quiet and soft, but as she spoke everyone turned to listen.

"Will the coastguard send a lifeboat?"

"It is doubtful that they will be able to launch a boat in these seas," answered the captain. "Now that they know we are in difficulty they will post men along the coast at intervals so that they can signal to the rescuers where we are. They have ropes and winches which can be used if we are near to the beach. We have a life raft and some belts, but I can't hide from you the fact that all our lives are in great danger."

There were many stunned and fearful faces in the wheelhouse as each person reflected on their fate. The realisation that they may never see their loved ones again was deeply distressing. They had not been prepared for this. They knew that they would never be able to say goodbye. Not a word was exchanged. The crew just stared into infinity. Then without cue or invitation, a solitary voice started to sing, hardly audible above the crescendo of the storm outside...

"Farewell to Prince's Landing Stage,
River Mersey, fare thee well
I am bound for North Cornwall,
A place I know right well"

Spontaneously, more voices joined the chorus with which they were familiar…

"So fare thee well, my own true love
For when I return, united we will be
It's not the leaving of Liverpool that grieves me
But my darling when I think of thee"

By the time the last verse was reached the whole crew were in full voice, singing their hearts out in defiance of the storm.

"Oh the sun is on the harbour, love
And I wish I could remain
For I know it will be a long, long time
Till I see you again"

***

During the morning the volunteer observers had watched from the cliff tops as the 'Mersey Rose' was driven inexorably towards the subterranean reef which ran out from the cliffs beyond Trebarwith Strand. Messages were passed from observer to observer until they reached the main body of rescuers assembled in Trebarwith Strand. In the howling, gusty wind, the cold and the rain they discussed launching a rescue boat, but gave up when it became obvious that conditions were too severe. A small boat would be smashed against the rocks before it could reach deeper water. In any case the men did not think it would be possible to row against the fury of the storm.

George stood outside 'The Strand', which was built on a terraced section of the cliff. Part of the building was used as the harbourmaster's office as it overlooked the quay where slate was transported from a nearby quarry. A large shed at the rear of the building housed the rescue equipment. He pulled his waterproof hood closer round his head. A mist of icy spray danced in the air, and everyone tasted salt on their lips. George knew that an inn had stood here from as far back as anyone could remember. He was aware that his family was distantly connected to the old inn and the stories his grandparents had told him flooded back. Standing next to the inn keeper in this emergency situation he was reminded of the brotherhood which always bound the locals together when times were hard or individuals were in trouble. They often worked together, drank together and today had come together to help those in peril on board the 'Mersey Rose'. Ropes, winches and the Manby's Mortar had been brought down the track to the rocky beach although the severity of the storm was going to make it difficult to deploy them.

Through the spray and the riotous waves the vessel came into view round Penhallic Point. She was in a sorry state, with her two masts gone, and her anchor chains trailing like pig tails. The rescuers saw that she was flashing a light to locate her position and they replied with a flare in acknowledgement. The vessel appeared and disappeared through the swell and the spray, but as she was driven between Gull Rock and the cliffs at Dennis Point, a huge white capped wave crashed across her decks ripping away the hatch covers and the wheelhouse structure. The vessel disappeared in a frothing, frenzied cauldron. There was a deep groan as if the vessel was sending out a last cry of pain. Then a spout of seawater as she took her last gasp and sunk to the bottom taking everything with her. It was five past two in the afternoon. The rescuers fanned out across the quay, scanning the turbulence for any sight of survivors. They searched for over an hour, but in vain. A combination of the raging sea, spray and the driven rain made visibility poor. It had been a fruitless search without sight of anything but bits of torn wreckage.

Eventually, Jake invited the drenched and freezing rescuers into the inn for shelter. The mood was sullen as they all slumped onto the wooden benches. Jake's wife, Vicky, had helped her husband run the inn for years. She had a convivial charm that endeared her to the customers and her personality suited her role in front of house. Today she looked around the room at the bowed heads and she saw the vacant sadness in the rescuers' eyes. She decided that it would be worth a trip to the cellar where she knew that they stored the brandy.

George sat solemnly with his elbows on the wooden table, his chin resting on his hands, gutted at his helplessness in saving the crew.

***

Whilst the singing was in full voice Coral made her way with great difficulty to her cabin. On the walls were strung some old floats which were intended to be a type of primitive decoration. Hurriedly, she emptied her rucksack and stuffed as many of the floats inside as she could manage. It was an awful sacrifice to jettison the books that were her resources, but she knew that they would be of little use if she was dead. She fastened the rucksack tight and secured the straps firmly around her shoulders. She looked like a turtle, and the bag was heavy, but hopefully it would provide buoyancy once she was in the sea.

Moving about the ship was dangerous, but so was staying in the cabin. She decided that the safest action would be to return to the wheelhouse. It was higher above the water and she would be in a prime position to hear the captain's instructions. Braving the violent movements of the ship and managing to defy the elements proved to be just as daunting as Coral anticipated. Soaked and breathless she scrambled into the wheel house wearing the cumbersome rucksack. Coral could see James gathering a length of rope attached to a lifebelt. Captain Stan stood legs braced fighting to control the wheel whilst issuing final directions for the crew to launch the life raft. Barely visible through the spray was John Kenyon valiantly helping to clear debris from the deck so that the raft could be accessed by the crew. Everyone knew that they had to abandon ship. It was obvious that the ship was abandoning them.

The turbulence from the ocean reached a crescendo as the vessel drifted into the shallower water where the submerged rocks formed a reef. Suddenly, with a deafening roar, a huge wave descended onto the vessel. In a cacophony of splintering wood, shrieking wind and pounding water the wheelhouse was torn from the vessel. The last thing Coral remembered was the sight of the granite mass of Gull

Rock framed in the starboard window of the wheelhouse before she was deposited into the sea. Gasping for air, shocked by the cold, and with a salty taste of the ocean in her mouth Coral realised that she was alive and afloat. The rucksack had proved to be remarkably buoyant, but she was being swept towards a high black cliff and felt powerless to change direction.

When the wave struck James was caught off balance. He glimpsed the captain gripping the wheel, his knuckles as white as the foam. There was the sound of rushing, thundering water and cracking timbers. The air was sucked from his lungs and James prepared himself for the end in the icy waters. Like a cork from a champagne bottle he was propelled upwards and found himself dumped alongside a section of the forward hatch cover. The rope he had been collecting was wrapped around his arm still attached to the lifebelt. Although numb with cold he managed to secure one end of the rope to a large bolt that protruded from the woodwork of the hatch cover. Using all his strength James slowly winched himself onto the wreckage as it was swept by the tide away from the quay and towards a dark cliff. The huge cliff was a menacing sight as it towered darkly above the crashing waves. It seemed to echo with a constant shriek as the wind howled around its rocky outcrops. A blowhole was acting like a lung as it sucked in the sea and then vomited a thunderous torrent of water back into the ocean. James had never been a particularly religious man, but like many before him when confronted with death he put his head down on the remains of the hatch, closed his eyes and prayed for salvation.

In the midst of this awful turmoil James had an impulse to look up. He could see that ocean currents were washing him towards the mouth of a cave. Each swell took him a bit nearer to the entrance as it broke with a foaming mass on a large, flat lip of rock. Slightly ahead and a little to one side James saw what appeared to be a bundle of wreckage from the stricken vessel. The bundle rose with the swell and was swilled into the entrance to the cave. As the water receded the bundle remained fixed to the flat rock with torrents of seawater streaming back from it. Watching, almost hypnotised, James suddenly realised that the bundle was not wreckage. It was a person. It was Coral, the passenger, and she was hanging onto the flat rock desperately trying to avoid being sucked back into the sea. Her ruck sack was snagged on a sharp section of the rock. Miraculously, she managed to claw her way over the slippery rock until she penetrated the part of the cave entrance sheltered from the turbulent waves. Seeing James on his splintered hatch approaching, she beckoned for him to follow.

James decided that the best chance he had of following Coral's example was to detach from the hatch and try to float with the swell as it swirled into the mouth of the cave. He convinced himself that it was just a matter of good timing. It was also a matter of grip. As the swell rose James floated with it above the flat rock and was slapped on it violently and unceremoniously. Instantly, he was sucked back by the retreating torrent, into the turbulent sea. Numb with cold, bruised, shocked and physically weakened by his exertions, James knew that he would not have many more chances to repeat this manoeuvre. The swell picked him up again and drove him back into the cave. As it started to drain back James saw that Coral had taken the line of floats out of her rucksack and tied one end to her leg. She was hugging a rock with both arms, the floats dangling over the edge of the slippery section of flat rock. As the swell retreated over the rock dragging James with it he managed to reach out and hold onto the last float on the line. It was enough to prevent his body being washed back off the rock and it gave him the time to haul himself off the rock and into the relative safety of the cave. He collapsed, exhausted, in a heap next to Coral. Spontaneously, they hugged each other, shivering uncontrollably, shocked, but relieved to have found sanctuary.

They were both suffering from the wet and cold and were covered in cuts and bruises after their battering on the rocks. Conditions just outside the entrance to the cave were unrelenting and so they decided to move along the passage, deeper into the cave to escape the wind and spray. There was just enough room to walk upright, but it was dark and slippery and their legs felt weak after their exposure in the sea. They were surprised that the passage maintained its height. It was not very wide and in some places there were marks which suggested that the rock had been quarried.

Gradually the sound of the storm faded and after about three hundred yards the passage ended. An old heavy wooden door was set into the rock face, its rusty hinges betraying its obsolescence. At least they were sheltered from the wind as they sat down, leaning against the walls, shivering with exposure to the cold. James picked up a flat rock from the floor intending to use it as a tool to prise open the door. His other hand gripped the rocky crevice above his head. As he pulled himself up his fingers detected a strange leathery surface which felt so different to the usual coarseness of the rocky walls. Intrigued and surprised by this unexpected texture James quickly pulled his fingers away. His clumsy movement dislodged the leathery object and it fell from the crevice landing on the floor in front of Coral. It was too dark to see what the object was let alone to inspect it, although it appeared to be an old leather pouch. The leather was partly covered in green slime, but a symbol of some sort was faintly visible on the front. James picked up the pouch and stuffed it in his jacket pocket before moving to the door.

"There's no way this is going to open," gasped James as he tried to lever the door open with the flat rock.

In frustration he started to pound the wooden surface of the door. Each blow emitted a dull thud which echoed around the passage.

***

Vicky never liked descending to the cellar on her own. It wasn't just the gloom. The whole area of the cellar had been in existence for hundreds of years. The inn had been rebuilt, but the cellar was original. It had a sort of silent ambience that made Vicky feel as if history had seeped into the fabric of the walls. She wondered about the people who had been in the cellar in past times and imagined that unseen eyes were watching her. As she descended the steps holding a candle before her, she could hear an unfamiliar banging coming from the far end of the cellar. Cautiously approaching the source of the noise, and initially thinking it was a rat, Vicky was alarmed when she realised that the sound was coming from the other side of the old, oak door. This was the door which had been used in the past as a portal for smuggling. She could not reach the door because heavy barrels stood before it. A wave of fear descended on her and she froze. It was being alone yet feeling as though an invisible force was pulling her towards the door. The others were not far away, yet she was temporarily immobilised, unable to communicate with them. Gritting her teeth, she forced herself to retreat to the bar where all the rescuers were gathered. For a minute she stood silent, her heart pounding. She knew that what she had to say would create scepticism, yet she felt a sort of frightened excitement. Finally, she uttered a blunt expression of her thoughts.

"There is someone banging on the other side of the old door in the cellar," she gasped.

There was just a faint hint of disbelief on Jake's face as he asked, "Do you mean the smuggler's door?"

"She's been drinking that brandy," someone shouted. "Come on let's go down and let them in."

They all followed Vicky down to the cellar which was in silence.

"I don't hear nothing," sarcastically remarked one of the men, cupping his ear with his hand.

"Quiet!" commanded Vicky.

The assembled crowd looked at each other in surprise at the unexpected ferocity of Vicky's retort. Then the silence was suddenly broken by a heavy bang on the door.

"Give us a hand George," shouted Jake as he started to shift the barrels which blocked the access to the door. One of the men picked up a heavy piece of timber to use as a lever.

They used a mallet to knock the rusty bolts back and tugged with all their strength on the large, iron ring attached to the latch mechanism. The door groaned, its hinges screeching until slowly, reluctantly, it ground open. Before them, in the flickering half-light of the candle two bedraggled faces looked out from the cave.

After their trauma neither of the survivors could find a voice.

James tried to speak, but his brain did not seem to be making his mouth respond. He knew that he was lucky to be alive and the only word that preoccupied his mind was 'Sanctuary'.

Coral dragged herself forward and strong arms pulled her into the comparative shelter of the cellar. She was closely followed by James. Someone went to fetch dry blankets and the local doctor who had joined the rescue attempts stepped forward to check their condition.

"Give us some space," snapped the doctor.

A quick inspection showed that the pair had not sustained any broken bones, but they were shivering uncontrollably.

"They are suffering from shock and exposure," explained the doctor, as he and George helped James remove his wet clothes.

Vicky helped Coral remove her clothing and she wrapped her in a dry, warm blanket. Together, they managed to reach a seat near the fire in the main bar of the inn. As James removed his jacket there was a damp slap on the floor as the leather pouch he had found in the cave dropped from his pocket. James, George and the doctor looked down at the curious object. George picked up the pouch and placed it on the pile of wet clothes without saying a word. The doctor's gaze seemed fixed on the object in a sort of dumb recognition.

"That is a most unusual pouch." George spoke excitedly and with a mystified expression on his face.

James was still trying to find his voice so he just nodded and pointed towards the cave before being wrapped in a blanket and assisted to the bar by the doctor.

The barman poured glasses of brandy and gradually the two survivors felt the effects of its restorative powers. Helped by the fire, functionality gradually returned to their bodies, including the power of speech. The rescuers crowded around, listening as James and Coral recounted their fortunes after the ship had sunk.

"Are there no other survivors?" asked Coral, perplexed that they seemed alone.

The rescuers looked at the floor and shook their heads. One of them placed a faded, torn and bedraggled section of the ships ensign on the bar.

"That's the only wreckage that came ashore," he said sadly.

The rescuers wished the two exhausted survivors well before they quietly left the inn. The loss of the 'Mersey Rose' would need to be reported to the maritime authorities. Jake and Vicky moved two bath tubs from the outside washroom and filled them with buckets of warm water that had been heating in the fireplace. To the survivors exhaustion was overriding the desire for hygiene, and modesty did not seem an issue. They were alive and that's what mattered. As the doctor had predicted, the warm water soothed their joints, eradicating the lingering embrace of exposure. Wrapped in dry woollen blankets the two uninvited guests were escorted to a couple of vacant rooms on the first floor of the inn. They flopped down on their beds with the blankets tightly tucked around their bodies and curled into a ball. Haunted by terrifying memories, but too drained to stay awake, sleep slowly enveloped their consciousness. Physically and mentally delicate, but mercifully warm and dry, they slept soundly and did not wake until the following day.

CHAPTER 4

The Quest

The next morning dawned grey and cold. The wind was no longer whistling around the corners of the building and the weather system which had wreaked so much destruction had moved away. James awoke and surveyed his unfamiliar surroundings as powerful memories flooded back, threatening to submerge him in a tide of anxiety. Opposite where he lay there was a small window covered by thick, red velvet curtains. They made the room dark and it was hard to estimate the time of day. Dragging his bruised legs out of the blankets, James staggered across the bedroom and pulled the curtains to one side. Peering out of the window he could see Gull Rock being pounded by a moderate swell under a slate grey sky. Outside the inn, Jake was talking to a man wearing a large hat and a brown raincoat. As the conversation ended Jake walked towards the quay, leaving the man scribbling something in a little notebook. Thinking it must be later than he thought James moved away from the window and noticed that a set of clothes had been left for him on a chair near the door. His body ached from head to foot as he dressed, but worse still was a feeling of acute hunger. James decided to go in search of food.

Seated at a table in the bar, Coral was enjoying a plate of bacon and eggs. The man in the brown raincoat, who had been talking to Jake outside, was now sat on his own in the corner, seemingly engrossed in his jottings. James looked over at the food enviously as Coral beckoned for him to join her at the table. As he crossed the room he saw Vicky drying glasses behind the bar and enquired about the time.

"It's nearly ten," replied Vicky cheerily. "Make yourself comfortable and I will sort out some food."

A large fire was burning in the hearth sending out a welcoming warm glow. James looked across the table to where Coral was enjoying her breakfast. Her brown hair was tied in a ponytail and her appearance was similar to when James first saw her on the dock at Runcorn. He hadn't really noticed until now, but seeing Coral close up, he found her natural appearance appealing to his eye. In the light from the window her brown hair had a golden sheen as it dropped to her shoulders. Aware that James was staring straight at her she stopped eating and their eyes met. They both knew that they had been lucky to survive the ordeal the previous day. Stranger still was the knowledge that they were the only survivors. They felt slightly guilty to be sitting eating, when everyone else had died. James recalled his mother once saying that the eyes are the windows to the soul. Looking across the table at each other, the couple knew that their relationship had changed. They were no longer strangers. Their traumatic experience had forged a bond between them.

Feeling fortified by the food, the couple began to feel more relaxed. Their thoughts turned to practical issues. They were both concerned to let their friends and family know that they were safe. Just as they were about to leave, the man in the brown raincoat approached their table. He apologised for disturbing them before introducing himself as a journalist from 'The Western News'.

"My editor has asked me to write a piece on the shipwreck that happened here yesterday," he explained. "I know that it will be stressful for you so soon after the event, but our readers will want to know what happened. Your accounts would be invaluable in ensuring that my report is comprehensive and accurate."

Describing their ordeal to anyone let alone a stranger was not what the couple were envisaging just now. The shock and pain were still acute. James stood up and was about to decline an interview when the outside door flew open and Jake barged into the bar.

"I asked you to go away," he shouted angrily at the journalist. "Now I am commanding you to leave right now."

The journalist stepped back as Jake rounded on him, intent on marching him to the door. James was just in time to intervene before Jake grabbed hold of the man's arm.

"It's alright Jake. Leave him be," said James suddenly. The sound of his own voice sounded detached from his brain. His every instinct was against raking up the events of yesterday and yet, perversely, something was telling him that his story needed telling. People had died and others had risked their lives in the rescue.

"We both appreciate your concern Jake," James continued. "I don't know how Coral feels, but I am willing to talk to this man under certain conditions. Firstly, that his newspaper makes a financial contribution to The Volunteer Life Saving Brigade, and secondly that they send a telegram to my brother in Cheshire confirming that I am alive."

The journalist appeared a little taken aback, but after a seconds thought he held out his hand.

"That is fair enough if I am to get an exclusive, but what about your friend?" he said looking towards Coral.

"I will talk under the same conditions as James, if you will also include a telegram to my professor. He was expecting to meet me today," said Coral with a hint of sadness in her voice.

Jake shrugged his shoulders and moved away to continue his work restocking the bar leaving the journalist alone with the two survivors. Recounting his side of the story was proving to be less stressful than James had anticipated. He found recalling the sequence of events was cleansing his mind. It was a release from his pent up emotions. At least this was how it felt, until he started to describe the door at the end of the cave. Something had been troubling him and it was concerned with the cave. Now it had returned with a jolt. It was the dream about the horse with the two riders inside a cave. This was the dream that he had experienced on Christmas Eve in Cheshire. James felt a chill run through him as he realised that his dream was more than a dream. Had it been a portent, a premonition, a glimpse of the future? The journalist had been scribbling notes in shorthand and he looked up as James paused. Feeling physically and mentally uncomfortable, James shifted position on his chair, and continued his story omitting the dream and his discovery of the pouch. It was something that he personally could not explain and he had no intention of telling a newspaper reporter.

Content with his exclusive, the reporter left the table explaining that he needed to ask Jake if he could use the telephone. Coral had noticed the discomfort that James had displayed whilst relating his story and she now took the chance to ask him about it.

"What's the matter? Coral whispered noticing that the startled look on James's face was still there. He looked like an animal caught in the glare of a lantern.

"It's the pouch that I found in the cave yesterday," whispered James. "It has a symbol on the front that I suddenly realised I had seen before."

"Where did you see it?" asked Coral.

James decided to confide his dream with Coral. "It appeared in a strange dream I had just before that last voyage."

"Are you sure?" said Coral as she considered this unlikely connection.

"The pouch fell out of my pocket when we were undressing in the cellar. We all saw the symbol."

"All?" asked Coral.

"All three of us," said James. "There was the rescuer called George and the doctor. George looked as if he had seen a ghost when he picked the pouch up."

"Where is the pouch?" asked Coral. "I think we need to take a closer look at it."

"It's with my wet clothes in the cellar," he said feeling a rush of adrenalin start to quicken his pulse.

Their conversation was abruptly ended when the reporter reappeared to tell them that their story would appear in the next edition of the newspaper. Coral accompanied him to the door and took the opportunity to remind him of his obligations under their agreement. As the door opened a blast of cold air rushed in. Coral glanced outside and noticed a figure leaning casually against a rock at the other side of the quay. The man looked like a shadow in his dark cape. A black, broad brimmed hat was pulled down low across his face. Smoke occasionally drifted up from under the brim as the figure enjoyed a cigarette. Coral shivered. Apart from his odd appearance there was something sinister in the man's demeanour. He seemed disengaged from the world, overtly casual, but covertly surveying the scene like an animal stalking its prey. Coral closed the door feeling slightly uneasy. The warmth of the room embraced her as she returned to join James at the table. Her discomfort quickly evaporated as Vicky brought them a pot of tea.

James started to tell Coral about life as a sailor and the Christmas he had spent in Cheshire with his brother. Recounting the end of Christmas Eve, he described his dream to Coral and the details flooded back. What really haunted him was the expression on the rider's face and the gesture he was making. A frown spread wrinkles across his forehead as he recalled the dream.

"It was as if he was desperate for me to follow where he pointed. The rider was pleading with me to follow his direction. I don't understand what it means and now that I have found the pouch I feel stunned," said James glancing towards Coral to see how she was reacting. "It must sound weird to you?"

Coral thought carefully. As a researcher she was cautious about accepting or rejecting any information without due thought.

"Well it is a bit strange," she said resting her chin on both hands. "I don't want to sound too much like an academic, but I remember a quotation from one of Shakespeare's plays. I think it was in Hamlet where one of the characters said, 'There are more things in Heaven and Earth, than are dreamed of in your philosophy'. When you think about it, we humans possess a subconscious mind, although as we sit here talking we are not aware of it. We can't see it, only feel it. Our physical survival depends on avoiding disaster by being able to see it coming. All the time we are receiving subtle stimuli that affect our senses."

James looked a bit perplexed. He remembered how vivid the

dream had been at the time. He had not mentioned that he had been drinking before falling asleep.

"I don't think my subconscious was working too well," he said cautiously.

Coral smiled, "Just because you had a drink doesn't mean your subconscious disappeared. It may have been heightened!"

"Really?" said James surprised by Coral's perceptive response.

Realising that James did not fully understand, Coral tried to give a clearer example of what she meant.

"I remember a story that my father told me about an incident on a trip he made in Africa. He recalled being taken into the bush to observe the animals. The guide needed to fill the water bottles. He stopped the transport and took a step forward before freezing, glued to the spot, listening. He retreated to the carriage just in time, as a leopard that had been completely hidden, charged forward from the reeds. My father asked him how he had anticipated the danger. He said that he had a feeling that all wasn't well. When he listened there was no birdsong and he caught a trace of animal scent on the breeze. In the same way, our subconscious minds may respond to signals from our surroundings leading to a vague awareness of what lies ahead. It could be something simple like an adverse weather report or recognition that something doesn't look quite right. In this context the future already exists."

James was impressed with Coral's story about a subject that he had never really thought deeply about. Leaning forward he spoke quietly, not wanting to be embarrassed should he be overheard.

"I did feel apprehensive about this trip. It may have been because I had enjoyed the company of my brother and wanted to stay longer with him. Another factor was that the captain told me it was his last trip. It may also have been the unsettled, dark, winter weather. The extra responsibility of being an officer weighed on my shoulders a little because I wanted to make a good impression."

"That could explain the cave part of your dream," said Coral. "The cave represented the unknown decisions that you were worried you might have to take as an officer. Anxiety was affecting your subconscious mind. You were in the dark as to what direction to take at this juncture in your life. Perhaps the rider was a symbol of reassurance as to the right path!"

"The rider was not reassuring anyone," replied James. "It was more like he was imploring someone to follow his directions. It was a look of desperation. He was compelling my attention to something unseen."

They were distracted by Jake who had come to collect their empty cups. He excused his intrusion, but was pleased that his guests seemed to be more settled.

"I can see that you two are feeling better," he remarked. "Sorry about that irritating reporter earlier."

"It's difficult to express how glad we were to see you last night," said James. "I don't think we would have survived much longer in the cold. My body felt totally numb. We are both grateful for the care and hospitality that you have provided. Telling our story was a small price to pay if it generates funds for your volunteers."

"It seemed as though the cold got worse when we knew that we wouldn't drown," Coral agreed. "I was so relieved when the door opened and you pulled us through."

"I have some money in my jacket pocket and will pay you for our rooms if it hasn't been washed away," James offered. He was worried about the costs of their stay.

"Those clothes that you are wearing were left by the last person who couldn't pay," snorted Jake. "I despise thieves, but you don't need to worry about money. It's not your fault you were shipwrecked. You are welcome to stay until you fully recover. There will be officials visiting from the coastguard and the board of trade to contend with. It's best that you make yourselves comfortable for the time being. Then if anyone wants to find you they will know where you are. We will sort out any debts later."

"That's very generous," said James.

Jake moved off with the cups towards the kitchen. He looked back over his shoulder and called for the couple to follow him. "If you want to collect your clothes go through the door at the back of the office. Take care going down the stairs because they are cut into the rocks and can be slippery."

Their clothes had been left in two neat piles on a table at the far end of the cellar near to the heavy, oak door through which they had entered from the cave the night before. The smell of dampness and beer drifted in the air. James went straight to his jacket and retrieved the pouch with the symbols.

"It is not an illusion", said James, holding out the pouch so that Coral could see the symbol on the front cover.

"Let's take our belongings back to our rooms upstairs," suggested Coral. "Then we can have a proper look at your discovery."

Coral sat on the end of her bed next to James as he opened the leather pouch. There was an old fragment of paper which looked as if it had been watermarked by vinegar. Whatever had been written on it had dissolved years ago. Behind the paper was a fragment of green cloth still intact, but damp and disintegrating to the touch. Coral laid an old newspaper on the bed and using a hair clip she gently prised the fragment out of the pouch until it lay face up on the newspaper. Although the wording was severely faded and discoloured it was just about legible. Copying the message letter by letter, numeral by numeral Coral managed to make a readable version of the fragment on a sheet of foolscap paper.

I fear for my life. Follow to complete mission.

44 23 15
13 23 15 43 44
43 24 44 43
45 33 14 15 42
44 15 32 35 31 15
13 23 45 42 13 23
32 11 42 44 54 42

Sholto Kelley. 1291. Mellifont Abbey Ireland.

James wasn't impressed and couldn't help voicing his

disappointment. "So all we have is an old pouch with a symbol, a rotted sheet of paper and this message that we can't read."

Coral was not listening, she was studying the numbers. After a while she looked up and said to James.

"This message looks like some sort of ancient code or cipher. It is the sort that in ancient times was used by the Greeks to keep their intentions secret. Whoever Sholto Kelley was it appears that he had something valuable that he wanted to protect until he completed his mission. We need to find someone who can decipher codes written in 1291 in order to make sense of it."

"Let's go for a breath of air while we have some time," James suggested after noticing that a watery sun was peeping from behind the grey clouds.

Coral carefully replaced the cloth inside the pouch which had been its home for six hundred years and put it in her bedside drawer, before following James to the front entrance of 'The Strand'. Once outside she looked nervously across the quay, remembering the man she had seen earlier, but there was nobody there. An onshore wind was tugging at their clothing and the couple were having second thoughts about venturing further outside when they met George. He was making a routine delivery of produce from his farm at Trebarwith.

"Glad to see that you two are making a quick recovery," said George. "So sorry about the rest of the crew. We just couldn't reach them in those awful conditions!"

George stopped as though in deep reflection before looking directly at the couple. He gave the impression of having made up his mind to ask them a question.

"To be honest I was hoping to meet you both when I made this delivery. My farm is just up the road. I have spoken to my wife, Catherine, and we would be pleased if you would join us for dinner tomorrow. Catherine is a superb cook," he added, as if he needed to further encourage them.

"We don't want to burden you with visitors," protested James. "We are already indebted to you and the other rescuers for saving our lives."

"It is an honour to entertain anyone who managed to survive the ordeal that the pair of you endured. Anyway, I have to confess that I do have another reason why I would like to meet with you. I hope you are not offended by this observation, he said nervously, but I couldn't help notice the pouch you dropped on the cellar floor last night. I was surprised to see the image on that pouch and I have something at the farm which closely connects to it," said George mysteriously.

"That sounds intriguing," said James as he turned towards Coral. "Do you think you will feel fit enough to visit the farm tomorrow?"

Coral trusted George. After all he had helped in the rescue. She was interested to see whatever he had to show them at the farm so she told him that she would be happy to accept the invitation.

"Then the matter is settled," replied George. "I promise that you will not be disappointed with what I have to show you. I will collect you from here at the same time tomorrow morning. Don't forget to bring the pouch with you."

During the rest of the day the couple explored their immediate surroundings, relaxing in the inn and enjoying Jake and Vicky's hospitality. Word had reached Coral from her colleague at the university expressing his sadness on hearing of the shipwreck and his relief that she was safe. He explained that he would be at 'The Stonemason's Arms' in Camelford on Friday and could meet her there if she had recovered sufficiently from her ordeal. So much had happened in so short a time that Coral was glad of the chance to resume the purpose of her visit. At least there was the prospect of restoring a little more normality and so she replied confirming the meeting.

Thursday turned out to be another cold, but dry day. The wind had dropped and George arrived at eleven o'clock to find the couple sitting on a low stone wall outside the inn looking out towards Gull Rock. They walked to the farmer's cart and climbed aboard, unaware that a shadowy figure, his face obscured by the brim of his hat, lurked, observing their movements from a gateway across the quay. He was a silent, watchful presence.

The road to Trebarwith farm led steeply uphill from 'The Strand' inn. After about a quarter of a mile, still going uphill, they made a sharp turn to the right. High banks obscured the view on both sides of the road. The couple still felt a little fragile and were glad that they did not have to walk up the steep track.

George pulled on the reins and they passed through a gateway which took them onto the farm. They could see the granite stone shape of the farmhouse ahead in a hollow amidst the fields. The grey green sea stretched out behind the farm buildings, contrasting with the green embankments which marked the perimeter of the fields. Cattle grazed in one of the fields enjoying their freedom after the storm. A man was using a fork to heap hay into the pens where the cows would be milked. He greeted George and the two men had a short conversation before George led them to the farmhouse.

"That was Thomas our trusty labourer," George explained. "He has been a long serving employee, almost like one of the family. Now in his later years, he just works part time."

The farmhouse was traditionally built with the front door constructed under an arch of stone. On each side of the door was a large, square window consisting of eight individual panels. The first floor had three windows with the middle one in a central position above the arch of the doorway. This window was inlaid with stained glass panels. When they entered the hallway the light from the stained glass spread a tapestry of colour onto an oak staircase that led to a landing area. Proceeding down the hall George introduced his guests to his wife Catherine, who was just closing the kitchen door behind her. She was a well-built woman who displayed the stature and demeanour of a person well used to physical work. She had a kindly face with a rosy complexion and retained a sort of plain attractiveness. Catherine warmly welcomed the visitors before directing them through a door to their left which opened into a large room that extended from the front to the back of the house.

"George told me that he was inviting you. He hasn't been able to settle since he saw you in the cellar," she said. "I was so sorry to hear about the wreck with all those poor sailors. It was a miracle that you both survived. I am glad that you were able to come so soon after your terrible experience in the storm."

They all sat down around the glow from the fireplace and George offered each of them a glass of elderberry wine. Half burned logs blazed away in the fireplace sending flickering shadows throughout the room.

"It is hard work here on the farm," said George reflectively. "I am glad that you could come today because with Thomas available to help with the animals I have more time to talk to you. Catherine and I enjoy the farming life well enough, just as our ancestors have. Our ownership goes back generations."

George dragged forward a small table, his eagerness to see the pouch barely contained. Coral took the pouch from her bag and laid it on the table. The symbol of the horse with two riders stood out clearly on the leather cover of the pouch. Carefully she extracted the piece of cloth from inside the pouch and laid it flat.

"It's very delicate and not easy to read," said Coral apologetically.

George inspected the fragment of cloth in silence before muttering one word; "Remarkable."

"We made a more legible copy of the wording," explained Coral as she showed George the handwritten copy they had made earlier.

George stood up and walked across the room to where a large bureau was displayed. He opened the front flap and took out a small square box. Returning to the table he opened the box and extracted a red book. James could see that it was an old Bible with a clip that held the front and back covers together. George offered the book to James making a turning gesture with his hand inviting him to open the Bible. James gasped as the contents were revealed. Inside the hollowed out Bible there was what appeared to be a key, the head of which displayed the one horse and two rider's symbol. The key was attached to a chain which formed a necklace.

"Now you can you see why I was keen to see the pouch," George sighed.

"Where did you get the necklace from?" asked James and Coral in harmony.

"It's a family heirloom," replied George. "It has been passed down to us from further back than anyone can remember."

It was now one o'clock and they were beginning to feel hungry when Catherine asked them to come to the table. She was a good cook and provided an excellent meal which they all enjoyed. Conversation flowed around the table as they discussed the meaning behind the strange symbol that had now appeared in two separate places. It also featured in the dream which James had experienced in Cheshire. Catherine explained that the necklace had been handed down from generation to generation within the family, but no one knew exactly what the origin was.

"I have to tell you that I think that there is something on this farm which links our key necklace to the message on the cloth fragment," said Catherine thoughtfully.

George spoke with a sceptical tone in his voice. "Well, what is it?"

"It's the old, granite gravestone on the edge of the western field," said Catherine sternly.

"Someone is buried on this farm?" asked Coral.

"The gravestone has been on the edge of the field for centuries and the inscription has been eroded. However, I have looked at the stone many times and a while ago, using a pencil and paper, I made a rubbing to see if anything showed up."

"You didn't mention this to me," said George indignantly.

"I didn't think it was worth mentioning," Catherine replied. "Anyway, you weren't around at the time. The only letters that showed anything were those on the right hand third of the stone. Look I'll show you."

Catherine left the room and a few minutes later returned with her pencil rubbings.

ELLEY

1291

GAVE HIS LIFE FOR A FRIEND

"The more to the left the more worn away the letters are. The fragment from the pouch has the name Sholto Kelley and the date 1291. I don't think it's a coincidence that the letters and date match and so I think that it is a strong possibility that the grave is that of the person who left the pouch," pronounced Catherine triumphantly.

James saw another connection and spoke excitedly to the group.

"The words at the top of the fragment state that the writer of the code was in danger of being killed. That's probably why he wrote the message in the hope that if he died someone else might find the instructions. He must have thought that it was the only chance of seeing his mission through." Although he said nothing James began to suspect that the man who pointed so urgently in his dream was probably Sholto Kelley!

"So he must have been in the cave connected to the inn," said Catherine. "We know there is a historic family connection between the farm and the old inn so that is most probably why we have the necklace."

"What we don't know, sighed George, is what the symbol represents, or who this person Sholto was, or anything about his mission."

Coral had been listening quietly to the conversation and decided that now was a good time to offer some positive help. "Tomorrow I intend to go into Camelford to meet the colleague who was expecting me. He is an authority on medieval history and I can ask him to take a look at the pouch if that would help?"

"It is certainly worth a try," said George. He might be able to shed some light on the artefacts. If you will let me take you and James to Camelford I will bring the necklace and key along with me."

By four o'clock in the afternoon, it was starting to get dark so Coral and James helped Catherine to clear the dishes and thanked her for her hospitality. Meanwhile, George brought the cart back round to the front entrance.

"Thank you for coming," said Catherine. "I am so glad to have met you. Take extra care until you get your strength back."

"Thanks again for that lovely meal," came the reply which echoed across the farmyard.

On the short journey back to the inn, George explained that he intended to write a letter to the Church of Ireland. He would enquire whether there were any records of people at Mellifont Abbey.

"I will check if there is a record of someone called Sholto Kelley who served at the abbey in 1291. It's a long time ago, but monasteries often keep records going back centuries," said George as he left his guests at 'The Strand' and turned for home.

CHAPTER 5

Camelford Reunion

As Jake had anticipated there was a visit from the coastguard early on the Friday morning. James and Coral were preparing for their visit to Camelford when they were met by the official. He explained to them that there would be a board of trade enquiry into the loss of the 'Mersey Rose'. They would be expected to attend the enquiry in order to give evidence as to the events leading to the loss of the vessel. Evidence would also be heard from the owners, the rescuers, the coastguard and the survivors. The meeting was set for the following Friday 16th January, 1891 and would be held in Trevena House, Tintagel, starting at 10:00 am. The official reassured the couple that they had nothing to fear as the purpose was to establish the facts and clear the way for the insurers to recompense for the ship and her cargo. He left them with a copy of 'The Western News' which carried a front page story under the headline ***'Trebarwith Shipwreck – Survivors Story'***. As he left he cautioned the couple about giving any further interviews before the enquiry. There was no contention about this matter. None of them wanted to prejudice the outcome of the enquiry.

Three hundred miles away, in Cheshire, William Cartwright had received a telegram message. The date always stuck in his mind. It was Wednesday 7th January, 1891. The message simply stated ***'Mersey Rose lost off North Cornish coast. The two survivors James Cartwright and Coral Byford are safe and well'***. Although he was shocked to hear such tragic news, relief poured through him in an emotional wave when he read that his brother was a survivor. He immediately contacted the shipping company who confirmed the names of the survivors as James Cartwright, ship's officer from Winsford, Cheshire and Coral Byford, a researcher attached to Manchester University. William was provided with the location where his brother was recovering and offered assistance with travel arrangements by a company representative. His immediate instinct was to be reunited with his brother. He wanted to support him personally and felt a compulsion to travel to Cornwall immediately. The shipping company responded by facilitating the transport arrangements for William and Jayne. The next morning they found themselves boarding the sleeper train at Crewe bound for Exeter.

Jayne Cartwright had been only too well aware that her husband had felt very uneasy the day before and had tried to reassure him. She now found herself accompanying William on the long rail journey to Cornwall. They passed through Bristol and continued along the Great Western Railway, eventually arriving at Exeter, Saint David's on the Friday morning. It was here that they changed trains connecting with The North Cornwall line. Unfortunately, the line ended at Launceston, but the couple were lucky to find two seats on the mail coach. The coach collected the mail from the station on its journey along the Post Road between London and North Cornwall.

It was afternoon on Friday 9th January before they crossed the River Camel. The driver pulled sharp left and through a wide arched entrance in the centre of a coaching inn called 'The Stonemason's Arms'. This was where the horses were swapped for fresh legs and was the final destination for William and Jayne.

The reception for 'The Stonemason's Arms' was really just the end of the bar. The barmaid was also the receptionist. As soon as she caught sight of the two newly arrived travellers with their luggage she spoke with the tone of someone who had answered the same question repeatedly and could hardly be bothered to answer. "If you've come about rooms we're full," she said curtly.

Stifling the impulse to retaliate with equal rudeness, William spoke calmly. "We have travelled for twenty four hours from the North of England. Can you check if one room is available for a couple of nights?"

The receptionist shook her head, "Fully booked I'm afraid," she repeated with just a hint of defiance.

William picked up the luggage with a weary resignation, but before he moved away, a voice from behind intervened.

"They can use the second room that I have booked under the name of Byford. My guest has been delayed and the room is unoccupied."

Jayne had been standing behind her husband and found herself next to this benevolent stranger. "That's very kind of you," she said. "We have travelled from Cheshire to meet with my husband's brother who was shipwrecked down here. Thank you ever so much."

Another voice, more familiar this time, came from the main entrance door. "William! Jayne! Good to see you!" James exclaimed on entering the bar accompanied by Coral and George. They had just arrived from Trebarwith for the meeting with the professor. "This is a surprise. How did you know where to find us?"

"We didn't," replied William. "We had a telegram from a newspaper informing us of the shipwreck. Your shipping company told us the rest. They explained to us where you were and with their help, we left home straightaway. It is such a relief to see that you are alright."

William and James hugged each other as if glued together. They were determined not to take each other for granted ever again. Having nearly lost each other they now valued being together more highly than they had done in the past.

The sound of Jayne's voice jerked James's attention back to the other people in the room. In the flurry of excitement and surprise the kindly gentleman who had offered his room had almost been forgotten. It was Jayne who first thought to include him in their introductions. "This is Mr. Byford, she explained. "He saved us from wandering the streets by giving up a room he had booked for himself".

"He gave up my room?" laughed Coral in mock indignation.

"Your room?" said Jayne with a puzzled look on her face.

"Yes, this is Ormerod Dymond, Professor of Medieval History from Cornwall University. He is the colleague I was scheduled to meet down here after you dropped me off in Padstow," she said looking over towards James.

"So you are Coral Byford. The girl who survived the shipwreck with James," said Jayne now realising why she had been confused.

"She saved my life," asserted James, fondly putting his arm around Coral's shoulders. "I would have drowned if it wasn't for this person. Coral is an absolute angel."

Ormerod stood listening, pleased to hear that one of his students was being described as a heroine. The professor was a tall slim man, but the years had taken their toll and his thoughtful, kindly face was etched with more than the odd line. His once long brown hair, now turned grey, still hung over his collar like a fleece. He wore a brown, corduroy jacket with various papers peeping out of the pockets giving the impression that the jacket was also a filing cabinet. A pipe and pouch of tobacco protruded from the breast pocket of his checked shirt. He had received a message that Coral was on her way to meet him, but had not expected to be in the centre of a family reunion.

He spoke with sincerity facing James and Coral. "I'm very pleased that you could come to meet me. I was distressed to hear of your misfortune on the journey and feared the worst when I heard about the shipwreck. It was a relief when the newspaper contacted me. It is a nice surprise to see that you have both recovered so quickly."

"Glad I was able to reserve a room for you both, he continued," turning to address William and Jayne. "I know that Coral has accommodation elsewhere."

"I'll help my brother and his wife to settle into their room after their long journey. Perhaps you and George can update the professor on recent events," said James winking at Coral.

Coral was thankful of the opportunity to introduce George as one of their rescuers and the owner of Trebarwith Farm. "We have some special items to show you," she said excitedly. " I am hoping that you may be able to help solve a mystery."

Looking a little intrigued Ormerod gestured for Coral and George to follow him. Addressing James he spoke in a quiet voice so as not to be overheard, "My room is number ten. Join us when you are ready. We will be able to talk in greater privacy than down here."

Unseen by any of them, eyes were watching their every move . A man dressed in dark clothes with hat brim pulled low, had discretely followed them into the bar and was sitting in a corner, smoke circling from his cigarette, one hand on a chilled pint of freshly poured ale. Unobtrusive and alone, this solitary figure observed in silence, content for now to watch his prey.

William and Jayne felt much more relaxed after visiting the bathroom and changing their clothes. They were hungrily eating a sandwich ordered from the bar earlier and listening to James explaining what had happened to him, what he had found, and how he had met George. More than an hour passed during which time James reminded his brother of the strange dream he had experienced at the house in Cheshire. The couple listened sometimes incredulous, sometimes mystified, often horrified, as James related his story.

"I had the most awful feeling that something was wrong the morning of your shipwreck," said William. "Then, as if to add to my sense of misgiving, the large clock on the mantelpiece stopped at five past two that afternoon. That clock has never stopped before and I remember thinking how odd that it had stopped. The next thing I heard was that there had been a wreck."

"It seems that it is not only me who has premonitions. I am not sure whether it's a gift or a curse," said James giving his brother a look of acknowledgement at their common experience.

Further down the landing in room ten, Coral described her

own experience in the cave and laid out the fragment of cloth contained in the pouch for Ormerod to see. George put the little Bible containing the necklace on the table next to the fragment and gave a summary of how it had been handed down within his family and his amazement when he first recognised the symbol on the leather pouch matched the necklace. The longer he listened the more absorbed Ormerod became as the stories unfolded.

The room Ormerod occupied was large, but when James, William and Jayne joined the others it was congested with people. William and Jayne sat on Ormerod's bed while the rest huddled around the little table, eager to hear whether he could throw any more light on their discoveries. Feeling as though he was about to give a lecture in a broom cupboard, Ormerod leaned forward and sucked on his freshly lit pipe. The rich vapours from his tobacco mix soothed him as he started to talk.

"I have to confess that I am fascinated by your discoveries. I recognised straight away the symbol of the two knights on one horse. This is a device of The Knights Templar and is thought to symbolise their collective ownership of property, and their brotherhood. The Templars were formed in Jerusalem during 1118 as a religious, Christian brotherhood of warrior knights. Their primary purposes were to protect Christian pilgrims on the routes from the coastal ports to the city of Jerusalem, and safeguard territory conquered from the Muslims during the first Crusade."

Ormerod turned towards George who was listening intently; keen to get some light thrown on a mystery that had been in his family for generations.

"Attached to your necklace is what could be a key. The round Templar symbol sits on a stem similar in appearance to an Egyptian Ankh, the symbol of life. The stem could be used to slot into a lock and the round Templar symbol at the top would provide the leverage to turn the mechanism. At a guess I would say that someone in your family has had a connection with the Templars."

"We have no knowledge of anyone," replied George with a frown. "There is an old gravestone on my farm that dates back to someone living in 1291. Would this be too late to be relevant?"

"If we consider the evidence," suggested Ormerod, while slowly blowing out a lungful of smoke, "the key has been with your family for generations. It has the same symbol as that on the pouch. The pouch was found in a cave near your farm. The document within the pouch is dated 1291. Someone with the same name as on the pouch document who died in 1291 is buried on your land. Therefore, it is highly probable that the key and the pouch are connected. The symbol connects them, the location connects them and the person named as Sholto Kelley connects them. This is more than just circumstantial evidence. The date is significant too, in that it was the year when the Templars left the Holy Land after the battle of Acre in 1291. It was not the end of the Templars just the end of their occupation of Judea. The Templar movement was ended in 1307 by King Philip 1V who accused them of heresy, confiscated their land and subjected those arrested to an inquisition."

Coral was looking at the fragment laid out on the table. "We know that Sholto Kelley was connected to an Abbey in Ireland and that he wrote in English stating that he was in danger of not being able to complete his mission. I think that if we can decode the message it will tell us more about what his mission was?" said Coral speaking her thoughts aloud.

Ormerod frowned as he pondered the numbers laid out on the table. "It looks like a numerical transposition code where the letters are substituted by numbers. If the message is written in English we should be able to decipher it without too much trouble using certain tried and tested techniques. The first thing we can do is to complete a frequency analysis of the numbers."

Coral picked up a pen and paper and listed each separate number in the left column. She then noted how many times each number had been used in the whole message.

Number	Frequency
44	5
23	4
15	5
13	3
43	3
24	1
45	2
33	1
14	1
42	4
32	2
35	1
31	1
11	1
54	1

"That's interesting" said Ormerod glancing towards Coral. "What do you think is the most commonly occurring letter in English?"

"Probably a vowel like 'E'," replied Coral.

"Exactly said Ormerod, 'E' followed by 'T' and then 'A' 'O' 'I' 'N' and 'S' from what I can remember. Next, you need to look at how the letters group together. 'The' is the most frequent three-letter group or word in English. More often than not 'N' will be preceded by a vowel."

"How did you remember all this?" James asked.

"It may seem a bit sad to you, but I have had to use these decoding mechanisms many times in my historical research," replied Ormerod peering back at the message.

The analysis revealed that the two most commonly occurring numbers were 44 and 15. These numbers appeared in the group of three at the start of the sequences. Without further prompting Coral inserted the word 'THE' at the start and used these letters to substitute for numbers throughout the message. The second sequence of numbers now had the most letters substituted and so it was a question of what letter could go before 'HE' and end with 'T'? Running through the alphabet Coral was excited to discover that the first match was a 'C'.

"This means the next sequence is probably the word 'CHEST', she said triumphantly. "Consequently, the number 43 can now be filled in as 'S'".

Coral used a little guesswork which revealed the words 'TEMPLE' and 'CHURCH'. The message now read as follows: 'THE CHEST S_TS U__ER TEMPLE CHURCH M_RT_R'

Feeling as though she was involved in some type of word game, Coral suddenly had an inspiration and exclaimed, "SITS UNDER!"

At first no one could think of what 'M_RT_R' could be until George had a brainwave and proposed 'MARTYR'.

Ormerod let out an audible sigh. "If this is connected to the Knights Templar then we need to think about the word Temple as designating a chapel. The usual pattern for the Templars was to establish preceptories which included a chapel, domestic and farm buildings. Produce from the land was sold to finance the crusades."

"I have lived in North Cornwall all my life," said George suddenly. "There is a place called Temple located six miles north east of Bodmin, but I don't think many people live there now."

As George was speaking Ormerod walked across the room and selected a book called ***'Medieval Cornwall'***. It was part of an untidy pile of material he had brought from the university. After flicking through the index and turning over a few pages he addressed the group.

"It would seem that we have found our Temple. It says in my book that Temple church was built in 1120 and was dedicated to St Catherine of Alexandria. It was linked to the Templar preceptory of

Trebeigh. Hospitality was provided to pilgrims crossing the moor and knights were trained there before leaving for the Holy Land. Apparently, the church fell into disrepair and was rebuilt in 1883 from the ruins of the original building. I think we need to pay this church a visit to see if it contains a chest."

George took out a battered map of the North Cornwall area from his jacket pocket and after folding it out on the bed he drew a circle around the location of the place called Temple. "I've carried this map around in my pocket for ages," said George with a smile, "and never needed to refer to it once until today."

"Would you be able to take us there?" Ormerod enquired. "I would like to help and can clear my diary for tomorrow."

"I have a cart with four seats and two strong horses," replied George. "The shortest way is across the moor, but it won't be a comfortable journey. The barometer showed that pressure was rising when I checked it at the farm this morning. If we went tomorrow it is likely that the weather will be dry, but cold."

"Aren't you forgetting something," asked Jayne indignantly. "There are six of us."

"There is only room for four and I will be the driver," repeated George. "It is important that Ormerod comes because he has specialist knowledge which will probably be needed."

"I think that James and Coral should go because they found the pouch," admitted Jayne. "It is better that we stay around here tomorrow and if you find anything you can tell us when you get back."

William felt uneasy about not going with his brother, but he could see that it would not be practical for them all to go together. They would be reunited by the end of the day anyway and so, reluctantly, he agreed to stay behind in Camelford.

Observing how weary William and Jayne looked, Ormerod felt compassionate towards them. He was well aware of how tiring travelling long distances could be, especially overland. It must have been an anxious journey for them and Ormerod wanted to restore their spirits.

"You two must be famished," said Ormerod warmly. "I don't do this often, but I'll treat you to a meal in the bar, courtesy of my expense account."

George stuffed his map back in his pocket and together with James and Coral they headed down the stairs towards the main door of the inn. Passing through the outer door which led into the street a man in dark clothing lunged into George knocking him off balance. The lingering odour of tobacco merged with the man's beery breath and George pushed him away in disgust.

"Careful, you drunken oaf," shouted George angrily.

The man staggered off up the street in what appeared to be a merry stupor. George turned to his companions, an embarrassed expression on his face. "Clumsy fool," he muttered, before turning to the arched gateway which led to the stables. It was not until later that night that he discovered that the map was no longer in his jacket pocket.

CHAPTER 6

The Hidden Crypt

TEMPLE CHURCH – CORNWALL

Saturday 10th January, 1891 was not a routine day for anyone. George had prepared a hamper to sustain the four investigators for the day. He hitched the horses to his cart, made sure that Thomas, the labourer, knew what needed to be done on the farm that day and collected James and Coral from 'The Strand'. There was room to leave the cart at the rear of 'The Stonemason's Arms' in Camelford before the three of them entered the building where the others were residing. William reminded his brother to be careful as he anticipated that there could be danger in searching for the chest.

The North Cornwall Volunteer Life Saving Brigade had a small fund which was used to support the victims of shipwrecks. As a member of the Brigade, George had been able to obtain the finance needed to enable James and Coral to buy some winter clothing. He had wisely insisted that they would need protection from exposure to the cold as they travelled across Bodmin Moor. After collecting Ormerod from 'The Stonemason's Arms' he pulled up outside the draper's shop on Fore Street. There were relatively few businesses along the street, but they included a boot and shoe dealer, a blacksmith, a sadler's, a grocer and a stationery shop. George knew that the draper, Mister Laxon, would probably be able to supply the clothing they required.

Laxon was a short, energetic fellow, with curly hair. A tape measure hung around his neck like a stethoscope. He quickly assessed his customers and repeatedly shot up and down a set of moveable ladders which gave access to tiered racks of garments. Within half an hour both James and Coral were transformed. As Coral climbed aboard the waiting cart James admired how attractive she looked in her green, hooded coat. She had never worn much make up, but she was no longer the bedraggled survivor in borrowed clothes. Her natural appearance seemed in harmony with the unspoilt moorland which bordered this Cornish town. James felt warm and content in his navy blue, weatherproof, double breasted coat.

Ormerod was full of enthusiasm as he took his place on the cart next to George. This was a little diversion from routine that he had not anticipated, but held the potential for some fascinating historical research. They looked a strange group with the two men perched high up at the front. George, the typical farmer, sporting dungarees over a thick patterned pullover and a scarf wound around his neck making him look like an animated scarecrow. In contrast, Ormerod, a brimmed hat that had strings which tied beneath his chin and a dark grey overcoat with toggle buttons. He could have been mistaken for a Methodist preacher. Behind the two men James and Coral sat comfortably in their new clothes looking almost too smart for a trip over the exposed moor.

The cart followed the main road through Camelford, scanned by the inquisitive eyes of local people. George turned left at a place called Valley Truckle. Having lost the map George was relying on his knowledge of the area to navigate, fending off questions about directions with an outward confidence not entirely matched by his memory of where Temple was located. He felt feckless at losing the map and did not want to admit his carelessness. They turned left again, crossing the River Camel at Trucking Mill and passed through Churchtown before traversing Bodmin Moor. The wild beauty of the moor appeared resplendent as it glistened with the pearls of half melted frost in the morning sun. The narrow track was uneven and the cart jolted uncomfortably over some of the ruts. James put his arm around Coral's shoulder and pulled her body towards him. Although his intention was to stabilise their position he was pleased that she did not resist. She was surprised that James was so concerned for her comfort. At the point where they had to cross the main Bodmin to Exeter road George stopped to ask directions from a farmer.

"Just down there on the other side of the main road," directed the man pointing to a typical narrow Cornish lane.

The lane was straight with high banking on one side and open moorland on the other. The journey had taken well over an hour and they decided to stop for a short break to indulge in food from George's hamper. Their appetites fulfilled, they continued down the lane for about a mile. George was beginning to think they were on the wrong track. His head was peering from left to right as though he was watching the ball during a game of tennis. Then, with miraculous luck, he caught sight of the top of a square tower located in a valley to their right. George turned first right down a steep downhill track and after a few yards Temple church appeared, from behind a row of mature trees. The building had been discreetly constructed on a sloping site. The moor reared up behind the church creating a lush, green background. Sheep were lazily grazing on the exposed moorland, their cream woollen fleeces protecting them from the weather.

George secured the horses to a tree on a flat patch of grass next to a small iron gate. There was just enough room so that the cart did not block the road. The gate creaked as it opened. To the left was a row of stone crosses and immediately in front a gravel path leading downhill to the church. The square tower of Temple church stood imperiously at the front of the building. The gravel path wound its way around the side of the tower to where an entrance door was sheltered in the recess of an elegant stone porch. This appeared to be the only external entrance and fortunately it was not locked. Opposite the porch was a small detached building which had the appearance of a storeroom. It looked as though it had been built using material from an earlier building on the site. Many of the blocks still retained marks and symbols from the time of the Templars. The door of this store was secured by a large padlock. George lead the group into the porch where a weathered sign invited visitors to close the door behind them in order to protect the interior from the elements. Inside the church there were signs that the building wasn't used very often. It was unheated and cold with few seats, but the decoration was well maintained. One of the stained glass windows depicted a knight seated on a horse displaying the distinctive Templar cross. Another showed St Catherine of Alexandria to whom the building was dedicated. A solitary large candle glowed on a simple altar. Behind the alter were two rectangular stained glass windows with another round window higher up. This was an east facing wall and the round window contained a red Templar cross. In front of the altar were two rounded, wooden seats, presumably for the clergy to use during services. The floor was quarry tiled with an alternating red and black sequence.

As the four visitors walked around the church their footsteps echoed around the walls.

"No sign of a martyr in here," said George as he rubbed his hands to keep warm.

"The message said the chest sits below the martyr. It may be that the martyr is in a stone tomb, but I must admit that I don't see any of those here," stated Ormerod.

James was standing with Coral in a wing of the church that protruded away from the nave. On the white plaster of the wall a Templar flag was displayed. The top half of the flag was black and the bottom half white. In the centre was a large, red, eight pointed Templar cross. James stood admiring the flag and his gaze fell to a small notice attached to the wall just below it. It read *'visits to the church to be made by arrangement with the warden, Temple village'*. George came up alongside and read the message. He then offered to go and find the warden leaving the others to continue their survey of the building.

After the gloomy cold interior of the church George was glad to be back outside in the morning sunshine. He took a deep breath and in so doing noticed something that seemed oddly out of place. It was the faint smell of a cigarette, but not any cigarette, a particular type. George couldn't just place where he had smelt that brand and seeing no sign of the smoker he retraced his steps back up the path to the little iron gate.

In the shadows by the gate George was startled to see the approaching figure of a man. He was walking slowly and his slightly stooped shoulders betrayed a lifetime of heavy work. The man was dressed like a farm labourer, wearing a flat cap over his dishevelled hair. In his hand he carried a large bunch of keys. As George approached the man stopped, put his hands on his hips and shouted accusingly.

"Are you the owner of that black mare that has appeared in my field?"

"My horses are there next to the gate," replied George defensively.

"That's the one I mean," snarled the old man pointing his grubby hand towards where a black mare was standing in an adjoining field. "It's not my horse. No one trespasses on Denzil Dibble's fields without asking first. It's rude, unacceptable behaviour."

George looked straight at the man, "Who are you?"

"I am Denzil Dibble, warden for the church, farmer and odd job man," replied the old man proudly. "No one visits for weeks and then two lots of you tourists arrive on the same day."

"Why do you say two lots?" asked George.

"Well first of all you, and then there's the trespasser with that black horse," retorted Denzil.

A sudden feeling of foreboding descended over George as he remembered the cigarette smoke. Now he knew where he had smelled that foreign brand. It was the drunken man from 'The Stonemason's Arms'. Was the man here today? Was he stalking them? Alarm was growing fast in his head as George realised that his map probably had not been lost by accident. It had been stolen and the culprit was here within the circle he had drawn on the map.

"Mr. Dibble," said George in a low voice, "Can you tell my friends and me more about the church?"

"Folk call me Denzil," corrected the man. "Can't see why anyone would be interested, but if that's what you want, I hold all the keys. Lived here all my life, so I know a thing or two about this place."

George followed Denzil back inside the church, furtively looking to see if he could see or smell the trespasser. There was no sign of anyone.

Shadows flickered as the branches of the trees waved in the breeze, giving plenty of cover as the hidden stalker checked that his targets had entered the church.

The musty smell of cattle seeped from Denzil's clothing. Coral sneezed and the sound echoed around the church amplified by the hollow, confined space. It made them all react with a jump, followed by nervous laughter.

"You'll be sneezing some more if you stay too long," said Denzil with a smirk. The only heating is these small stoves and they only operate when there is a service."

Denzil gave the visitors a short history of the church in a voice which betrayed the fact that he was repeating a script he had delivered many times before. "Temple Church was originally built in 1120 as part of the preceptory of Trebeigh." His expressionless address continued with hardly a pause. "It was handed to the Knights Hospitallier in 1314 after the Knights Templars were suppressed. Rebuilt from derelict ruins in 1883 and is now linked to the Parish of Blisland. Did you notice the old Norman font near the entrance doorway? It was recovered from the original church," said Denzil answering his own question.

Ormerod had a question of his own. "Sorry to interrupt," he said apologetically. "I notice that the storage building outside retains some of the original blocks of stone."

"Yes, I always thought it wastful to use such historic blocks for a store," replied Denzil.

"Would it be possible to look inside the store?" asked Ormerod. "I have a particular interest in the marks and symbols from medieval times and there may be more to see on the inside."

"Nobody has ever asked to go in there before," replied Denzil with thinly veiled suspicion. He scratched his head thoughtfully. "I don't see any objection if that's what you want."

Denzil led the way out of the church through the porch. The store building which was built parallel to the church was only divided from it by the width of the pathway. After fumbling with his keys Denzil unlocked the door and reached around in the darkness with the assurance of someone who knew the layout well. Selecting a candle holder containing a large candle from a dusty shelf he handed it to Ormerod.

"You'll need this to see anything in detail. Just be careful you don't set the place on fire. I'll be back in a few minutes. Need to find that trespasser." Denzil shuffled off, heading back up the path towards the gate.

Ormerod kept a box of matches in one of his pockets. His pipe and pouch of tobacco resided in another. He struck a match lighting the large candle and it proved sufficient to illuminate the relatively small area of the store. At first sight the interior was a disappointment. No symbols, just gardening tools leaning against the walls, dust and cobwebs. Stretching out his arm so that the light from the candle shone on the far wall of the store Ormerod noticed that the blocks in the centre of the wall were built around a rectangular granite lintel. The lintel was only a few inches above ground level and directly in front of it, set in the floor at right angles to the wall, was a large paving slab inscribed with one barely decipherable word – 'Crypt'. The slab must have been relocated to this place because it had been worn away by the regular passage of feet at the part where it met the wall. This worn, concave part of the slab had probably been in a well-trodden part of the old church. It was now in a position impossible to walk on. The group looked at the slab and then at one another. George grabbed a shovel from the assortment of garden tools and prised the corner of the slab upwards.

James found a pick axe and used it to help lever the heavy slab to one side. A set of stone stairs led down into a dark void. There was just enough space under the granite lintel for a person to descend with bowed head.

"This must be the entrance to the crypt from the original 1120 building," said Ormerod excitedly. "I wondered why the new builders had gone to the trouble to create such an impressive store."

Without further hesitation, he led the way down the stone steps, candle in hand, into the vaulted chamber of the crypt. There were only four tombs in the crypt and the group nervously huddled near Ormerod to read each inscription in the flickering light from the candle. The suspense was soon broken when they saw the word 'MARTYR' on the second tomb from the left. 'SEPULCRUM PROTI MARTYR' was inscribed on the stone side of this sepulchral monument. The coffin, or sarcophagus, was hollowed out of rock and had a solid flanged lid. The masons had crafted the lid to fit snuggly over the tomb.

"There are few circumstances when I think desecrating a grave can be justified, but I think that this is one of them," James pronounced. "I think that we need to open the tomb now before Mr. Dibble returns." The urgency in his voice reflecting what everyone was thinking.

"We need a tool to prize open the lid of the tomb," said Coral as she looked around for something suitable.

She was about to give up the search when she noticed in the gloom that leaning against the furthermost section of wall was a corroded metal bar. It had faded green paint which betrayed its origins as part of a garden tool. Next to it was a rusty spade and a discarded broom handle. The items didn't seem very old in comparison to the rest of the items in the crypt.

"They must have been left here after the church was rebuilt," Ormerod speculated. "If I use the metal bar and James synchronises my efforts with the spade we may just be able to prise the lid up at one end."

Ormerod wedged the candle in a gap, which had at some time in the distant past, held a bracket for a flaming torch. The lid was heavy and reluctant to be moved after remaining in position over the past six hundred years. The old tools were inadequate for the job and James noticed that the blade of his spade was bending as he feverishly levered on the handle. Eventually, after much exertion, the lid groaned and lifted slightly at one end. Quickly, George inserted the broom handle as a wedge. The four of them gently slid the heavy cover to one side. Not sure what to expect, but seeing a chest resting in the tomb they resisted the impulse to drop the lid and go straight to it. A bead of sweat dropped from James's brow and landed silently on the top of the old chest making a watery pattern in the dusty surface.

"Easy now," panted George. "Take it steady," he blurted as they pivoted the lid on the edge of the tomb and lowered it to the floor. It landed with a dull thud which reverberated around the walls of the crypt.

The tomb contained an ancient bundle of cloth and the old, dusty chest. The chest had a metal construction and was rectangular in shape. Although dusty, it was generally in good condition. There was a film of rust on the outer frame. It had a carrying handle at the top and was of similar size to a large brief case. A seam ran around the perimeter of the chest where the sides were separated from the top. A reinforced metal flap containing a keyhole held the lid to the base of the chest.

"Surely this must be the chest described in the coded message," gasped James.

"I would leave the sack," warned Ormerod. "It may contain the remains of the martyr called Proti. Have you remembered to bring your special key George?"

"This key has stayed firmly buttoned in my inside pocket," replied George indignantly. He decided it would be better to keep his suspicions of the stalker to himself. It would be embarrassing to admit that he had lost the map and that his carelessness had resulted in them being followed. Anyway, there were four of them and only one stalker. He felt confident that they could deal effectively with a solitary intruder.

George retrieved his key from the little hollow Bible and inserted it into the lock. The stem of the key fitted perfectly. George turned the key and the lock grated slightly in resistance. After a bit of extra pressure it gave a satisfying click before releasing the flap from the side of the chest. The thirteenth century lock had evidently been engineered with precision. Coral pulled the handle and the top of the chest opened easily sending up a small cloud of dust. Through the dust the contents of the chest were revealed. Inside were two scrolls resting in simple wooden cases and what appeared to be a gold drinking vessel.

Meanwhile outside, Denzil Dibble did not have to look far to find the trespasser. After leaving the entrance to the store he was confronted by a man who stood on the pathway legs apart blocking the route to the gate. He wore a dark cape and his broad brimmed hat was pulled low shading his features. A cigarette hung from the side of his mouth and Denzil caught the aroma of the smoke as it circulated around the man like the atmosphere of a small planet.

"I would ask you to remove your horse from my field," commanded Denzil with a politeness that he found hard to muster.

The man blew a new cloud of smoke out of his mouth and brushed past Denzil, ignoring him as though he didn't exist. Seconds later he was in the storeroom.

"Now look here….." protested Denzil, but he was cut short by the sound of the heavy grass roller being moved against the door on the inside. Ignored and out manoeuvred, Denzil found himself locked out of his own store room by the ignorant trespasser.

In the crypt everyone was absorbed by the contents of the chest. Ormerod had carefully lifted one of the scrolls out of its case and was trying to check the written symbols to see if he recognised the language. James and Coral were surprised at the weight of the gold cup and were excitedly running their fingers over the patterns embedded on the side. George carefully extricated his key from the lock and replaced it in his pocket. They were all so preoccupied and flushed with the euphoria of their discoveries, that they did not hear footsteps on the stone steps. None of them noticed the shadow which eclipsed the wall at the bottom of the steps until it was too late.

"Put the items back in the chest and move away from the tomb,"commanded the shadowy figure.

All four were startled and looked into the gloom in the direction of the voice. The dark featureless, silhouette of a man was just visible leaning casually against the first tomb. The man held a pistol in one hand and with the other he discarded his cigarette stub, which flickered to extinction across the stone floor of the crypt.

"Who are you?" asked Ormerod.

"It doesn't matter who I am. I have instructions to return these items to their rightful owner," growled the man.

"You have no idea what these items are," said Ormerod in an attempt to undermine the credibility of the man's demands.

This provocation was too much for the stranger. There was an explosion as he fired the pistol into the ground. Trickles of dust fell like tiny waterfalls from the ceiling. The bullet hit the stone floor with such violence that part of the surface chipped away sending a shower of granite particles blasting around the confines of the crypt. Everyone ducked instinctively to protect themselves as the ricochet from the impact sent the bullet zipping upwards. Coral let out a shout as the bullet grazed her cheek causing a gash which quickly turned red. A trickle of blood started to run down her face and dripped from her chin onto the floor. James was incensed at this violation against his friend and companion. He had not realised it fully until now, but he felt very protective towards Coral and reacted with fury at her injury. She was precious, a fellow survivor, someone who had shared the trauma of the storm. To be blasted by some imbicile cowering in the dark was an intolerable assault. A savage vengeance raged through him overcoming rationality.

George grabbed hold of James as he tensed to move forward, forcing him to listen. "If you kill yourself you will not be able to help Coral. Help her and leave me to deal with this situation."

George waited and slowly he was able to release his grip on James as his words sank in. James diverted his attention to helping Coral.

Turning towards their assailant George spoke decisively.

"You give us no choice, but to comply. The chest is not worth dying for."

"That's not what the Templar's thought," scoffed the man.

George overtly and with slow deliberation, returned the gold cup to the chest. Taking advantage of the distraction Ormerod discretely opened the matchbox in his jacket pocket and after fumbling for a few seconds with one hand, took out a match. He struck the match against the side of the crypt and it flared up instantly. The lighted match was like a beacon and attracted the attention of everyone in the crypt. Ormerod looked towards the shadowy figure and spoke with intent.

"If you try to take this scroll off me I will burn it," he threatened. As he spoke he moved the lighted match close to the scroll and the document started to smoulder at one end.

"This is the property of more worthy people than a gang of treasure hunters like you," shrieked the gunman as he watched the end of the scroll turn brown. Suddenly, but with decisive intent, he lunged forward and grabbed the chest. The lid snapped shut with a resounding clump as he retreated to the stairs.

"You had better guard that scroll carefully," threatened the gunman. "You will be hearing from us again."

He climbed up the stone steps holding the chest under his arm and his shadow evaporated as he departed. There was a loud explosion as he fired a warning shot which echoed around the room above.

"I would not advise that you follow me too closely," he shouted back down the stairs.

Without a word, Ormerod quickly extinguished the flame. He smothered the embers of the smouldering material with two of his fingers. Next to him the open tomb yawned in the gloom, robbed of its chest, its integrity violated, but its custody of the martyr intact.

CHAPTER 7

Rescue and Recovery

William had been unable to settle, not knowing what was happening in Temple. He had been considering hiring his own transport, but his thoughts were interrupted by the clatter of a wagon entering the yard at the back of 'The Stonemason's Arms'. The wagon had damaged a wheel. Repairing wheels was something that William knew a thing or two about having gained this skill as part of his work in Cheshire. Leaving Jayne inside the comfort of the inn, he offered to help the drayman change the wheel. During their conversation William mentioned that he and his wife were staying at the inn, but wanted to join his brother who was in a place called Temple. It transpired that the drayman was on his way to 'Jamaica Inn' with a delivery of barrels. He would be prepared to transport William and Jayne to Temple as it was near to the route he was taking across the moor. In return William agreed to repair the broken wheel the following day. This fortuitous encounter enabled the couple to reach the village of Temple seated uncomfortably between the barrels on the back of the delivery wagon. The drayman continued towards 'Jamaica Inn' promising to collect the couple on his return within a couple of hours. After thanking him, William and Jayne headed towards the church to find a very angry churchwarden strutting around the porch entrance.

"He's locked himself in the store," said Denzil indignantly and without introduction.

"Who is locked in there?" asked Jayne gently, recognising that the man was stressed.

"The bastard who trespassed on my land with that horse," snapped Denzil pointing towards his field.

"We'll go and find the keeper of the keys," offered Jayne trying to be helpful.

"I am the keeper of the keys," replied an exasperated Denzil. "I can't believe this is happening. I have two lots of visitors in one day with one man trespassing on my land then pushing past me. Not content with that he has locked himself inside the store room building. Now you have arrived. I suppose you want to climb up the tower to get a better view of the moor!"

Not reacting to the sarcasm William stepped forward to address the man directly. "How many have you let into the store?"

"Four," replied Denzil. "I told them not to………"

William cut into the sentence. "Is the man who locked the door not part of the group?"

"No. I told you he's a trespasser, and an ignorant slob," asserted Denzil. "He has wedged the grass-roller against the door on the inside and I haven't the strength to dislodge it."

Their attention was diverted by the unmistakable sound of a gunshot. They all ducked and crouched down in a defensive position. When they recovered the roller had moved and the door opened to reveal a man in a dark cape, brimmed hat pulled low to disguise his face, carrying an old chest under one arm. In his other hand he brandished a pistol still smoking from its recent discharge.

Denzil took a step forward and shouted, "Thief!"

"Back off," shouted the gunman as he threatened him with the loaded weapon.

Denzil quickly backed away, but in his haste to escape the gunman had not noticed William standing against the side wall of the store. William picked up a thick branch, which by good fortune lay invitingly by his feet. A single blow from the improvised truncheon whipped across the gunman's head. Unfortunately, the man's large hat cushioned the blow and he staggered to one side stunned by the force of the blow, but still on his feet. Denzil, who was in an angry frenzy, jumped on the man's back. He managed to land a punch on the man's head knocking off his hat to reveal a bald, fat head with a scar raking from one side to the other. Distorted by the scar but easily identifiable was a large tattoo displaying a black and white flag. The hat skimmed down the gravel path like a piece of litter in the wind. Enraged by the assault, the man acted like a caged animal, throwing Denzil off and dumping him heavily on the ground. He turned the pistol towards William, a confused expression on his face, and William thought for a moment that he was going to squeeze the trigger.

"Stop," screamed Jayne, seeing the resilience of the assailant and fearing he would execute her husband.

The gunman turned to face Jayne with a look of confused bewilderment. He appeared stunned, momentarily unable to cope. He lowered the gun and shot into the ground. The explosion echoed all around the surrounding land. The sound startled a flock of nesting rooks who took to the air, screeching like excited banshees above the violence below. William and Denzil were immobilised as each turned to look at each other to check for injuries. This was just the distraction that the assailant needed and he lumbered unsteadily up the path.

"Do not follow me if you want to see your friends," shouted the retreating assailant as he staggered to the gate.

William went to help Denzil dust himself down.

Bruised, but otherwise intact, Denzil tried to compose himself. "I don't want that ugly brute on my land," he grumbled.

"He won't be coming back," asserted William confidently. "Not today anyway. It is urgent that we check the whereabouts of your other group of visitors. One of them is my brother."

They followed Denzil into the darkness of the store. Towards the back of the building there was movement. A shadowy figure was emerging from an opening in the floor close to the rear wall.

As George emerged from the crypt he spoke from the gloom, "Who is there?"

Half expecting a gunshot he was relieved to hear familiar voices.

"It's William, and Jayne. We are with the warden," William replied.

"The others are down here," George said pointing back down the steps. "They found the chest, but Coral has been hurt."

Down in the crypt Coral was sitting with her back to the wall. James had used water from his drinking bottle and a handkerchief to clean the wound on her face. He had stopped the flow of blood, but it was obvious that she was still in shock as she sat pale faced, holding the cloth against her cheek. It was an odd reunion in the dismal atmosphere of the crypt, and they all realised that they had been lucky that there hadn't been more casualties.

"Did that monster shoot you?" Jayne asked as she looked anxiously at Coral's injury.

"He needs locking up before he kills someone," mumbled Coral.

George, William and Ormerod struggled to heave the stone cover back on top of the open tomb. They knew that they needed to get Coral some medical attention.

"That cover was heavy. I was beginning to think that we would never get it back in place," sighed George.

"You have desecrated a grave for that old chest?" said Denzil in disgust.

Speaking his thoughts out loud Ormerod replied so that all could hear. "We owe you an explanation."

Denzil looked puzzled. "What is there to explain?"

"Help us to get our friend outside and as soon as I have a chance I will tell you why we came here," replied Ormerod.

James and Jayne supported Coral back to the cart and sat her down on the front seat. James put a blanket round her shoulders and she leaned against him resting her head on his shoulder. Colour started to return to her face as the moorland air refreshed her lungs. She looked up and spoke to Jayne.

"It's good to see you and William, but how did you get here?"

"William negotiated a lift on the back of a beer wagon," replied Jayne. "We arrived just as that maniac was leaving."

"A piece of bad timing," said George unhelpfully as he climbed aboard. Graciously, he opened the hamper and offered around the remains of the food. "We don't want to suffer hunger as well as humiliation," he remarked to the group.

The other three men emerged from the store and Denzil locked the door. Turning to Ormerod he said, "It just shows how easy it is to become complacent. I have been in the store many times, but never did I suspect that there was a crypt underneath, let alone an ancient chest."

"Well you had no reason to look," said Ormerod sympathetically.

"You do realise that I will have to amend my tours to include the crypt!" Denzil reflected.

As they walked back to the gate Ormerod wrapped the scroll in his overcoat to protect it until they reached the cart.

Denzil hung precariously onto the back of the cart, one hand pointing as he gave directions to George. "There is a doctor who lives in the village just two hundred yards down the road. He is a friend of mine and will treat the young woman's wound."

William and Jayne walked back to the road through the village to await the return of the drayman.

Guided by Denzil, the cart stopped outside a stone cottage which doubled as a home and a surgery for the doctor and his family. After placing a clean dressing across her wound the doctor told Coral that the cut would not require stiches. "Fortunately, it is not a deep cut and should heal naturally without leaving a scar," he said reassuringly, before turning to get an antiseptic cream from his cupboard.

"Thank you for seeing us," said James "We are all grateful to you for helping our friend."

The doctor just waved his hand and said without ceremony "Glad to help." He never asked what had caused the wound, but James thought that he was suspicious as to its origin. His association with Denzil probably meant that it wouldn't be very long before he got updated on the whole story.

Whilst the doctor was explaining to Coral how to continue to treat her wound Ormerod took Denzil to one side and told him about their quest. Denzil listened and his frown grew more pronounced as the story unfolded. As Ormerod finished telling the story of the shipwreck, the pouch and the message, it was time to leave the surgery. Denzil expressed his regret that James and Coral had been exposed to another ordeal so soon after their rescue from the sea.

Once outside, Denzil sighed with weary resignation. "It seems that you have found me another room to clear out! If you manage to interpret that scroll let me know," he said looking towards Ormerod. "Meanwhile, I think you all need to take care. The curate from Blisland administers the religious services in the church, but there is someone in Tintagel who overseas proceedings here. He belongs to some sort of ancient Order. Sometimes members of the Order dress up in white gowns with a large red cross on the front. They always strike me as a bit menacing and so I never ask questions. I just think you need to be careful not to antagonise them."

They thanked Denzel for his advice and bade him farewell. Even though he had been grumpy for much of the day they had gradually warmed to his dubious charms.

"Sorry, for the trouble we caused today," said George. "Thanks for the history lesson though."

The cart headed for home. James felt content to be returning to Trebarwith knowing that they had been correct in decoding the message. They may not have acquired the chest, but at least they had custody of one scroll. As they sat huddled together in the back of the cart he was glad to be physically close to Coral. She looked up at him with a warm smile. She didn't need to say anything. James knew that she cared about him too. Ormerod sat in a contorted position next to George with one sleeve of his grey overcoat containing his arm and the other sleeve held in front of his chest with the scroll pushed up it for protection. During the journey Ormerod invited Coral to accompany him to the university the next day. The whole reason she had come to Cornwall was to involve herself in ancient studies. It was her interest and her occupation. She was flattered by the invitation, but couldn't help wishing that she could stay with James instead.

It was another uncomfortable journey for William and Jayne in the drayman's wagon. They were preoccupied with their own reflections of the dramatic events at the church and time seemed to pass quickly. By the time they reached 'The Stonemason's Arms' in Camelford it was dark and they felt physically and mentally exhausted. Although it was only the previous day, it seemed a long time since they had all sat in Ormerod's room deciphering the message.

When George delivered James and Coral back to 'The Strand' the bar was buzzing with activity as regular patrons and music lovers savoured the delights of 'The Rum Runners', a folk group specialising in sea shanties. Vicky was shocked to see Coral had injured her face.

"Just a flesh wound," said Coral trying to avoid a full explanation.

Vicky looked at her sceptically, "Better duck more quickly next time my dear," she said, not wanting to spoil the atmosphere. "Hunting can be a dangerous activity."

The couple found a table and listened to the entertainment whilst enjoying a chicken and mushroom pie. Jake was an experienced landlord and he knew that a combination of beer and music were a volatile mix, but it never ceased to surprise him how the most placid individuals seemed to find full voice after a few pints of ale. For James and Coral it was a relaxing diversion from their eventful day and after their meal they found themselves engaging with the crowd in some familiar songs until the evening ended at about eleven o'clock.

"What a day of contrasts," said James as he and Coral eventually reached the first floor landing. "Triumph followed by near tragedy, treasure found and lost, was it worth it?" Looking into Coral's eyes James looked concerned. "It has been a good evening, but you were close to disaster earlier today. I realised that I would have been desolate without you."

Coral leaned forward and as their lips met they kissed passionately. "I never thought I would meet someone as kind as you when I booked that voyage," said Coral. James pushed the door open and they fell on the bed in a warm embrace. Jake would only need one room for them in future.

CHAPTER 8

Dubious Proposal

Coral felt relieved to be safe and warm next to James in the bed they had shared last night. She felt happier and more relaxed than for a long time. The year had not turned out anything like she had imagined. The shipwreck had been a nightmare, but she felt lucky to have met James. They were so different, yet in things that were important, they were in harmony. A feeling of optimism flooded through her as she contemplated the future. James still lay asleep and Coral gently brushed her hand over his hair. Eventually, her thoughts turned to her work. She remembered that today she would be assisting in the dissemination of an ancient scroll.

Investigating historical mysteries was an activity that particularly appealed to Coral. Discovering new facts by scientific study could be quite exciting. There were moments, after long and critical investigations, when suddenly something new materialised. These moments gave immense satisfaction and drove the researcher forward. She had read in a journal of cryptology that if you were to select any English book and list all the words it contained in order, from the most commonly used to the least, you would find 'the' at the top. Moving down the list you would eventually arrive at the long tail of words that had only been used once. The rate at which the most common words give way to the least common, or the rate of decay as the author called it, was a calculation which could be applied universally to all languages. Different languages all followed the same pattern, without any producer of the language setting that as a purpose. Coral made a mental note to remind Ormerod about this as being a possible method of checking that any text written in the scroll was a genuine language. They would not want to waste time on aimless gibberish created by a medieval hoaxer.

During breakfast Jake stopped by to ask Coral how she was feeling, after noticing the scar on her cheek was inflamed. Coral had decided that after she had applied the cream it would be better to let the air get to the wound. She told Jake that she was looking forward to meeting Ormerod in Camelford as they had work to do. Jake had business in Camelford that morning and he offered to stop outside 'The Stonemason's Arms' as it was on his route. She would then be able to travel on to the university after she met with Ormerod.

"Just promise that you won't return with any more injuries," said Jake. "This is the West Country, not the Wild West, although I must admit that it does look wild out there this morning!"

Coral exchanged a furtive glance with James who was sat opposite. Smiling at Jake she promised to be careful. It was clear that Jake was suspicious as to how Coral had received her injury, but he carried on with his jobs without another word.

"I've been thinking," said James between sips of a large mug of tea. "I was trying to work out how that stalker knew so much about us. It could be that he just overheard our conversations and decided to try his luck, but it was the way he mentioned the Templars that troubled me. Almost as if he was one of them. He used the word 'us' when threatening further trouble. He seemed to be passionate about the ownership of the chest as though it was a violation that we should have found it."

"He did seem very possessive about the chest," added Coral. "There was no other person outside our group who knew about the pouch so how would he know we were searching for items related to the Templars?"

James finished his tea and sat back. "There was another person who saw the pouch. Do you remember the night we were rescued in the cellar and I dropped the pouch when I was changing out of my wet clothes?"

"I remember seeing you with George and the doctor as I was taken to the bar," Coral responded. "You were shivering uncontrollably like me."

"That's it," said James, giving Coral's hand a squeeze. "The doctor was the only person close enough to see the detail on the pouch apart from George."

After considering this for a minute Coral asked, "Do you think that the doctor became involved in a conspiracy to possess the chest as a result of recognising the symbol on the pouch?"

James remained silent for a while trying to remember the incident. It was not a time he wanted to recall, but it did appear to be significant. "Well he did show a reaction when he saw the symbol."

"You mean like a raised eyebrow," said Coral thoughtfully.

"Yes, just like that, but he made no remark. There is a possibility that he may be implicated in the drama that we endured yesterday. I think I will pay George a visit to see if he can tell me more about the doctor. They are both on the rescue team and have known each other for years, so he may be able to give me some background."

"It may be that George has been thinking on the same lines. After all, he was there too!"

They both stood up and Coral put her arms around James's waist. She fondly kissed him goodbye. "Be careful," she said. "I have to go now because I think Jake is waiting to collect me. See you later."

The walk to Trebarwith farm from 'The Strand' was short and steep. It was cold and the wind tugged at his clothing, but James felt quite hot by the time he approached the farmhouse. There was no answer to his knock on the front door so he walked round to see if there was anyone working in the other farm buildings. He soon met with Catherine who was loading hay for the cattle in the cowshed. She explained that George was still out on his milk deliveries.

"Do you know when he is due back?" James enquired.

"Anytime now," Catherine replied after checking her watch. "He's supposed to be helping me muck out this cow shed. I hope you have recovered from the ordeal yesterday at Temple. George told me about that poor girl getting shot and the man running off with the chest. He was lucky not to lose the necklace key. Anyway, how is Coral today?"

James response did not disguise the anger he still felt. "She's alright, no thanks to that maniac with the gun. I am sorry to trouble you when you are working. I just wanted to ask George a few questions about the doctor who helped with the rescue on the night we were shipwrecked."

"That will be Doctor Sherwin. He has been on the rescue team with George for years." Catherine sounded a little breathless after launching another bale of hay onto the shelf from which the cows fed. She leaned on her pitchfork and asked, "Is it something specific that that you want to know about him?"

James hesitated for a moment. "I know that this must sound a bit paranoid. It's just that the doctor is the only other person outside our group who saw the pouch and it occurred to me that he might be connected to the events yesterday."

"I don't know the doctor very well," said Catherine. This is partly because we have been fortunate to have had good health and haven't had to call on his services. I have heard that he is a good doctor, but he is also a private person. He keeps himself to himself and doesn't interact much with community events."

The clatter of a horse and cart entering the farm interrupted their conversation. It was George accompanied by the doctor. They pulled to a halt and both men jumped down from the cart. The horse dragged a hoof, kicking up a small clod of earth and then nonchalantly sauntered off to nibble on a bale of fresh hay, pulling the empty cart behind.

"I didn't expect to meet you here today," said George. "You were due to visit William and Jayne in Camelford weren't you?"

"What happened yesterday has been preying on my mind," explained James. "I thought you and the doctor might be able to clarify something."

"What happened has also caused me some concern," said George. That is why I am here with doctor Sherwin. I called at his surgery to check something that was troubling me all last night."

"If it's the same thing that has been troubling me you will have asked him whether he is connected to the drama at Temple yesterday," James asserted with obvious tension.

Looking straight at the doctor James spoke with the intensity of a detective. "That night in the cellar you and George were the only people to see the symbol on the pouch. How odd that yesterday a complete stranger stalked us across the moor and declared our discoveries to be sacrilegious. He was genuinely indignant, accusing us of violating the Templar Order. I don't believe the man just stumbled across us. I think he must have been informed about the pouch and I can only think that his informant was you."

The doctor listened impassively. "If you think that I am connected to the drama at Temple Church then you would be correct," he replied honestly. My organisation has possession of the chest and its contents. I have explained to George about my involvement and he has brought me here because he holds the key needed to open the chest. We do not want to damage it."

A flush of anger descended over James. "The key is nothing compared with someone's life. My friend was within a whisker of being killed yesterday."

Realising that a confrontation was brewing George intervened and asked the two men to follow him to the farmhouse. "We can't sort this out standing here in this gale, we need to discuss it calmly inside."

"Don't expect dinner to be on the table if you are leaving me to clean out the cow shed," shouted Catherine. It was a job that George would normally have done and whilst Catherine was willing to help, she had no intention of being taken for granted.

"Sorry," George replied. " I promise that I'll be with you as soon as I can." It was probable that George was going to suffer an empty stomach that lunchtime.

The three men sat down in the room that James recognised as being where George had first shown him the necklace key. Through the window the fields looked barren today with misty sea spray drifting over the undulating landscape. Occasionally, a glimpse of the grey green sea emerged from the gloom. There was a log fire burning, but the atmosphere was frosty. The doctor sighed heavily and with a weary look of resignation he sat down at the table facing the other two men. He placed his hands together on the table as if he was about to pray. A sprig of his well-groomed, black hair, fell forward as he leaned forward to speak.

"As I have explained to George I am not just the local doctor. I am also preceptor of the modern Knights Templar. My members represent the ancient Preceptory of Trebeigh of which Temple Church is a part. We newly formed Templars are called 'The Preceptory of King Arthur' and we meet regularly in Tintagel. We are pledged to pursue excellence in work and daily life. We are committed to provide humanitarian help to the poor, and the sick. To help those on a pilgrimage, and to preserve Christian places in the Holy Land. We also aspire to be a chivalrous, inter denominational, Christian society providing practical charity."

James could not help interrupting. He could not let this hypocrisy continue unanswered. "There was no Christian chivalry yesterday when you condoned lethal force in order to get what you wanted."

"You should be careful of what you say when you do not know all the facts," snapped the doctor.

"The facts are that you employed a killer to enforce your wishes," asserted James.

"The killer you refer to is a long standing member of our preceptory. He fought in the first Boar War in the British Naval Brigade. He was seriously wounded in battle at Majumba Hill on the Transvaal border. The Brigade suffered a forty six per cent casualty rate that day and the man you call a killer incurred a serious head wound risking his own life to save a wounded comrade. His injury does sometimes affect his judgement and I admit that he was ill advised to carry a gun. His instructions were to observe and report back on your activities which I knew would be connected to the symbol I saw on the pouch. I can assure you that he is not a killer in the way you describe."

"Well that may be so, said James, but the fact remains that you have taken advantage of our research, stolen the very items we were searching for and nearly got my friend killed."

"I am very sorry about your friend," replied the doctor. However, you have to realise that the objects you found were not yours to possess. You trespassed on Templar land without authority and removed property of which we have been the custodians for six hundred years."

James sighed with exasperation. "Without my discovery of the pouch in that cave they would have stayed there for another six hundred years."

Doctor Sherwin's patience was being severely tested, but he remained calm. "You speak without knowledge of the historical context which pertains to the property deposited in the crypt. The Templars fought a decisive battle in a place called Acre in 1291. After that they had to evacuate from the Holy Land. Two hundred years of occupation ended following that battle and many documents and ideas were brought back to Western Europe by knights who had fought there. The persecution of the Templars did not end with their return from the Holy Land," the doctor continued. In a voice that did not disguise his contempt, he explained, "On Friday 13th October, 1307 the Templars were charged with heresy by the Pope. The Templars had obtained a cache of writings during their time in Jerusalem and they had also gleaned knowledge after living amongst different cultures for centuries. This had changed the way they thought and the way they worshipped. Unfortunately, Pope Clement V felt that the authority of the early church was being undermined and in collaboration with the greedy French King, Philip IV, he had the Templars arrested en masse. Most of their land and wealth were confiscated by the crown and some of it handed to the Knights Hospitallier. So perhaps you can begin to understand why we consider the chest to be lost Templar property."

"It was lost property," said James.

"That does not mean that the finder is entitled to keep it," replied the doctor.

Sensing that the conversation was deteriorating again George interrupted. "James, do you remember that letter I sent to the church in Ireland? Well, I received a reply this morning. Their archivist confirms that there was a person who worked at Mellifont Abbey in 1291. His name was Sholto Kelley. He left Mellifont on a pilgrimage to the Holy Land, but there is no record of him returning."

"That name confirms the letters on the gravestone on your farm," exclaimed James. "He must have died the same year that he went on his pilgrimage."

"That is one reason why I asked Doctor Sherwin to accompany me back here," said George. "I asked him the same question you did about his involvement with the Templars. We have worked together many times for the coastguard, and I was shocked when he confirmed that he was a preceptor of the modern Templar movement. Similarly, he had no idea that my family has a connection with Sholto Kelley or that we have held the symbolic key for centuries. I wish that we could have shared our common interests without confrontation. We can't undo what has happened, but we should try to reconstruct our relationship. I think we need to think about ways to resolve the issues which are causing division."

A pensive doctor Sherwin leaned back in his chair and spoke slowly choosing his words carefully. "It seems to me that your recent letter confirms the connection between the Templars and the chest in the crypt. Fate provided you with the pouch left centuries ago by a person who most likely was linked to our movement. He may well have risked his life to bring the chest home and I am sure he would not want his loyalty to be betrayed by petty rivalries."

Looking at James he continued. "You were expeditious enough to locate and retrieve Sholto Kelley's chest. However, I do not think that you were the intended recipient. Most of the old Templars could not read and needed to find members of the clergy to decipher written materials that came into their possession. The scroll was probably destined to be delivered to a monastery. The scrolls may contain information important to the enrichment of our movement and that is primarily why it matters that we access them. This is not about money, or possession, or ownership. It's about knowledge. I have the chest, one of the scrolls and a solid gold cup. You have the key, the pouch and the other scroll. Since yesterday my experts have been busy deciphering the scroll. I presume that you will be attempting to do the same with the scroll in your possession."

"Do you have a proposal?" enquired George hurriedly. He wanted to prempt any provocative comment that James might be about to utter.

"Firstly, we try to co-operate rather than confront," said the doctor grandly. "I am prepared to invite you to a special meeting of 'The Preceptory of King Arthur' where I will reveal the results of our research team. In return you would provide your findings to my members."

"You say that the knowledge is what matters most, but what happens to the scrolls, the chest and the cup after the meeting?" James asked with a hint of scepticism.

"The chest and its contents were intended for the Templars. They put in the research, the effort and the initiative to obtain these items six hundred years ago whilst in hostile territory, so I do not feel there is any injustice in us retaining them. I would be prepared to return the gold cup to your group in exchange for the missing scroll. You keep the pouch."

The doctor looked across to where George was sitting. "I am looking forward to seeing the key to the chest. Obviously, this item will stay with you as it has been in your family for generations."

"So those are your final terms?" James interjected.

"There is one other matter that might help to confirm my good faith," replied the doctor. "I will make a search through the old records pertaining to the 'Preceptory of Trebeigh' in the hope that more can be discovered about Sholto Kelley. There are records going back to the thirteenth century in our archives. If you accept my offer I will be pleased to share any details with you."

Rising from his seat Doctor Sherwin walked over to the window and looking out across the farmland with his back to the room he asked, "Do you accept my proposals?"

Both George and James stood up as if choreographed. George was the first to speak. "You will get an answer after we have spoken with the other members of our group."

There was still something troubling James about the terms. "From what you have told us I do have a better understanding of why the scrolls are important to you. None of us know the contents at this moment, but let's presume that they contain something sensational. Under your proposal there will be a total lack of dissemination outside the people at the meeting. Why should these potential revelations be locked away in your preceptory and denied to historians or other interested parties?"

Doctor Sherwin turned from the window and fixed his gaze on James. "You make a good point and one that deserves consideration." He pondered for a while whilst James headed for the door. He needed to get back to 'The Strand'.

"Much depends on what is in the scrolls," said the doctor. "There may be things that can only be understood by those with the means to understand. To the uninitiated certain information could be dangerously misconstrued. Bearing this in mind, I can arrange for the chest and the scrolls to be deposited on long term loan with the museum in Truro if that would satisfy you."

"It may well help our group to view your proposals more sympathetically when we meet to discuss this later tonight," James replied cautiously.

As he left, James arranged for George and Catherine to meet with him and Coral that evening at 'The Strand'. On his way back from Trebarwith Farm he had time to reflect. He still felt angry about Coral's injury, but from what the doctor had told him he could understand why the sight of the pouch on the night of the shipwreck had been of such interest to him. Perhaps the proposal they had to consider was reasonable, although he suspected that the doctor expected the contents of the scroll to be digested only by his disciples. He would have to wait to see what the others thought.

CHAPTER 9

Unexpected Revelations

For William and Jayne what had started as a routine day eventually turned out to be quiet exciting. The drayman had been so pleased with the repairs to his wheel that he had asked if the couple, 'from up North' as he referred to them, would like to accompany him to Tintagel. He convinced them that it was not too far from Camelford and that the ardour of the journey would be more than compensated for by views of King Arthur's Castle. William suspected that the draymen enjoyed company on his delivery journeys because he talked incessantly until they alighted from the wagon outside the 'Old Post Office' in Tintagel village. Following the drayman's directions they proceeded down a narrow lane that twisted, turned and undulated, until the sea appeared over the brow of a hill. The Parish Church of St. Materiana, surrounded by a cemetery, occupied a plot on the cliff top. They had been told by the garrulous drayman that the church dated back to the eleventh century and was located where they would have good views of Tintagel Island.

As they stood outside the lynch gate to the church they had a panoramic view of the Atlantic Ocean. Heading towards them from across the open sea was a shroud of grey mist which heralded an imminent downpour. Thinking it would be prudent to take shelter, William suggested that they enter the church until the weather abated. They were fortunate to meet the long standing vicar of the parish who was sitting in a pew, busily writing the parish notices. After explaining that they were sheltering from the elements outside and hearing that they were visitors from Cheshire, the kindly vicar treated them to a tour of the church. It was when they entered the vestry and saw volumes of church records that Jayne had an inspiration. She explained that they knew George Denke from Trebarwith Farm because of his role in helping her brother in law after the recent shipwreck. George had told them that someone called Sholto Kelley was buried on his farm and there was a gravestone inscribed with the date, 1291.

"I don't suppose that you have a record going back that far?" Jayne asked the vicar. "George told us that he had never found out who Sholto Kelley was?"

The vicar explained that the Parish Records for Births, Deaths and Marriages only went back as far as 1538. Seeing the disappointment on their faces he suggested that they would need to check the land registry or tax records to find out who was responsible for the farm in 1291. They were about to leave when the vicar beckoned them to the large painting of an ecclesiastical figure mounted on the oak panel wall of the vestry.

There was a click as the vicar pulled the side of the painting towards him. The panel behind the painting was hinged and it opened to reveal a cavity full of documents.

"This cavity contains an assortment of old parish leaflets, service sheets and a diary for the year 1310, presumably kept by a member of the clergy at the time. The diary just seems to have been placed in here and the writer forgot to remove it. It is possible that there may be something relevant amongst these items," suggested the vicar.

William was aware that they would not have time to meticulously search through all the batches of papers, because they had promised to meet the drayman back in the village. Explaining their predicament, William asked if it would be permissible to glance quickly at the diary. It was not the year they were interested in, but it might provide names of local people and life in the parish around this time. Keen to oblige in a little piece of historical research the vicar dutifully placed the diary on the vestry table. William opened the cover carefully, and the diary fell open sending out a little puff of dust. The date, 9th April was displayed complete with beautifully neat handwriting, testament to a very meticulous author.

"Perhaps I should explain about that particular date," said the vicar as he looked across the table. "Saint Materiana was a Welsh saint who lived in the fifth century. Apparently, she ruled Gwent with her husband Prince Ynyr and her feast day is 9th April. She had a tomb in this church until the reformation."

The page was full of information about activities surrounding the feast. William slowly turned the pages back towards the start of the year. He was just about to close the diary when he noticed that a silk marker had been left in the page for 17th March. There was to be a meeting with two people due to be married that coming weekend. As William's eye scanned the page a flush of excitement enveloped him.

"Look," he exclaimed as his finger pointed to an entry half way down the page. *"Meet Sholto Denke and Charlotte Lursk at Trebarwith Farm 2pm".*

"Sholto is such an unusual name and to be linked to the Denke name, which is George's surname, must surely be significant," said Jayne thoughtfully.

They both thanked the vicar for his patience and left feeling quite elated. The vicar was satisfied that their visit had enriched their knowledge of the Denke family history. He promised to forward any new information about the Denke or Lursk families that he unearthed in the future.

After hurrying back to the village, they joined the drayman seated imperiously on his wagon, waiting patiently for them outside 'The Old Post Office'.

"I was beginning to think you'd got lost," he retorted. "Did you say that you wanted to alight at the end of the lane that leads down to Trebarwith?"

"Yes that would be ideal. We are meeting my brother at 'The Strand' down at the bottom of the lane." William replied.

By the time they reached 'The Strand' William and Jayne fully appreciated a comfortable seat in the warmth of the bar. It had been a long downhill walk from the main road linking Tintagel and Camelford. James was already there looking at his pint of ale pensively as though all the answers to his problems lay somewhere inside the glass He still felt tense after his anguished conversations at the farm and was glad to be joined by friendly faces.

"Did you manage to fix that wagon?" asked James.

"Not only that, but we went to the church in Tintagel," laughed William. He couldn't wait to tell James about their discovery.

William described their venture at St Materiana's church. Jayne was conscious of the conversation taking place across the table, but she was preoccupied with thoughts about the connections between names. When William had finished speaking she was ready to voice her conclusions.

"This information may explain how the little Bible, the key and necklace came to be an heirloom in George's family," she added triumphantly.

"Precisely," replied William. "The link that George talked about between the old Trebarwith Inn and his farm was probably forged through the marriage of Sholto Denke and Charlotte Lursk. The farm could have been inherited by them and then by their children through the successive generations."

"George will be fascinated when you tell him what you found," said James. "It is possible that Sholto Denke could be related to Sholto Kelley. Do you think that Sholto Denke could have been the son of Sholto Kelley?"

"I don't think that we will ever know what happened," said William sadly. "It must have been Sholto Kelley who left the pouch in the cave. If you remember, the message inside said that he felt that his life was in danger. Perhaps, he was trying to escape from his enemies through the cave. All we know for certain is that he is buried on Trebarwith Farm".

"I agree that all the circumstantial evidence points that way. However, it seems odd that a person from a monastery, returning from the holy land and entrusted with Templar property should have formed a relationship and produced a child," mused James.

"Who would have thought that a merchant seaman delivering salt would have formed a relationship with an academic person studying legends," said Jayne with a wry smile.

"Strange things happen," James agreed. "Just think about events less than a week ago. What were the chances of me finding the pouch in the cave? I could have been shipwrecked anywhere along three hundred miles of coastline. Why that cave, and why exactly six hundred years since the pouch was left there? Is all this just chance, or is it some sort of weird coincidence? I find it rather unsettling."

"Maybe there isn't anything to understand except that it was your destiny," Jayne reflected. She touched James on the arm and whispered, "In any case I'm really glad you have found someone you care for and she obviously cares about you."

James sucked in a deep breath. "Thanks for bringing me down to earth. You're correct. What matters most isn't why those things happened. More important is the result."

Quickly changing the subject James continued, "George is coming here this evening and you will have a chance to talk to him about his family genealogy. Let's eat and then after lunch I can tell you about what happened this morning at the farm."

The light soon fades in Cornwall during the month of January, but from the garden of 'The Strand', looking west, out across the Atlantic, James, William and Jayne watched the last embers of light fade behind Gull Rock. This evening the weather had calmed and the dark silhouette of the rocky island was encircled with white surf cascading around its base. The rhythmic pulse of the ocean continued unabated, orchestrated by the thunder of breakers dispatching themselves against the rocky headlands.The gentle swish of each wave sent out a soothing resonance as it unravelled across the beach. Seabirds hovered around their nests, their calls announcing the onset of night. They could all smell the fresh salty air and couldn't help reflect on the natural beauty of this place.

The tranquillity was interrupted by the pounding of hooves. A pony and trap that Ormerod had borrowed from the university was the first to arrive. Coral jumped down and hugged James. He put his hands on her shoulders and kissed her forehead. Her hair was fresh and scented even though she had been working all day. Before they could speak George and Catherine arrived on the scene. The group entered 'The Strand' and George had a quiet word with Jake about using a small private room adjoining the bar. It was barely big enough for seven people, but Jake grandly referred to it as the conference room. It wasn't used often, but earlier that day a meeting had been held by a group of weekend visitors. The fire was still burning and the room provided them with more privacy in which to disseminate their findings.

"I hope this conference room will prove adequate for a meeting of the history detectives," announced Jake. He knew that Ormerod and Coral were academics interested in the King Arthur stories. He could not resist gently mocking the fact that they were spending so much time investigating what he believed to be a myth.

George ordered drinks and it wasn't long before they all relaxed, helped by the excellent beer and wine. There had been so much recent drama that it was good to sit and talk without the threat of some dangerous intrusion. If conviviality had been a liquid, the room would have flooded. Hearing William describe the information from the church in Tintagel was a revelation to George and Catherine.

"This confirms the old family connection between this inn and the farm," said Catherine. Looking at George she added, "It appears that you could well be a distant blood relation of Sholto Kelley. You have become the custodian of the key left by your ancestor!"

The word 'custodian' troubled George. "When I showed doctor Sherwin the key this morning I did feel a sense of mission regarding the chest and its contents. Whilst he was emphasising the chest as a legacy bestowed to his movement, I started to realise that I had become responsible for an important family artefact."

"We don't know much about what Sholto's mission was," said James thoughtfully. "When we know what the scroll contains we might get a better idea. This may give you a better perspective as to how important your responsibility is."

Ormerod sat casually in his seat with his long legs sprawled under the table. He put his beer down on the table and lit his pipe as William went to replenish the drinks. Smoke puffed out from the pipe forming a blue haze in the small room.

"The scroll that Coral and I have been examining at the university is proving to be a valuable source of new information related to our study of the Arthurian stories," pronounced Ormerod. "I know you are anxious to hear about its contents, but you are going to have to be patient. It will take another few days to fully disseminate the details. Remember it is an ancient, delicate item and needs to be treated with respect."

The disappointment in the room was palpable and a hushed silence descended on the gathering. Sensing the negative atmosphere, Ormerod quickly resumed speaking.

"If Coral would be so kind as to update you with the situation I can enjoy a smoke of this excellent tobacco mixture."

This was a surprise to Coral who was feeling a little heady having consumed her glass of wine more quickly than was her custom. She rose from her chair to gain a bit more space. James admired the soft curves of her body as she stood up and steadied herself against the edge of the table. Ormerod winked at her as she shuffled through some notes made at the university. How she wished she had written larger and more spaced notes. The wording was slightly blurred as if she needed spectacles. This address was going to be more spontaneous than autocued.

"The scroll has revealed some missing pieces of an ancient jigsaw puzzle," she began. Her voice sounded strangely loud as if it belonged to someone else. "The scroll is written in Aramaic on parchment and was written in approximately 63AD. It describes the evangelical travels of Joseph of Arimathea. He was a rich, educated and well-connected individual who was involved in the tin trade.

"Is that all?" said James expectantly.

Coral sat down and took another sip of wine. Normally she

would have been irritated by what she perceived as a silly comment. The wine had soothed her and she remained unruffled. "That may be a little writing, but it is a lot of information. It is like a few small pieces in a larger picture. When you add these extra pieces the overall picture becomes clearer."

"I wish I knew more about the bigger picture," James replied.

"If you have not studied history then it is harder to get an overview of how these pieces of information interlock," said Coral patiently.

"The scroll does not appear to be complete," added Ormerod leaning to knock his pipe out on the hearth. "Some of it has disintegrated over time and some of it has been damaged by weather and rough handling. What we suspect is that it was hidden under the Temple in Jerusalem round about the time of the Jewish Revolt against the Romans in 66AD by a sect called the Essenes. The Templars could have discovered it and the other scroll during their excavations under the Temple during their time of occupation. They may have moved the scrolls to the safe crusader stronghold in Acre. In 1291, when the city fell to the Muslims, Sholto Kelley must have been entrusted with the scrolls at the time he was evacuated."

"It's a pity that we weren't able to keep the other scroll," said James. It would have been interesting to discover whether it complements, supplements or duplicates what is in our scroll."

"Coral and I have a meeting with Professor Forest, the University translator at The Old Grammar School, in College Road, Camelford, on Wednesday 14th. If you are all in agreement, I can reserve a room in the school so that we can give you a more comprehensive idea of the scroll contents," suggested Ormerod.

George and Catherine apologised that they would not be available to attend on that day. They knew that they would be occupied with work on the farm. The other members of the group had no other business to attend and nodded their agreement. They promised to update George and Catherine at the earliest opportunity.

"Alright then, we will meet at two o'clock on Wednesday," said Ormerod decisively.

Talk of meetings suddenly jolted George's memory about the deal that Doctor Sherwin had offered them.

"Earlier today Doctor Sherwin offered us a proposal concerning access to the other scroll. It may be our only way of gaining entry to the contents," George suggested.

A chorus of voices echoed spontaneously around the table. "What proposal?" There was a tone of both surprise and anticipation in the air.

George, assisted from time to time by James, revealed the discussions that had taken place at the farm. The group listened carefully, absorbing the details of the deal offered by Doctor Sherwin.

Ormerod leaned his elbows on the table and addressed the group.

"I don't know what the rest of you think, but from what I have just heard it seems a reasonable deal under the circumstances. We get access to the contents of the other scroll and George recovers the cup left by his ancestor."

As nobody could see how the offer could be improved they all silently nodded their agreement.

In the corner of his eye George noticed that Coral had remained passive. Her head had remained still and she seemed transfixed by some distant object on the far wall as if hypnotised in her own thoughts. She looked slightly forlorn.

"Everything alright", George enquired worried that the discussion may have brought back the memory of her injury in the crypt.

Stung back into reality by the sound of George's voice Coral felt embarrassed that her detachment had been noticed.

"Sorry, to be so distant," she said. "I was just thinking how much the scroll could add to my study of the King Arthur legend. Of course I would like to know what was on the other scroll, but who will be invited to this meeting? I'll bet The Preceptory of King Arthur is just a secret society for men who like to dress up. They will exclude me just like the men who selected stories for the Bible excluded Mary Magdalene."

"I am told by the preceptor," George replied pedantically, "that they are not a secret society. They are a society with secrets. If you are not invited then none of us will go. I plan to meet Doctor Sherwin tomorrow and will make your invitation a condition of our acceptance. I understand that the meetings of 'The Preceptory of King Arthur' are on the third Sunday of each month, so the next date will be a week today on Sunday 18th January."

"William and I would have liked to have come with you," said Jayne. "Unfortunately, we have to return to Cheshire the day before. William has commitments back at work on the Monday morning. We were so relieved to find James safe when we arrived a few days ago, and never anticipated that he would be connected with a mystery. We will be returning knowing that James has such good friends around him."

"That means that you will still be here when the Board of Trade meeting is held in Tintagel next Friday 16th January," said James.

"They have been quick to organise the hearing considering the shipwreck only happened a week ago. When did you find out about it James?" asked Coral.

"After talking to Jake earlier this evening. Apparently, an official called at the inn while I was at George's farm this morning and left a letter summoning us to attend the hearing at Trevena House. Sorry I didn't mention it before, but there's been so much happening that it slipped my mind." James fumbled in his jacket pocket and handed the letter for Coral to read.

Coral shrugged her shoulders and took in a deep breath before handing the letter back to James. They both knew that they would have to be at the hearing for the sake of the people who died. It was just that they dreaded having to relive the tragedy of the shipwreck again.

"I am glad that we will still be here to support you both," said Jayne. "The sooner the hearing is completed the sooner you will be able to rebuild your lives."

"You have a settled, busy life in Cheshire," said Coral. "I have spent so much time in libraries and lectures doing the research that

I enjoy, I didn't consider the future very much. This terrible accident has changed my life dramatically. It has made me realise that there's more to enjoy than just developing a career. I'm grateful that I'm still alive and have been lucky in having met James."

Jayne smiled and spoke sincerely in response. "I'm so pleased for you both. It will be a new dawn for James. He's been a bit of an adventurer, but since he's met you he seems much more content. I hope that we will see more of you in the future."

"I hope that you will," Coral replied. "We just need to emerge from this tragedy. Then we can move forward with greater clarity."

"You are welcome to stay with us in Cheshire until you decide what direction to take next," said William.

Fond memories of the recent Christmas holiday spent with his brother emerged for James. It would be tempting to return home to Cheshire. He had been born and bred there amongst the green fields, the farms and the winding lanes. He had friends, relatives and contacts with the shipping line in Cheshire. Circumstances had changed now that he had met Coral and he felt differently about where home was. The whole reason why Coral had made the journey to Cornwall was because of her work and James knew that she would want to stay and complete her research. His heart was strongly telling him that he wanted to stay in Cornwall, but he did not want his brother to think that he did not appreciate his offer.

"That's a really generous and tempting offer," replied James. "My family roots are in Cheshire and I will always have fond memories of it, but right now I want to stay down here for a while to help Coral complete her research."

"I thought you were sceptical about my research," said Coral with a reproachful expression. "You said that you were more interested in the future than the past!"

"Well, I said that before I got to know you better," James replied truthfully.

Coral kissed James affectionately on the cheek. "See he can be charming," she said to the others, who smiled politely. They knew why James wanted to stay.

There had been many important and absorbing subjects to discuss and the time had slipped by unnoticed. The group had needed to recount the events and discoveries of the last couple of weeks. The evening had been valuable in consolidating the disparate pieces of information that had evolved. Everyone in the group was relieved that there was a potential way to avoid further conflict with Doctor Sherwin's modern Templar group. Ormerod and Coral felt the most exhilarated by the unexpected disclosures gleaned from the scroll because it related to their work. Even George and Catherine had gained satisfaction from learning a little more about their family history.

Ormerod had arranged to take William and Jayne back to Camelford and had gone to the yard to fetch the pony and trap. Jayne put her arms around James and Coral's shoulders. She knew that she would not be leaving until Saturday, but she realised that she was going to miss them if they stayed in Cornwall.

As George and Catherine bade them all goodnight and headed up the narrow track towards Trebarwith Farm, William, Jayne and Coral squeezed aboard Ormerod's university transport. It quickly disappeared into the night, bound for 'The Stonemason's Arms' in Camelford. James returned to the bar. It was warm and cosy inside the inn and he felt relaxed in the surroundings which had become familiar to him. He wished that Coral could have been with him, but understood that she had to continue work on the scroll.

CHAPTER 10

Visitor from the East

It was a long walk to Camelford. Even though Jake had transported him to the main road before turning towards Tintagel, James knew that it would take all morning to reach Camelford. Mercifully, it was a dry day and he was able to walk in comfort, reflecting on the relaxing time he had spent over the last couple of days in the company of William and Jayne. As he headed towards Camelford he could see the rocky crag of Rough Tor rising imperiously behind the town.

The imminent enquiry into the shipwreck kept returning to trouble him. It was like a dark cloud and James would be glad when Friday was over. On the other hand, he had been looking forward to this Wednesday afternoon because he knew it would occupy his mind. It would also be nice to be reunited with Coral who had been busy over the last two days helping Ormerod with preparations for the presentation. He reached 'The Stonemason's Arms' just after one o'clock and joined William and Jayne in the bar where they enjoyed a plate of sandwiches. The Old Grammar School was just across the river and they did not want to arrive feeling hungry.

Just under an hour later they entered the old, red bricked grammar school through the main entrance. It looked more like the council offices than a school and it was gloomy in the foyer. Visible through a sliding glass panel, an elegant grey haired lady sat working at her desk. A lamp illuminated the desktop which was piled high with folders leaving only a small square of space to work in the middle. Seeing them approach, the lady looked up and removing her half rimmed spectacles she opened the glass panel. She spoke with a friendly, soft spoken voice.

"I presume that you are the visitors that Professor Dymond is expecting," she said in anticipation. "I will lock the office door and then you can follow me to his room."

The group wandered down the corridor trailing silently behind their guide. They could hear distant, muffled voices reciting Latin verbs. James shuddered at the thought of being a pupil in this academic environment. It was not for him. There were windows along the corridor side of the classrooms and it wasn't long before they saw the professor and his team seated around a group of desks that had been pushed together. Coral welcomed them in. James embraced her warmly, before she showed them to their seats.

It was a square shaped classroom with windows set high on the outside wall. Shafts of light from the windows made it feel bright. It felt a bit cramped at the desks which were designed for the teenage pupils. Next to Ormerod sat an attractive young woman who James noticed had distinctive blue eyes. She was wearing a dark brown waistcoat over a light grey jumper. As Ormerod introduced her she stood up.

"This as Professor Helen Forest, the university's translator," said Ormerod. "She is going to reveal the story we have gleaned from our work on the scroll."

Professor Forest stood up, her attractive blue eyes surveying them.

"Please call me Helen," she smiled. "You couldn't have come at a better time. We finished our work on the scroll only yesterday. I have to say that what you found has turned out to be a very significant addition to our historical knowledge. It is a just reward for the dangers that you were exposed to in retrieving the scroll. I know that both Coral and Professor Dymond have found the contents to be particularly exciting and relevant to their field of study."

Helen was obviously not a person to waste time with small talk. Speaking in a fluent, articulate voice with just the hint of a West

Country accent, she began with what she called – 'novel revelations'.

"The scroll describes a journey along the traditional Phoenician trade routes at a time just after the death of Jesus. Joseph of Arimathea accompanied by Mary Magdalene, Lazarus, St Philip and some others left the Holy Land and arrived at a place called Saintes-Maries-de-la-Mer, near where the river Rhone is received by the sea. Then, after leaving Mary in the South of France, Joseph continued his journey to the South West of England. His joint aims were evangelism and trade although not necessarily in that order. Realising the former aim he founded a Christian church near the River Brue in Somerset. The scroll mentions the place named 'Glestingaburg' in this location. This is where the wisdom taught by Jesus was disseminated to the Pagans. The scroll describes Joseph as travelling on to Tintagel where he paid for a consignment of tin which he shipped back to the Middle East".

"The contents of this scroll are very interesting for a number of reasons," she explained. "In the Saxon language 'Glestinga' means a group of kindred people and 'Burg' means a monastic enclosure. It doesn't require much imagination to surmise that the place named in the scroll as Glestinga is probably Glastonbury since it is recorded as near the River Brue in Somerset. The Romans left England in the fifth century and in this vacuum of power the Saxons invaded the area from their strongholds in eastern England. We know the Saxons were Pagans, but it appears that the monastic enclosure of Glastonbury survived, being both patronised and protected by local Celtic Barons. Eventually, in the seventh century, Glastonbury Abbey was built and the first Patron established there in 676AD. Medieval stories describe one of these Barons as a great British leader, a commander who was born in Tintagel and who was eventually buried at Glastonbury."

"Is that the person we all know as King Arthur?" asked James, amazed at his own initiative in making the connection.

"He fits the jigsaw neatly doesn't he?" Helen replied with gusto. "During the Middle Ages King Arthur was made a member of the 'Nine Worthies.' They were chosen to represent a group of heroes who it was thought embodied the qualities of chivalry. Three of the worthies were Christians, three were Pagans and three were Jews. The Christian 'Worthies' were King Arthur, Charlemagne and Godfrey of Bouillon. You can still see the thirteenth century statues of all nine 'Worthies' on the wall of the City Hall in Cologne, but the key factor is that they depict Arthur as a Christian. It can't be a coincidence that he was a leader who defended the area where the Glastonbury community was situated. I think that he adopted the Christian philosophy, ideals and wisdom left by Joseph and forged them into his army. This explains how the principles of chivalry became embodied as the operational code of the Knights of the Round Table. If you recall the story, the round table signifies the equality of the knights each of whom was pledged to eighteen virtues or wisdoms".

"I thought that the story of King Arthur was just a myth," Jayne enquired.

"It is not unusual for medieval writers to couch real events in mythical formats," Helen replied. "They sometimes used analogies as a way of portraying ideas or events. For example when they want to convey the idea of genealogy they sometimes talk about viticulture and grapevines. When they want to describe family connections they may allude to intermarriage by a story about alchemy. It doesn't mean there is no truth in the myth, just that it is a cover story for something else. It's not always easy for us to interpret their symbolic stories when we live in a different era. We have to decode the data. Our lifestyles and culture have evolved dramatically, yet traces of ancient wisdom are everywhere. They are in the days of the week, the months of the year, in stories told to children, in statues, in art and in literature."

"Why bother creating such elaborate stories when it would be easier to just state the facts?" William was obviously less than impressed by complicated myths that required special knowledge to unravel.

"It was often too dangerous to express the facts outright, especially if they contradicted the teaching of the church or were perceived as undermining the state. The writer had to convey the facts covertly to protect against being accused of heresy or sedition," Helen said assertively. "Even Galileo felt threatened by the established church when his calculations proved that the Earth revolved around the sun."

Ormerod had been listening as the conversation progressed and remembered that there was something else important that was mentioned in the scroll.

"I apologise for interrupting," he said to Helen. "Before I forget, do you all remember the beginning of the scroll when it described Joseph of Arimathea arriving in the Camargue region of France with Mary Magdalene? Well every year on 22nd July the local people celebrate Mary Magdalene's Feast Day. Her skull, encased in a golden mask, is paraded through the town of Saint-Maximin-La-Sainte Baume. The skull may be a fake, but the interesting fact is that she is revered in this area even today. The historical story has left such a powerful memory in Provence that it would suggest that it is based on a real event."

There was a knock on the classroom door and the grey haired lady from the office entered with a tray of tea and biscuits. Ormerod thanked Helen for her clear and concise exposition. The meeting then disintegrated into an informal gathering as they enjoyed the refreshments.

Eventually, Coral got the chance to talk directly with James.

"There is something that you need to know," she whispered discretely. " When I was working with Ormerod deciphering the scroll he told me that a new research post had been created in the History department at The University of Cornwall. He wanted to know if I would be interested in filling the post. He told me that he would be prepared to support my application. I felt unsure about leaving the Manchester area where my friends and family are based, so I asked Ormerod to give me time to think it over. The other day in 'The Strand', I remember hearing you say that you wanted to stay down here. I would be much happier to work in Cornwall if you were here too."

A look around the room confirmed that the others were occupied in conversation and so James felt able to express his feelings.

"I want to be with you," said James. "You could have come to Cornwall by train or coach, but you chose to come by sea, and on my ship. We were fortunate to have survived the shipwreck. The disaster brought us together and I want us to stay together."

"Won't you miss your job working at sea?" asked Coral.

"I still love the ocean. It is like a living thing that breathes and moves. I have always wondered at its scale and power. It gives me a sense of freedom. I know that I don't want to go back to my old job though. It is not what I want to do any more. It is not that I am afraid to go back to sea, but the wreck has been a turning point in my life. Since those events I have lost my lust for adventure. I feel a need to spend time with the person who matters to me," James replied.

"The wreck has changed the way I feel too," said Coral thoughtfully. "I have gained a fuller perspective. The experience has made me aware of how precious time is. Things that seemed vital before appear trivial. I have been too busy focussing on myself and material things that don't really matter. Of course, I am still interested in my work, but that is not everything. Do you think you can put up living with someone who is always investigating history?"

"I will find things to do to take my mind away from King Arthur," said James with a smile.

"If I managed to be successful in applying for this job it would mean we could support ourselves in Cornwall. The job comes with a small apartment which we could rent from the university. It doesn't preclude a return to the north in the future if we want to."

James was not sure how he would get work in Cornwall. He knew that in the summer there were jobs attached to the tourist trade. He might be able to take people on fishing trips around the coast. That would be one way to use his seaman's skills. As long as he was with Coral the details would work themselves out.

James took hold of Coral's hand and gave it a squeeze. "I think it is a great opportunity and I know we can make things work if we are together."

It was after this conversation that Coral made her decision. She would accept Ormerod's offer and send in her application for the research post.

CHAPTER 11

Time Warp

James and Coral had decided to start Friday 16th January with a walk on the beach. This was the day of the enquiry. It was not a day that they had been looking forward to. Standing outside 'The Strand' they could see the solid block of Gull Rock firmly protruding from the sea, resilient against centuries of wind and tide. Beyond, the sea stretched out to the horizon moving to the rhythms of nature as though nothing had happened here. There was no physical trace, yet the memory of what had happened, less than a mile from the shore, would always linger in their minds. For the two survivors it was still a sensitive memory which could easily be invoked, bringing back the trauma, the regret, and the terror of the shipwreck. This unwelcome enquiry was just such a trigger and both of them felt sad and daunted knowing that they would have to remember events that they would rather have suppressed.

This morning the tide was out and a beautiful sandy beach was revealed, framed between dark outcrops of rock that extended from the shoreline cliffs. Feeling the need to gather their thoughts before leaving for Tintagel, the couple carefully picked their way along a deep gully which had been worn through the rock by the tide. It was the only easy route from the end of the track down onto the beach. Many deep rock pools left behind by the outgoing tide obstructed the route over the rocks and the pair had to constantly look down to check their footing, alert to the hazards presented by the wet surfaces. They could hear water cascading down to the beach from a stream that bubbled swiftly a few yards away to their left, but invisible on the other side of the gully. Rather than feeling cheered by the natural world around them their sense of depression seemed to increase with each step.

James reached the sandy beach first and waited as Coral jumped from the last outcrop. The glistening water from the stream surged past a peninsular of rocks on the left of the beach fanning out across the flat wet sand on the last stage of its journey to the sea. They had the beach to themselves. It was deserted apart from the gulls that strutted about in search of food. James took in a lungful of fresh air and looked up into the hazy sky. Suddenly, the beach was lit up in a golden glow as the sun penetrated a gap in the opaque canopy of cloud. A hint of warmth swarmed around them as abruptly as if someone had switched on a heater. James turned to speak to Coral, but he could see that she was distracted. Her eyes were tracking something beyond him. He looked in the same direction and saw two figures in the distance running towards the sea. The figures were now a few hundred yards to their left. James sensed that his field of view had become strangely distorted, although it was clear that there was a man and a woman. The man was wearing a green jacket which hung over a pair of brown jodhpurs. He was holding the woman's hand as they ran, urging her towards the sea. She had long brown hair which trailed back over a blue tunic. There was something odd about the urgency of their movement, an anxious furtiveness, as though they were being chased into the sea by an invisible assailant. The whole scene was reminiscent of a mirage with vision reduced to shimmering, grainy images. When the couple got to the edge of the sea the man looked towards them. His bearded face was tense and he opened his mouth as if to speak whilst spontaneously shoving the woman into the surf. His body jerked violently backwards before collapsing in a heap on the wet sand. A surge of the tide surrounded him, turning his green coat as dark as an emerald. The woman raised herself from the surf dropped on her knees, and cradled the man's head in her lap. Shock and grief convulsed her body, her hair hung straggled and dripping, as she looked down at the man's lifeless body. Both James and Coral were imbued with a deep sense of sorrow, induced by the emotions of the couple. James moved towards the distressed female closely followed by Coral, but they stopped short when they heard a voice shouting from the rocks at the top of the beach. Distracted, they both turned to respond. They saw Jake signalling for them to return, his arms waving like the branches of a tree.

As quickly as the sun had warmed and illuminated the beach it disappeared behind a bank of cloud. The change of temperature introduced a hazy mist which drifted in patches over the beach. They both rushed to the edge of the sea in search of the tragic couple, but the figures were nowhere to be seen. They had vanished. Moments before there had been drama, now there was just the lonely sea surging back and forth within the grey curtain of mist. Perplexed, they returned to where Jake was waiting with his cart to transport them to Tintagel. He had left Vicky in charge of 'The Strand' so that he could escort his guests to the enquiry. They asked Jake what he had seen on the beach. His response to what he perceived as a stupid question gave them the answer they already suspected. Looking at each other with raised eyebrows, the couple now knew that only they had seen the drama. They needed to focus on the hearing which was now imminent, and so did not pursue the subject any further. The events they had witnessed on the beach were burned into their memory. This was not the moment to reveal their weird experience, but it would continue to haunt them.

Coral's face still bore the scar from the encounter in the crypt, but it was healing quickly and was not causing physical pain. Now that it was less apparent she did not feel as self-conscious in public. On arrival there was a notice outside Trevena House in Tintagel which read 'Board of Trade Enquiry into the loss of The Mersey Rose – Sixth day of January, 1891.' The three of them were shown to a series of wooden benches upon which sat the witnesses to the disaster. James immediately recognised George sitting next to Doctor Sherwin a couple of rows to the left. Coral turned to look behind and saw William and Jayne at the back of the room seated next to Ormerod. Amongst the other officials, there were representatives of the Board of Trade and the managing director of the shipping company that owned the vessel. A man from the insurers dressed in a formal suit, sat with a notepad in his hand. In front of them was a table containing files, papers and a large water jug. Positioned behind the table were the wreck commissioner, a vice admiral and a sea captain who would hear the evidence and act as assessors. The meeting started promptly at 10.00am in the main hall. The wreck commissioner gave a summarised description of the events leading to the sinking of the ship. The officials from the Board of Trade then directed questions to the owner. Was the vessel in good condition? Was the cargo stowed and secured properly? Were the crew properly trained and certified? Was the vessel and cargo insured and for what value? Then it was the turn of the coastguard to explain what had been done to assist the stricken vessel? Why had it not been possible to send out a rescue boat? Had everything possible been done to rescue the crew? The coastguard described the horrific weather conditions and the frustration of the team of rescuers in not being able to save anyone.

James was asked about the training and experience of the crew. He felt numb as he relived the terrifying events on board and gave a heartfelt tribute to the skill and bravery of the crew. Finally, he looked round and raised his arm towards Coral expressing his view that it was miraculous that anyone had survived. She in turn gave testimony to the dedication of the crew in doing everything they could to save the vessel.

After what seemed an eternity there was a short adjournment as the three assessors discussed the evidence. The time then came for the wreck commissioner to give the report of the court. He spoke clearly so that everyone in the hushed, tense, atmosphere of the room could hear.

"The court, having carefully considered the circumstances, finds that the loss of the 'Mersey Rose' was due to the extreme violence of the gale encountered on the sixth of January, 1891."

James and Coral embraced. It was such a relief that they and the crew were exonerated from blame. They had just been unfortunate to have been caught in the worst weather conditions for years. The enquiry closed a dark episode in their lives and it now opened the prospect for them to put the dreadful experience behind them.

Emerging from the court into the winter sunlight James and Coral were reunited with William and Jayne. They hugged each other warmly. The verdict was like a breath of fresh air. Happily they made their way back towards Jake's cart. Just before they reached the cart James felt a tug on his sleeve.

"Can you spare a minute before you leave?" It was the managing director of the shipping company.

"I'll join you at the cart," shouted James to the others, as he took a seat next to the director on a low stone wall outside Trevena House.

"The company would like to thank you for the work you have done for us and also to express regret for the ordeal you have endured. This cheque is to cover your outstanding wages."

He handed a business card to James with his name and the company address details.

"If you ask your landlord to forward the bill for your accommodation to this address we will settle your account. Have you had any thoughts about resuming your work with us?"

It was a question that James had anticipated, and he felt relieved to bring his decision into the open.

"Thank you for your consideration, but I have decided to stay in Cornwall."

This was not the same James of old. Not the restless, single minded adventurer. Having faced death and survived James was now far less concerned with himself or his career. More important was what he could give back to people in his life. He felt a greater sense of responsibility towards his family, friends and Coral.

"I understand," said the director as he stood up to shake James by the hand. "If you change your mind you know where to find me." He turned to leave and then stopped as he remembered something. "You and Miss Byford will receive compensation when the insurance claims are settled. I wish you luck in the future." With that he turned away and disappeared back into the court room.

On the way back to 'The Strand' Coral enquired, "What did that man want to talk to you about?"

"You will be pleased to hear that we are going to receive compensation from the shipping company," James said. He leaned towards Jake and passed the business card to him. "The shipping company address," he explained as Jake read the card. "They want you to send the bill for our accommodation to them."

"In that case a round of drinks on the house is in order," shouted Jake. "To both exoneration and solvency!"

Inside the pub a roaring fire sent a warm glow round the room. Ormerod and George were sitting opposite each other at a long table, chatting over a pint of ale. They had been the first to return from Tintagel. Doctor Sherwin had arranged to meet with George at the inn and was preoccupied searching for something in his bag. Jake brought a tray of drinks for his guests as they took their places around the table.

"You may remember," said Doctor Sherwin still fumbling in his bag whilst looking up towards George, "that as part of our agreement I promised to return the cup which was in the chest."

The doctor extracted the gold cup from his bag and placed it on the table. The light from the fire reflected on its gold ribbed contours. Its handle, decorated with double grooves, was riveted to the body through lozenge shaped washers.

"My sources tell me that the cup originated from the Middle East," explained the doctor rather proudly. "It has been hewn from a solid ingot of gold at some time between 800 and 950 AD. The quality in the craftsmanship and the purity of the gold are exceptional."

George picked up the cup and was surprised at its weight considering its relatively small size. The cup was passed to Coral and she held it firmly with both hands as if about to drink. "I'm just trying to imagine the person who drunk from this cup," she said. "It's amazing to think that the cup is still here centuries after the death of its owner."

"Doctor Sherwin wants us to meet with the council members of 'The Preceptory of King Arthur' on Sunday evening at 6.30pm inside the old castle on Tintagel Island," pronounced George. He winked at Coral as he anticipated her next question. "You are all invited."

"Since we last met," said the Doctor. "I have accessed and searched the archives of the Preceptory of Trebighe. Records were always kept of visitors who sought sanctuary as they passed along the old 'Saints Trail' to Fowey. Most of the records are intact and well preserved. They have been meticulously stored by our brothers. Each record is stored chronologically, by day, by month and by year."

"Did you find anything about Sholto Kelley?" asked George impatiently.

"Better than that," announced the Doctor. He delved into his bag and extracted a ledger with a red marker clip indicating the relevant page. "This is the log for May, June and July 1291." He opened the ledger and flicked to the page with the marker. Running his finger down the page was an entry which stated:

'Sholto Kelley – arrival 10th June, 1291 – knight's squire *– en route to Mellifont, Ireland from Acre, Outremer – convalescence interrupted by incident on moor- departed 12th June, 1291.*

The group leaned across the table to view the record. As they read the entry Doctor Sherwin discretely pulled out a faded sketch from behind the log book page, his movement and expression reminiscent of a smug magician pulling a rabbit out of a hat. Faded, but clearly legible, was a pencil drawing showing the head and shoulders of a man with a beard. The letters S K were written at the bottom of the page. There was something familiar about the contours of the man's face. Coral looked across the table to where George was seated and her thoughts were confirmed. George had the same eyes and facial expression. There was a clear family resemblance between the figure in the sketch and George Denke. Nobody spoke. They just gazed at the image. James was stunned as he recognised that the sketch was of the man he had seen on the beach that morning.

"Are you certain that this sketch was done in 1291 and has been in the log over since?" asked James.

"Nothing is certain, although it is known that occasionally our brothers would make a drawing of a guest if there was no objection. Sketches were included with the Preceptory records if the subject did not want to keep it. The doctor's mouth opened to continue his exposition, but before he could utter another word there was a sudden grinding crash from behind the bar. Vicky who had been working there let out a shriek of terror which reverberated around the room. A sword which had been clipped to the wall just above the main bar had somehow come loose and dropped blade first. The bar room which had been filled with voices in conversation became as quiet as a mausoleum. The silence in the room was deafening as all eyes were fixed on the sword. It stood quivering, its blade embedded in the polished wooden surface of the bar.

Jake moved to comfort Vicky who was visibly shaken. "I could have been killed," she said in a faltering voice.

Grabbing the handle Jake pulled the sword free leaving a deep cut in the surface of the bar. As he rested the weapon on the bar he thoughtfully ran his finger over the damaged area. A few muted voices began to punctuate the unnaturally quite atmosphere of the busy inn. A man wearing overalls and a leather apron walked across the room and introduced himself to Jake as a builder. The two men inspected the clips which had been used to secure the sword to the wall. Both clips lay sprung open and dislodged from their mounting, apparently wrenched by some invisible force. Jake could not understand it. He knew that the sword had been firmly secured in the same position for years. The man in overalls declared that he could find no technical fault in either the materials or the method of fastening. Scratching his head he returned to his table as mystified as everyone else as to the cause of the accident.

Gradually, the inn was restored to normality. Doctor Sherwin left the table leaving the log book open with the sketch lying like a discarded napkin across the top.

"Do you mind me having a look at the sword?" he asked Jake.

Jake held out his hand towards the weapon in invitation. He was preoccupied consoling his wife.

Returning to the table the doctor examined the sword. It had a double edged blade about three feet long. The sword was a single handed type with a cross guard which sloped slightly down at the end to give it balance. A shaped wooden handle provided the best evidence as to its origin. Emblazoned onto the top of the handle was the symbol of the Templars, two knights on one horse.

"It is absolutely exquisite," exclaimed the doctor. "This is a Templar sword without any doubt. It's not just the symbol, but look at the cross guard. It forms one half of the Templar Cross and the steel is hardened to enable it to cleave chain mail."

Looking towards where Jake was standing behind the bar the doctor asked him if he knew the origin of the weapon.

"It's a mystery to me," replied Jake. "As far as I can remember in my years as tenant, it has always been there. The brewery paid to rebuild the inn and they must have placed the sword above the bar as a decoration. Perhaps it came from the old building!"

"Well, I wish they had fixed it properly," said Vicky. "It could have killed me," she repeated in an aggressive tone. Obviously, the initial shock had worn off.

The doctor walked across to the bar and laid the sword flat. "If you are ever thinking of disposing of this weapon let me know. I will give you a fair price," he said to Jake.

Returning to the table he replaced the sketch in its position between the pages of records, closed the log book and tucked it back into his bag.

"I am glad that you have found the old records helpful, but I am afraid that I have to leave," announced the doctor. "Can you tell me which of you will be coming to the meeting on Sunday? I need to make sure that suitable arrangements are made."

"There will be four of us including me," George replied.

"We always try to make full provision for our guests," replied the doctor imperiously. "In addition to our expert dissemination of the scroll, we will serve a meal and provide you with entertainment. Just remember that when you enter the old castle through the arch in the wall, turn to the left. You will see a large millstone leaning upright against the embankment. Knock on the stone twice with the wooden stake which you will find on the ground next to it." The doctor gave just the hint of a bow, but his face remained impassive as he strode from the inn without another word.

James exchanged glances with Coral. They wondered what sort of odd meeting they had let themselves be invited to.

The gold cup still sat regally on the table amongst the tankards and empty glasses. Ormerod pushed it towards George. "I think that you had better look after this. After all it belonged to one of your ancestors."

George held the cup in front of him with outstretched arms, turning it from side to side in admiration of the craftsmanship. "I expect it has been a witness to many events in the past. I will give it pride of place on the mantelpiece in memory of Sholto."

Ormerod collected his coat from the back of his chair. It was getting late and he had promised to give William and Jayne a lift back to Camelford. It would be the last day that that the couple would be in Cornwall before their return to Cheshire. As they left the inn with Ormerod, they arranged to meet with James and Coral the next day to say goodbye.

It was late and the inn was emptying rapidly. Jake came over to the table to talk just as George was preparing to leave. He slumped in one of the spare chairs, his body language showing his tiredness. "It's been a long day," he sighed. "Strange chap, that Doctor don't you think? Tonight is the first time he has really spoken to me and it was all about that sword."

To James and Coral it was uncomfortable that they had accepted Jake's hospitality for so long, but had never really talked to him about their quest. Coral had not even been forthcoming about her injury .They both knew that Jake was a perceptive person and that he had probably picked up on some of the things that they had been doing. Jake saw them every day, but he was invariably busy running the inn. He had never been intrusive, or asked embarrassing questions. It was the incident on the beach this morning and the drama with the sword during the evening, that finally made both James and Coral agree that Jake deserved an explanation. It wouldn't be easy to explain something that they didn't understand themselves, but they wanted to try.

"There's something we need to talk to you about," said James and Coral in harmony. "Do you remember when you called to us on the beach this morning?"

"I certainly do," replied Jake looking puzzled. "You were both absorbed looking at the tide and I couldn't make you hear my calls."

"We weren't watching the tide," said James. "There were two other people on the beach near the edge of the sea. A man and a woman. Something tragic happened to them as we watched. This evening when the doctor showed us the old sketch from his record book we recognised that it was the man on the beach. Looking at that sketch and recognising the person numbed us with shock. It was just then that the sword fell off the wall. There may be no connection, but it is really strange, especially now we know that it is a Templar sword."

"How can that be possible?" snapped Jake. When you were down on the beach I saw just you and Coral."

"We don't understand what happened either," said Coral in support. "We were both feeling apprehensive about the enquiry. The weather conditions made the light variable and I felt that my senses were sharpened. James has told me that he felt the same. There's no mistaking that we both saw the man in the drawing with a woman on the beach and they were in obvious danger."

"It was like watching a replay of a bygone time," added James.

Jake was perplexed. He was hearing things which were odd and as a practical man he did not readily accept things not supported by a rational explanation. To Coral there was no alternative but to tell Jake about the history of the people from the old inn. It was the only way that she could think of which would encourage Jake to give credence to their experiences.

Addressing James and George she said, "I think Jake deserves to hear the full story."

They nodded in acquiescence. "I agree that now is the time to confide in Jake," said George quietly.

Coral explained how the pouch from the cave had led them to find the chest, the relevance of the Templar symbol and the link between Sholto and the Denke family. Slowly, Jake began to fit the pieces of the puzzle together.

"So this fellow Sholto escaped through that cave and you found the pouch he had hidden there six hundred years ago. Then you saw him on the beach today?" There was a long silence and Jake's expression was one of bewilderment as he struggled to reconcile all the facts.

Coral tried to help him, although she felt perplexed as well. "Imagine normal white light which is all around us," she said. "Under showery conditions the sunlight passes through raindrops and is transformed into a spectrum. We see a rainbow. It is still light, but it has been changed by the conditions. It is possible that the conditions on the beach this morning interacting with our charged emotions resulted in a physiological change sufficient to induce an altered state."

"You mean that you went into some sort of trance," asked Jake.

"Possibly," Coral agreed. "It is similar to what happens when people meditate. Both of us were subject to the same conditions. Perhaps, we unintentionally connected to another wavelength. One which, in our altered state, enabled us to read back traumatic events that happened in history. How do we know that our minds cannot be manipulated to transgress natural laws?"

"How do we now that they can?" countered Jake.

George had been listening intently to Coral's reasoning and something she said reminded him of an item he had read in a newspaper article. Rather sheepishly, he related the story to the group.

"A few years ago I read an article in the newspaper about a couple on holiday in France. They were travelling after the bereavement of a close relative who had died at the age of one hundred. Consequently, their emotions were raw. They made an overnight stop in a small rural town in order to break their journey south. Everyone in the hostel was dressed in what appeared to be period costumes. They even used old French coins. They continued their holiday, but were increasingly mystified by their strange experience. At the end of their holiday the couple retraced their route trying to find the hostel, but it seemed to have disappeared. Enquiries at the Hotel de Ville revealed that the hostel in question had been demolished one hundred years before their visit. The report suggested that the couple had experienced some kind of psychological phenomenon. They had connected to the past in some kind of time warp."

Looking across the table George concluded, "Your experience on the beach may have been similar. There may be another conduit through which we can connect to the past. However, I do not think it can be physical. It is more likely to involve some intangible aspect of the mind. In your case the detonator must have been the shipwreck enquiry. It would seem that Trebarwith Strand has been the scene of tragic events separated by centuries."

"Yes, and the consequences are that I have become the landlord of a haunted inn," complained Jake.

"Think of the extra trade that a haunted inn could generate," said George in an attempt to lighten the conversation.

"That's all very well," replied Jake, "but Vicky and I have to live here. We don't want to be surrounded by groups of ghost hunters every day."

"Not just ghost hunters," smiled George mischievously as he got up to leave. "Modern Templars too!"

Jake picked up the Templar sword and brandished it towards George feigning to threaten him with it as he opened the door. "Mind as you go!" he shouted with undisguised sarcasm.

Slightly embarrassed, George left hurriedly, but this did not save him from hearing raucous laughter drifting from the bar.

CHAPTER 12

The Den

James had valued the company of William and Jayne. Their presence had been reassuring and they had been a significant influence in his swift recovery from the shipwreck. Since they had returned to Cheshire, James was warmly reflecting on his joy at their unexpected meeting in Camelford. So much had happened since then, but he knew that their experiences together had strengthened their relationship. As he sat in the cart trundling down the steep track heading towards Tintagel Island, James pondered when he would next meet his brother.

The group all felt apprehensive and did not know quite what to expect when they met the Templars. James considered the Templar group to be a club of eccentric people trying to embrace parts of history that were now just memories. The cart jolted and lurched over a rut where rainwater had eroded a channel into the surface of the track. Nervously, Coral ran her finger across her cheek remembering the injury she got the last time she came into contact with the Templars. Although her wound was now just a red mark, she couldn't help wondering how comfortable she would be in a forum dominated by men. Only Ormerod had any realistic idea about the purpose and rituals of the group and this knowledge did not particularly inspire him as to how productive the evening would be. However, true to his word, he had brought along the scroll for the council members to view. George just felt glad that the end of this unexpected ordeal was in sight. He put his hand in his pocket to check that the little Bible that contained the key to the chest was secure and felt a flush of satisfaction knowing that he was now more aware of his heritage.

The track came to an end at the point where the steep valley terminated and dropped away until it became a sheer cliff. At one side of the track a torrential stream continued its journey to the sea, pouring over the edge of the cliff to form a spectacular waterfall. Straight ahead moonlight reflected over the sea in a monochrome carpet of silvery light. It illuminated the narrow bay where a large rock protruded from the beach like a discarded chunk of coal. This was the place where boats had been tethered whilst they loaded and unloaded their cargoes. The rust encrusted on the remains of mooring rings showed that this port had been made redundant a long time ago. Coral imagined what it would have been like when Joseph of Arimathea visited all those years ago forging the first trade links with the Mediterranean. Tintagel Island scarred by the ruined remains of an ancient castle loomed large to the left of the bay. Deep, shadowy caves were bored into the base of the island cliffs like hollow portals. This was a magical place and Coral could see why it had inspired the story of Merlin the wizard. She could almost visualise the Knights of the Round Table thundering down the narrow track on their way to meet King Arthur's court.

George ensured that the horse and cart was secure in a little dell sheltered from the elements by an overhanging outcrop of rock. A narrow path on their left snaked its way around the contours of the mainland cliff and George ignited a flaming torch which he had brought from the cart. Immediately, they were able to see the precipitous route that they would need to navigate. They followed in single file as George led them along the path to a point where a rickety wooden bridge constructed of rope and wood joined the mainland with Tintagel Island. The bridge spanned a distance of about a hundred yards, but it seemed longer as the structure swayed with every step. Glancing down through the wooden slats between each footstep, a vertical chasm appeared where the sea was swamping rocks a hundred feet below.

After crossing the bridge the path continued to wind sinuously as it ascended the steep contours of the island cliff. It was a narrow and treacherous route which eventually led to a gateway in the ruined walls of the ancient castle. The exertion meant that there had been little conversation. The journey had been accompanied by the background thunder of the ocean and the cascading torrent of the waterfall. Inside the castle wall there was an immediate feeling of security. In a strange way the darkness had protected them from a full view of the dangers this path presented to the unfamiliar walker.

Now they all looked towards the left for the millstone which Doctor Sherwin had told them lay nearby. Sure enough the round shape of the millstone came to view, shadowy with the light from the flaming torch flickering over its rough surface. It resembled a large abandoned wheel slumped against the soft grassy embankment.

"No wonder they only meet here once a month," James whispered flippantly.

The castle stood in darkness completely deserted, empty and uninviting. Ormerod picked up the large baulk of timber that lay next to the millstone and knocked with two deliberate heavy blows as the doctor had instructed. At first there was no reaction, but then they noticed that the stone was gradually rolling to one side. It grated abrasively against stones in the embankment until eventually there was a gap just big enough for a person to enter. Framed in the dark portal of the entrance appeared a man dressed in a white mantel. He had a bald head on which there was a nasty scar and a tattoo of a black and white flag. He smelled of tobacco and George suspected that this was the man who had confronted them at the church. A red, eight pointed Templar cross, was sewn over the area of his left breast. In the gloom he looked like a spectre as he bent forward to usher them inside. The man led them through a short passage which opened into a large chamber cut out of the rock. George decided not to convey his thoughts about the identity of the man to the others. He was conscious of the ill feeling that James still harboured and did not want to ignite a confrontation before the meeting had even started.

The chamber was circular in shape with a domed roof cut from the rock about thirty feet above the floor. The rock hewn surface area of the roof had been painted over dark blue and overlaid with gold painted stars. It was reminiscent of the night sky, similar to the view in a planetarium. At one end of the chamber a large fire blazed with smoke billowing up a stack that protruded through the roof. Blackened stonework above the fireplace evidenced that it had been frequently used. This is where the hot food was being prepared with a hog turning on a spit. Tonight, the smell of meat and burning logs mixed with the scent from enormous candles created an ambience of embracing warmth. At the end of the chamber opposite to the fireplace the floor was higher forming a raised semi -circular shelf across the chamber like the segment of an orange. In this part of the room the floor was patterned with alternating black and white quarry tiles. At each side of the raised floor area were two sturdy pillars, one Doric and one Corinthian. Placed centrally between the pillars, abutting the rear wall was what appeared to be a stone altar. A large tapestry on the wall behind the altar displayed a red solar cross below which the words 'Not to us O Lord, not to us, but to Your Name give the glory' were woven into the material. Ormerod whispered to James that the pillars represented the duality of severity and mercy. He explained that the floor tiles were symbolic of both the days and nights of time. Positioned in front of the altar was huddled a group of entertainers called 'The Troubadours' who were in the midst of performing a version of the song 'Green Sleeves'. The three male musicians wore black tights below yellow and purple tunics. The female singer was adorned in a gown of the same colours. The gentle melody drifted around the hall creating an authentic medieval charm.

In the centre of the chamber the floor was hollowed and furnished with a large, round, granite table. There were twelve wooden chairs equally spaced around the table. One of the chairs was bigger than the others with arms and a high back into which was carved the symbol of the two knights on one horse. This chair was reserved for the preceptor, but six of the other chairs were occupied by the committee. They were all members of 'The Preceptory of King Arthur'. They looked regal in their white mantels decorated with the Templar cross.

Doctor Sherwin in his role of preceptor strode forward to welcome his guests, before introducing them to each of the six seated members of his committee. Working clockwise around the table they were identified by their titles, almoner, chancellor, chaplain, marshal, seneschal and finally, the clerk. George was now convinced that the bald clerk with the tattoo was the man who had stalked them. He also remained certain that it would be expedient to keep this information quiet. Seated at a chair alongside where the preceptor would chair the meeting was a woman dressed in a blue cassock. She wore no make-up and had a plain ecclesiastical appearance. Ormerod was not surprised when she was introduced as Sister Grace from The Convent of Mercy. An intrepid woman he thought to himself, considering how she must have braved the precipitous route to the castle dressed in a cassock.

Sister Grace bowed slightly when introduced to the new arrivals and smiled.

"We have spent many hours deciphering the first scroll. It has proved to be a profound and informative archive. We are intrigued as to the content of the second scroll which I am told you have brought with you," she said expectantly.

"The contents of that scroll have been a fascinating addition to my research into the Arthurian Legend," Coral replied. She felt relieved not to be the only female at the meeting.

"Perhaps we will be able to talk about it later," suggested Coral.

Doctor Sherwin shepherded them to the four empty chairs. James observed that there were no windows, the walls being decorated by tapestries depicting scenes from the Arthurian legends. Each tapestry portrayed one of the main virtues which the Knights of the Round Table agreed to observe. From where he sat James could read a few of the tapestry virtues quite easily: love, purity, faith, courage and loyalty were written on the tapestries hung nearest to his position at the table. In front of each table position, pewter plates and chalices were arranged for each individual person of the assembly.

James still did not feel well disposed towards Doctor Sherwin. He had not forgiven him for being implicated in the shooting incident at Temple church. He might be the preceptor and appear the generous, hospitable host, but to James he was also a man partly responsible for Coral's injury.

Carefully, Ormerod extracted the scroll from his case and passed it to the preceptor in accordance with their agreement. The preceptor laid it on the table in front of Sister Grace who partially unrolled it and glanced at it with raised eyebrows. She knew straight away that it was not connected with the scroll that she had expended so much effort interpreting. Discreetly, she folded the scroll and asked for it to be taken to a safe place where it would not get damaged at the dinner table. Meanwhile, a valet serviced the table, filling each chalice with wine.

'The Troubadours' came to the end of one of their songs and their melodies were replaced by the low volume hum of background conversation. This was abruptly interrupted by the crude sound of plates being drummed on the table by the Templar members seated around the table. Everyone naturally fell silent and looked to where the preceptor was standing in front of his chair.

"You are dining with a group of people here today who embrace the knowledge which the Templars acquired and melded with Christianity. That is why we are not bound by the literal meaning of everything written in the Bible. Whilst we believe that the Bible contains much wisdom, we recognise that it is composed of selected fragments of scripture. These have been edited and amended, leaving an account of events relying more on faith than knowledge. Spiritual resurrection is still an important ingredient of our creed, and I hope that the content of these scrolls will enhance our understanding of this mystery. Sister Grace represents the team from the convent who have spent many years researching the scriptures in a search for historical accuracy. I am honoured that she agreed to come here tonight to disseminate what her team learned from reading our particular scroll."

Doctor Sherwin raised his chalice. "A toast to Sister Grace and her team," he announced.

The assembly responded with one voice which echoed round the chamber with an eerie hollowness.

Showing perfect manners Doctor Sherwin proposed a second toast, "Welcome to our learned guests."

As James raised his chalice he had to stifle a feeling of resentment. It was like being welcomed to the house of the person who had robbed you and thanking them for showing you the proceeds of the theft.

CHAPTER 13

Secrets

After a furtive glance at her notes Sister Grace stood and faced the assembly. She spoke in a clear, audible voice. She may have had a plain appearance, but she was obviously an intelligent and articulate person. Thanking the preceptor for his hospitality she continued by saying that she would be as brief, but as accurate as possible. She invited the assembly to interrupt if they had any questions and then began her address.

"It would appear from my discussions with the preceptor that two scrolls were left in the crypt below Temple Church on Bodmin Moor in 1291. Evidently, the scrolls were deposited there by a person connected to the Templars called Sholto Kelley. Preceptory records confirm that Sholto was returning to Ireland following a pilgrimage to the Holy Land. The date 1291 is significant because it is the year when the last crusader city in the Holy Land fell to Muslim armies. This may explain why the scrolls are not in their original containers. It is with the utmost respect that I regard Sholto Kelley for his tenacity in returning with these fascinating treasures."

Sister Grace took a deep breath before continuing.

"I have only just had a brief glance at the second scroll, but that is enough to tell me two things. Firstly, it relates to a different period of history, and secondly, it is written in different languages to the first scroll. It is possible that in the turmoil, panic, and utter chaos during the evacuation of Acre, as the battle drew nearer, valuables were thrown together in a jumble. The only aim being to save them from falling into the hands of the enemy. The scroll that my team have examined is in reasonably good condition although there are sections that are illegible due to the effects of confinement for centuries in a damp, dark environment."

There was a pause whilst Sister Grace checked her notes.

"The scroll we worked on was written in Hebrew using a reed pen with an iron oxide based ink. Hebrew text is written from right to left and each letter has been substituted using a cipher called Atbash. We know that Atbash substitutions are found in at least two places in the Old Testament and it was used when the documents contained sensitive information. Our team decoded the cipher and were then able to translate the Hebrew into English".

"Did it reveal anything new?" The marshal interjected with an air of disrespectful impatience.

"It consists of a collection of ethical teachings about life and death, so in that respect it is not new," said Sister Grace glancing sternly towards the marshal as though he was a naughty schoolboy.

"However, the teachings are fascinating because they do not conform to traditional Jewish or Christian belief systems. There is no clue as to who the writer was, but they are monotheistic and non-doctrinal. The writer describes the universe as composed of physical matter that can be held, touched and weighed. In addition, he states that there are non- material, ephemeral aspects to the universe. One example is gravity, another is magnetism, but most important in this context is spirituality. The human body is an example of the material aspect and the human soul the spiritual. Whoever wrote the scroll believed that the material and spiritual aspects were integrated."

Sister Grace glanced around her audience as if sensing hostility to her presumption that the writer was a man.

"Forgive me for describing the writer as a male," she implored. "It is just that most of the writers of this type of document were monks?"

"We are not concerned about the writer's gender," replied Doctor Sherwin. "We are only interested in what the writer says."

Feeling reassured by this comment Sister Grace continued.

"He states that body, soul, spirit and matter are not designed to be independent, but interconnected. We are part of the universe and the universe is part of us. The writer describes God as being part of the universe in the form of pure spiritual energy. It is from this energy that both spiritual and material aspects of the universe emanate. The spiritual energy of God existed first in another dimension. This means that before matter there was no matter only spiritual energy. God is the alchemist, the creator of physical effects. Everything has come from the mind of God and when the material body dies to return to the physical world as dust the spiritual aspects return to God. Nothing disappears it just changes."

The chaplain who was sitting next to the preceptor interrupted, "Is the writer saying that God is not a person?"

"My interpretation would be that the writer is describing God not as a person with a material body, but as spiritual energy. I think that this energy could be described as the mind of God because it was directed towards the aim of creation. In my opinion it is the human spirit which mankind has in common with God rather than his physical body. That is what I think the writer is trying to convey. If the real 'us' is spiritual, then the real God is spiritual. In order for us to survive in the material world our spirit is embedded in our physical body. The result of this combination makes humans greater than the sum of their parts. They gain the capacity to love, to overcome adversity, to think and act according to their consciences."

"In fact," added Sister Grace, "there is no contradiction with the Christian Bible (Genesis 1:26) where it is stated 'that man is formed in the image of God'. If God is a spirit then man must be too."

"What does God get out of this connection with mankind? I mean, why has he bothered to create mankind in his own spiritual image with the added difficulty that this happens in a material world?" The chaplin spoke awkwardly and with a perplexed expression which showed that he was having difficulty adjusting to the concept of God as a form of spiritual energy .

"The answer to your question can be summarised in two words. Spiritual growth," said Sister Grace. However, referring back to the writing in the scroll it does say that as a form of spiritual energy, God becomes enriched as each human spirit goes through a refinement process. This refinement comes through living a virtuous life on earth, acting wisely, and attaining inner enlightenment. The scroll writer describes examples of the virtues as wisdom, truth, honesty, kindness, justice and humility. Spiritual purity is enhanced after an individual applies the virtuous principles in practical situations experienced during life on earth. This is the point of Gnosis or knowledge when the spirit is enlightened sufficiently to be reunited with God. God as spiritual energy is enhanced by this reunion when the human spirit is resurrected after the body dies. This suggests that the whole object is to increase spiritual purity through the practical application of particular virtues in the laboratory of the material world."

The hall was filled with an expectant silence, before Sister Grace continued, adding her own thoughts about wisdom. She wanted to link the ideas written in the scroll to the more traditional beliefs held by the audience.

"In the Bible an example of wisdom is represented by Solomon. The story of the dispute between two women as to who was the mother of a baby is an example of wisdom applied in practice. (1 Kings iii, 24-27). We could say that wisdom is the combination of knowledge and experience and its deliberate use to promote well – being. In fact, an understanding of God and individual salvation can be achieved through personal experience. The Bible is an illustrated code for virtuous living. Live by the code and gain wisdom. Live by the code and increase sensitivity to enlightenment. There comes a moment in life when enlightenment leads to an understanding of God. Some people describe this moment as being born again."

"Sorry to interrupt", said the almoner, "but it doesn't sound easy to reach the stage of enlightenment".

"In my experience nothing worthwhile is ever easy," retorted Sister Grace.

"Self- improvement requires dedication. People are inspired towards a virtuous life by different means. Some find it through their religion, some through learning and education, some by individual experience, some by quiet reflection, and some by imitation of the wise. Meditation is a technique often used to tune into the mystical wavelength. It facilitates spiritual enlightenment by clearing interference from cluttered minds, wiping them clear and making them receptive to spiritual values. Other people have visions which inspire them, like Joan of Arc for example. As a mere peasant girl she was able to persuade the King of France to appoint her to head the army in a crusade to regain control of the country from the English. Occasionally, the influence of the church may provide the inspiration for a secular leader to rule with conviction. Spiritual enlightenment can emerge during the principled exercise of state responsibilities. In the final analysis it comes down to living according to the code of practice detailed by the stories in the Bible."

The seneschal was an old man with a beard as white as his mantel, who had sat listening in silence, but now spoke to ask a question that was troubling him. "Does the scroll explain what happens to those souls who never become refined enough to be reunited with God?" he asked.

"That is a good question," replied Sister Grace, and one that I pondered myself until our forensic experts rescued a section of the scroll that had become faded and was barely decipherable. It describes a process of reincarnation. The impure spirit would need to be recycled in order to have a second lifetime to achieve enlightenment. No soul recycled back to earth could be worse than its first existence so any change in the second life must represent an improvement. That is why the Holy books like the Bible, and the Koran are important. They provide the code required for living life directed towards enlightenment."

Sister Grace paused and for a moment she looked up towards the ceiling as if searching for inspiration. Returning her attention to the assembly she finished her discourse.

"Finally, I leave you with this thought as we dine at this symbolic table. The Knights of the Round Table did not adopt the codes of chivalry by chance. They embraced the codes because they knew that this would lead them in their quest for enlightenment."

The preceptor stood and raised his hand. "Remarkable," he said with genuine enthusiasm. Turning to Sister Grace he said, "It is going to take us a while to fully assimilate what you have discovered from the scroll. Not many years ago you would have been denounced as a heretic for airing the matters expressed tonight." Nervous laughter rippled around the table. The preceptor smiled warmly as his eyes met those of Sister Grace. "Thankfully, you are amongst friends. We value the integrity of the scroll message and the work that has gone into translation. Thank you, and now let us all relax and enjoy good food and entertainment."

The hall echoed with applause as the preceptor sat down. Coral glanced around the table as the murmur of conversation started to bubble between the diners. There was something about the content of the scroll that troubled her. It was not that she had found the content disagreeable to some of her own beliefs, but she could not reconcile the idea that it was the mind of God that was responsible. Why had the writer presumed that all creation was the result of a Grand Designer? All the effects would be the same if creation had just been the result of a chance coming together of all the ingredients. She leaned over to James and quietly passed on her thoughts.

"You have to remember that Sister Grace is a Christian so she is bound to have presented the details accordingly," said James cynically. "Especially, when addressing the modern Templars. I think that the odds against everything being the result of random chance are too great to be credible."

Coral remained sceptical. Some of her friends were Humanists and they lived by a moral code without believing in a God. Her thoughts were interrupted by the start of the entertainment.

'The Troubadours' resumed their repertoire as seamlessly as an orchestra after an interval. One played acoustic guitar, another played a flute whilst a harpist strummed away behind them. The female singer gave soul to the lyrics, sometimes tossing her hair to one side, sometimes provocatively running her hands down her thighs in harmony with the rhythms.

Emerging discretely from a shadowy recess, the valet circled the table like a bird of prey, occasionally swooping to ensure that no chalice remained empty. The soothing effects of the music and inhibition from the wine were complemented by sumptuous portions of a traditional a roast meal.

Half-way through the meal the music stopped abruptly, and James noticed that the guitarist was placing his instrument on its stand. The man bent down on one knee and with a sweep of his arm in the direction of the assembly he spoke in a tone laced with intrigue.

"I have a story to tell about a man called Sholto Kelley. Sholto went on a pilgrimage from Ireland to Outremer. En route he befriended a knight called Trevaie who made him his squire. The two men fought side by side in the city of Acre in the year 1291. They developed a bond, but Sholto never knew that Trevaie had been entrusted with a special task. This was to return home with scrolls recovered from Jerusalem. Trevaie was killed and in the eleventh hour, as Acre was falling to the Muslims, the task passed to Sholto. Eventually, Sholto came to take sanctuary in the Preceptory of Trebeigh. He was persecuted by a gang of thieves for protecting a woman from their vengeance. Fearful for his life he hid the scrolls in the crypt below the preceptory church. Six hundred years later we read the scrolls and are enlightened." The story was abruptly ended by a small explosion followed by a plume of smoke.

The music resumed only this time it was a distinctive Middle Eastern strain. Next to where 'The Troubadours' were performing was a pod about the size of a bath only it was shaped like a large egg. Through the clearing smoke, the top of the pod was suddenly ejected and water spilled down the side in little rivulets. A beautiful young woman, naked apart from a small yellow thong emerged. Her body was soaked by the water and she glistened like a seal. A purple ribbon held her dark hair in a tail. Only after this dramatic entrance did a member of 'The Troubadour's introduced her as 'Zodiac'.

"She is born to be the purveyor of the elements, earth, wind, fire, water and spirit," he proclaimed grandly whilst throwing a large yellow ball to her.

Zodiac caught the ball and bounced it on the floor as she danced to the music. Then she lit a flaming torch from a huge candle set on a stand. She thrust the flame against the ball causing it to explode like a balloon. Nine small balls cascaded from the disintegrating orb. They were all black except one which was blue and green representing the earth as part of the solar system.

Gyrating to the rhythms of the music she carefully let the flame burn up the length of her arm. The reflections from the flame highlighted every sumptuous curve of her body. When the flame reached the top of her arm she moved it in front of her face and blew hard. A jet of flame spewed from her mouth almost reaching the diners.

A combination of the wine, the music, and the food, supplemented with Zodiac's erotic performance was having a hypnotic effect on the guests. James felt that the room was beginning to slowly rotate, but managed to whisper to Coral.

"We've seen earth, wind, fire and water. What about the fifth element?"

"I'm sure that it will be included if you continue to concentrate," she replied with just a hint of sarcasm.

Moving with sensuous abandon Zodiac stroked the flame slowly up her leg until it licked her thigh. She leaned backwards until her hair almost touched the floor. She continued to move the flame up her body until it momentarily caressed her breasts. Leaning forward she blew strongly and a jet of flame shot forward lighting five small candles which were standing in a rack just in front. The music stopped right on cue as Zodiac ended her performance by plunging the flaming torch into a large trough of water. Steam hissed up creating a temporary cloud of mist. She disappeared through the vaporous, foggy veil and returned to her pod. Moments later she reappeared with a Mexican style poncho draped over her body. Collecting the five lighted candles she gave one to each guest. Symbols of the living spirit.

Zodiac bowed and lifted her hands above her head turning full-circle to applaud her audience who responded enthusiastically.

"Bravo! Symbolic, profound, and exciting," exclaimed Ormerod.

George said nothing. He had just enjoyed the cabaret. He felt totally ambivalent about symbolic aspects.

The leader of 'The Troubadours' stepped forward to explain the symbolism. "The five elements represent the material world. The flames from the candles portray the spirit we all share. The erotic dancing simulates the sexual energy needed for procreation. You are more likely to become receptive to the connections between the elemental and spiritual aspects of existence when your senses are stimulated. The conduit to enlightenment is lubricated as your senses become focussed and perceptions elevated."

We hope that you enjoyed our entertainment, but it is now time for the finale. This last song is a completely different tempo and is called 'Pasterela'. It recounts the tale of a love request from a knight to a shepherdess. Enjoy."

Once the music had finished the buzz of conversation enveloped the room. George was intrigued by the details about Sholto as revealed by the storyteller. "Where did he find out about Sholto being a knight's squire and those details about the woman and the thieves?" he mused.

"He must have been given the information by Doctor Sherwin from the preceptory archives," Ormerod speculated. Let's not forget that this group of musicians was not just any random group, but a group selected by the preceptor specifically for this occasion."

Ormerod explained to George that troubadours were historical characters who travelled widely like gypsies. Unlike many gypsies, they traditionally attended the courts of kings and powerful family dynasties. Their associations imbued them with information not generally available. As they travelled they cascaded this knowledge from town to town, country to country. Their lives revolved around an early form of networking.

The wine was having a profound effect on James who was finding it difficult to retain his concentration. Seeing that James was comfortable, Coral made her way around the table. She was keen to have a word with Sister Grace who happened to be sitting on her own. Doctor Sherwin had moved to talk to Ormerod and George about the key to the chest.

As Sister Grace turned, Coral noticed that she had striking eyes that seemed so intense that they almost burned through her.

"I think that your scroll and ours have similarities," said Coral. "I thought it would be useful to compare notes."

"They represent different periods, but I am intrigued that you think they relate," said Sister Grace. She gestured for Coral to sit down.

"But that's the preceptor's chair," Coral reminded her.

"It's only his chair if he's sat in it," smiled Sister Grace nonchalantly. "Tell me, what do you see are the similarities?"

Coral felt quite imperial sitting in the high backed chair, but was able to summarise the results of her work on the scroll. "When you described the virtues and how they could lead to enlightenment. It made me think that King Arthur may have learned about the virtues from contact with Glastonbury Abbey. Both scrolls emphasise the importance of a virtuous life and how this enriches the spirit. There is a trail of connections. They start with the ancient scroll, the teaching of Jesus, the evangelical mission of Joseph of Arimathea to Cornwall, the foundation of the Abbey in Glastonbury, and finally King Arthur embracing the values in the chivalry by forming The Knights of the Round Table. I don't think that they were searching for a material object like a cup. The Holy Grail represents the search for spiritual enlightenment."

"I see your point," said Sister Grace thoughtfully. "How ironic that we should be here as guests of the modern Templars when we discover these revelations. Did you know that the Templars have a structure? After acceptance and initiation, spiritual knowledge is disseminated from master to disciple? Access to spiritual knowledge is only accessible to those who have reached the designated grade. It works on the esoteric principle that if you cannot understand these matters, then you know enough."

"Well I hope that these scrolls have added to understanding tonight," said Coral looking across the table to where she noticed James chatting with Zodiac. "There is something else I wanted to mention. You talked about different avenues to enlightenment and one of those was personal experience. The man over there talking to that girl is called James. He and I were shipwrecked and nearly drowned a couple of weeks ago. Since then we have both felt greater contentment and a more proportionate view as to what is important and what is trivial. We are happier now than before the tragedy. In a strange way I think the shipwreck was our route to enlightenment."

"You have described a form of enlightenment, replied Sister Grace. Love is also a spiritual value. Your body language as well as what you have said gives it away."

"When you have had a chance to read through the second scroll, perhaps you would like to meet our team at The University of Cornwall," said Coral while handing over an address card.

"I will look forward to that," smiled Sister Grace graciously. "In the meantime, you had better go and rescue your friend."

Seeing a disapproving look from Coral, James curtailed his conversation with Zodiac. Coral quickly reclaimed her seat next to him. She noticed that Doctor Sherwin had taken a mould of the symbolic key. As he was the declared owner he wanted to make sure that he could access the chest when required. True to his word, he reaffirmed his commitment to loan the artefacts to the museum in Truro. George was replacing the original key in the hollow Bible and Ormerod had moved across to talk with Sister Grace. They were all absorbed in conversation. There was analysis, synthesis and evaluation of the information divulged from the scrolls. Without anyone realising, the night passed very quickly and it was dawn before they thanked Doctor Sherwin for his hospitality. Once outside the shelter of the island castle, the cold morning air embraced them. The coastal scenery looked so beautiful in the tranquillity of first light. Sheer rugged cliffs cloaked in lichen green. Grey rocky stacks, little protruding islands, dark peninsulas of land all caressed by the restless ocean. This was the backdrop to the precipitous path that led from Tintagel Island. The visitors silently retraced their footsteps from the previous night until they found their horse and cart under the outcrop of rocks.

CHAPTER 14

Aftermath

None of the visitors to the meeting with the modern Templars would have described themselves as deeply religious. They were not regular church goers. In the days following the meeting they had each reflected on the revelations from the scrolls to assess the impact on their current thinking. They had grown up and been educated with traditional Christian values and so some of the revelations, such as the recycling of the spirit, they had found hard to absorb. Yet nothing they had heard had really changed their fundamental beliefs. The new information was more supplementary than contradictory. Their perceptions of God had been amended and their understanding of human beings as spiritual entities enhanced. Resurrection and rebirth were fundamental Christian principles. The concept of reincarnation just seemed to be another facet of rebirth. James did feel that his overall understanding of the purpose of life had been clarified to some extent. It was comforting that the scroll harmonised with his new found feelings resulting from his experience of the shipwreck. George had cemented a new relationship with Doctor Sherwin distinct from their membership of the Life Saving Brigade. Ormerod and Coral were eagerly disseminating all the new data as part of their ongoing academic work.

As winter turned to spring James and Coral started to reflect on the recent changes that they had made to their lives. They had established themselves in the university apartment in Camelford and Coral was enjoying her new post. She was pleased that her article entitled 'Joseph meets Arthur' had been accepted for publication in the university magazine. Her memory of her brush with death in the crypt had faded to be replaced by the flush of acclaim from her fellow academics. The near disaster in the shipwreck had turned out to be fortuitous in more ways than one.

Word had reached the couple that the villagers in Trebarwith had raised enough money to provide a lasting tribute to those lost on the 'Mersey Rose'. The village leader had received permission from George to erect an inscribed granite shard next to Sholto's grave. This weekend James and Coral had made a special visit to view the new monument. As they approached they could see the shard standing gaunt, grey and gracious against the green and blue of the sea. It complemented Sholto's weathered and eroded stone, and did not appear incongruous. The panorama of the ocean and the blue canopy of the sky encouraged a feeling of freedom and infinite space. James looked up towards the heavens and took a deep breath, before bending to read the inscription below the names of the crew: *'For those in peril on the sea'*. The two survivors spent their time in silent reflection at this permanent memorial to the victims of the tragedy. Coral laid a wreath on the grass between the two stones. Eventually they made their way back down the steep path to meet George in 'The Strand'. Unknown to them it was the same path trodden by George Lursk six hundred years ago in pursuit of the murderous member of The Lamphill Gang.

They entered the inn through the front door and immediately saw George Denke. He was leaning against the bar talking to Jake. Obviously pleased to see them Jake welcomed them with his news.

"Do you remember the sword with the symbolic handle?" he asked.

"How could we forget after it fell off the wall," said James.

"Well, I sold it to Doctor Sherwin," asserted Jake proudly.

"Was that wise?" asked James. "It was an unusual artefact."

"Well, Vicky wouldn't have it in the inn after the events that night when it fell off the wall. I received a handsome price and the brewery has let me keep the proceeds," said Jake triumphantly. "It has returned to the Templars where it belongs."

After Jake went to the other end of the bar to serve a customer James quietly asked George if he minded that the sword had been sold.

"Not really," came the reply. "I already have the gold cup, the necklace and the pouch. I don't want the house to look like a museum."

George pointed in the direction of an empty table. "Let's sit down and you can tell me how you are both settling down to life in Cornwall."

James had received his compensation from the shipping company. He enthusiastically described his ambition to acquire a second hand fishing boat. He wanted to renew his acquaintance with the sea and intended to apply for a licence to carry passengers. The plan was to use the boat for fishing trips during the summer months. It was heartening to hear George offer the chance of some work on the farm during the winter months. The extra money would be welcome.

George looked over the table towards Coral. "I read your magazine article," he said with a smile. "I met Ormerod a couple of weeks ago in Bodmin and he gave me a copy of the university magazine. I expect you raised a few traditional eyebrows with the piece about Joseph and Arthur!"

"It's surprising how much controversy it has aroused," replied Coral. "It certainly seems to have touched a nerve."

"Talking about nerves, I had an odd experience in the farmhouse a couple of weeks ago," said George.

From the expression on his face James and Coral could tell it was something serious. George shifted uneasily in his chair. He felt slightly self-conscious knowing that what he was about to say would sound incredible.

"I was in the hallway and had just put my coat on. It must have been soon after midday because I remember the clock chiming as I was preparing to leave. It was cold outside and I realised that I had left my cap on the mantelpiece in the living room. Catherine was out in the barn and so the house was empty. The only object we keep on the mantelpiece is the gold cup. The one that Doctor Sherwin returned to me from the chest. It always reminds me of

Sholto Kelley when I see it there. I collected my cap and although I knew that I was alone in the house, I had a strange feeling that someone else was there. It felt like I was being watched. I pulled on my cap and glanced up into the mirror just above the mantelpiece. Standing behind me I saw an image of a man with unruly hair and a beard. He just stood immobile, erect like a statue, with eyes that stared straight back into mine. He wore a green jacket which hung from his shoulders, ill fitted and faded. It was clothing from another age. I froze with surprise, and then I realised that I was seeing the image of Sholto Kelley. I recognised him from the sketch we saw in Doctor Sherwin's record book."

"Did he speak?" asked Coral.

"He was totally silent. It was very odd. In a strange way I felt that I was seeing myself in his image. The face had a similar look to mine, but it obviously wasn't me. I closed my eyes for a moment and when I looked back into the mirror the figure had just evaporated into thin air."

"Well if it was Sholto that you saw it wouldn't be surprising that he had a familiar look. After all you are distantly related," said James.

It sounds similar to our experience on the beach before the shipwreck enquiry," said Coral thoughtfully.

"There was something else though," George interrupted. He was excited to tell the end of his story. "I noticed that a symbol had been smudged on the surface of the mirror. It didn't mean much to me, but I made a sketch which I can show you."

George extracted a shabby piece of paper from his pocket and laid it on the table. In the centre was the handwritten symbol that he had copied.

"That looks like an Egyptian Ankh," said Coral. "It represents eternal life," she added excitedly. "In many ways it makes a lot of sense."

"What do you mean?" asked George.

"We all share connections with Sholto. You are his ancestor. Some of his belongings are in your house. James and I nearly died on the beach where Sholto was killed. We found the pouch he left in the cave. The three of us helped to complete his mission by delivering the contents of the chest. Perhaps Sholto exists in some other dimension, but we see him when something causes his world and ours to meet."

"It's possible," added James in support. "The ingredients are the people, the place, and the objects. What I don't understand is why we sometimes see his ghost."

There was a short interlude whilst everyone absorbed the implications of the incident. Coral eventually broke the silence.

"I think that the two worlds are fused when there is a strong emotional current which links with the ingredients described by James. On the beach we were very anxious about the forthcoming enquiry. In the pub we were excited by the sketch before the sword fell. I don't want to pry George, but were there any circumstances in your farmhouse that day which could have resulted in heightened emotions?"

George pondered the day when he saw the apparition.

"It could be that he sensed that a new life was about to start. Knowing that his mission had been completed, it was his way of saying farewell."

James and Coral exchanged curious glances. "Do you mean a new life for Sholto?" enquired Coral.

"In a way," said George. "I shouldn't be telling you this now, but that same morning the doctor had confirmed that Catherine was expecting a baby. We were so pleased and had been talking about it before she left the house that day."

"Congratulations," said James. "That is really good news."

"Your family tree will need updating again," Coral added.

"Keep it quiet for now," George requested. "We haven't told anyone about it yet."

The three of them chinked their glasses in celebration. James put his glass down with a thump on the table. He leaned back in his chair and sighed reflectively.

"Sholto was killed six hundred years before the tragedy of the 'Mersey Rose'. The odds against us surviving and finding the pouch in the cave must have been very high. Trebarwith was a sanctuary for Sholto and it was certainly a sanctuary for us. I would have liked to have met him. The more we learned about his courage and behaviour, the more I admired him."

Coral nodded in agreement. "Trebarwith will always be a special place for the two of us. It is good to think that times are changing for the better."

ACKNOWLEDGEMENTS

Thanks to my wife, Carole for her clear opinions and patience in the preparation of this story. Also to the team at Troubador who have contributed to the successful publication of this book.

BIBLIOGRAPHY

Code Breaker. By Stephen Pincock and Mark Fravy. Published by Random House Books 2007.

The Templar Revelation. By Clive Prince and Lynn Picknett. Published by Bantum Press. 1997.

The Tutankhamun Prophecies. By Maurice Cotterell. Published by Headline Book Publishing. 2000.

The Hiram Key. By Christopher Knight and Robert Lomas. Published by Arrow Books Ltd. 1997.

Supernature. By Lyall Watson. Published by Hodder and Stoughton. 1973.

Life after Life. By Raymond A Moody Jr. Published by Bantum Books. 1975,

The Rise and Fall of the Knights Templar. By Gordon Napier. Published by Spellmount Ltd. 2007.

Gods War. By Christopher Tyerman. Published by Penguin Books. 2007.

Byzantium. By Judith Herrin. Published by Penguin Books. 2007

The First Crusade. By Thomas Asbridge. Published by the Free Press. 2004.

The Secret History of the World. By Jonathan Black. Published by Quercus. 2010.

King Arthur Country In Cornwall. By Brenda Duxbury and Micheal Williams. Published by Bossiney Books

The Holy Blood and the Holy Grail. By Michel Baigent, Richard Leigh and Henry Lincoln. Published by Corgi Books. 1982.